Claire Johnson's dedication to sex—the cornerstone of her ca-reer—led her to help found the Center for Sexuality and Sex Practices. Now in her fifties, she knows the Center must keep pace with the rapidly growing Baby Boomer market, so she agrees to go back on camera for a series on sex and aging. But work with her nemesis?

Former English Professor Max Wilson has championed the cause of the Center ever since his now deceased wife sought the Center's help to rekindle the nearly extinguished sexual flames of their relationship. He loves working on camera and welcomes the challenge to perform with the svelte but icy temptress.

Sparks fly immediately on and off camera. The jury is out on whether either Max or Claire can transform those sparks into a fire of sexual desire for their viewers—let alone for each other.

Ripening Passion
Copyright © 2023 Adriana Kraft
ISBN: 978-1-4874-3814-2
Cover art by Martine Jardin

Published by eXtasy Books Inc

Look for us online at:
www.eXtasybooks.com

Ripening Passion
Passion 2

By

Adriana Kraft

DEDICATION

The Passion series is dedicated to a favorite aunt, a free spirit and early pioneer in research on human sexuality.

CHAPTER ONE

Prone on the king-size bed on set one at the Center for Sexuality and Sex Studies, Claire Johnson tried to fight off a sudden wave of panic. The cameras weren't going to stop.

"Ouch!" She clawed at her partner's bare back. "You're pinching me. Stop fucking me this instant!"

Satisfied that Max Wilson at least had the grace to cease pounding her body and pleased that his glistening bald head had turned dark red, Claire whipped her glare over to Melissa Hopkins-Gage—the mastermind behind this debacle. Claire ignored the surprised cameraman and directed her venom at Melissa.

"This is not working." Her voice rose, then faltered. "I feel like I'm being fucked by a robot." She glowered at Max, who was propped above her on his hands and knees, breathing hard. She tried her best to ignore his hard cock still twitching inside her, seeking release. "A robot that's missing some parts. Get your damn cock out of me."

Inhaling deeply, Max did as she demanded.

Claire scooted out from beneath him. She leaned against the headboard of the bed, bringing her knees to her chest and wrapping her arms around them. She probably looked like she was protecting her virginity, which she could hardly remember yielding decades earlier.

"I always thought you were a bitch," Max said dryly, peeling off the shriveled condom before moving to sit beside her with his back likewise against the headboard. His breathing still came in short bursts.

Maybe she'd saved his life by stopping him before he climaxed.

"And I wasn't pinching you," Max added. "You just didn't find the rhythm."

"That's a joke. You wouldn't know rhythm if it smacked you in the face."

"Children, children!" Melissa's arms flailed as if she were flagging down a runaway train. Maybe she was.

Claire winced at the pain on Melissa's young face. For a moment, that look reminded her of a former lover — Melissa's aunt Phoebe. Claire blinked. The resemblance between Phoebe and Melissa was at the root of her current problem. The niece, like Claire's former lover and professional partner, could wheedle more out of her than she liked.

Claire glanced quickly at Max. His cock lay shriveled almost to a nub between his legs. She smiled to herself. She did get a perverse sense of pleasure out of seeing men cringe before her fury. She looked up at his face. He wasn't cringing. If anything, he was laughing. Laughing at her? *The bastard.*

"Put these on," Melissa commanded, tossing a Center bathrobe to each of them. "We have to talk. Now!"

"I want that tape erased," Claire demanded, standing to punch an arm through one armhole. She reached for the other repeatedly without finding it. She felt Max hold the robe for her. Claire closed her eyes, muttered a couple Hail Marys under her breath, and pushed her arm through the sleeve.

With a tinge of remorse, she peered back at Melissa. For a diminutive woman, the dark-haired beauty could certainly look furious.

Melissa came to a standstill at the foot of the bed. She crossed her arms under her breasts.

Claire thought she grew taller by at least three inches.

"I will not erase the tape." Melissa's mouth turned into a twisted grin. "Maybe later. If you two ever get it right. Or" —

she smiled brilliantly—"we might want to include this little scene in our instructional materials. It might help some of our viewers to see situations between a man and a woman that don't work out, that don't lead to orgasm."

Max ignored Claire. "If that's what you're looking for, you sure as hell got it."

Claire knotted the sash of her robe. "This is not going to work, Melissa." She sighed heavily. "All right, I admit he's not a Neanderthal lout, but we can't get into sync." She scowled. "And I doubt we ever will."

She plopped back down on the bed, hoping Melissa would give up on the entire idea of pairing her with Max to demonstrate options for how older couples could maintain their sexuality. She didn't question the Center's mission in this area—she'd helped champion the cause with foundations and private donors.

Max was the problem. She winced as he sat back down on the other side of the bed, doing a good job of avoiding eye contact with her and Melissa.

"Nonsense." Melissa's features softened. "Maybe we expected too much out of the two of you too quickly. Claire, you haven't worked in front of a camera for years. And I know from personal experience"—Melissa arched an eyebrow—"that Max is anything but a Neanderthal." She pursed her lips. "You remember, Max—the morning before we first worked on camera? We met for breakfast because you wanted us to get to know each other a little before meeting on set."

Max nodded cautiously. "That was my idea. I didn't want you to think of me as some old guy conveniently attached to a cock."

"You succeeded. And I don't think of you as an old guy. And you, Claire." Melissa blew her a kiss. "It took time for us to be around each other before you mesmerized me with your tongue, and it took longer still before I worked up the nerve to reciprocate." Melissa paused for breath.

Claire knew she wasn't going to like what would come out of the young woman's mouth next.

"You two simply need more time—time to be together off the set. You need to get to know each other before we can achieve what we want for our viewers."

"What?" Max looked shocked.

"Impossible!" Claire interjected quickly. "We don't have a single thing in common."

"You don't know that," Melissa insisted. "You don't know each other. Not really. Max only works for us occasionally. You've seen him working with me. And I know you have a lot in common."

Claire's heart tripped. How much did Melissa know? Melissa hadn't started working at the Center yet when Max's wife had come through the door like a lost waif looking for help with a nearly broken marriage. Melissa hadn't been there to offer a shoulder and share part of her heart with the red-head. Agnes had been insistent about what she required. She'd been the eager, able student. Claire had been the dedicated, capable teacher.

Agnes had become extremely devoted to the cause of educating others about the potential of human sexuality. She became an ardent advocate for the Center. If the Center could save her marriage, then it could work its miracles for many others. Agnes had cajoled Max into working with her on camera to offer hope to midlife couples who had suffered like them from discouragement and lack of knowledge.

Claire had never been present on set to watch them work together, and she'd only reviewed one of their tapes. That had been emotionally wrenching.

Claire knew Max shared his wife's passion, but he'd always resented the coach—*her*, the one who had taken on the responsibility for ushering Agnes into the varied arts of lovemaking. For her part, Claire had stayed away from Max. She'd supported his work with his wife, and after Agnes died, when he was ready, his work with others — particularly with Melissa, with whom he'd developed a curious bond. The two of them had been glorious together, along with Melissa's then-future husband and Center codirector, Harry Gage.

She'd known Harry since he first joined the Center staff. She was alarmed when he hired Melissa, a carbon-copy of Phoebe in her twenties. Neither he nor she had realized at the time that he'd just hired Phoebe's niece. Phoebe — Claire's lover since college days; Harry's lover until she left the Center to die.

Claire had vivid memories of the day Melissa first worked with Max and Harry. The two men were so tender with Melissa, and the girl responded so naturally, so genuinely. Claire shivered. The three of them had mesmerized even her, and she'd thought she was far too jaded to experience that kind of voyeuristic glow again.

"Are you listening, Claire?"

Claire shook her head at Melissa. "What? Sorry. Oh. I've seen him work. Just because he worked out well with you doesn't mean he will with me."

"I'm sure you share many things in common." Melissa pushed back strands of hair from her brow, then widened her stance. "You share a commitment to creating superb educational materials for older adults who may be in danger of losing touch with their sexual potential. You both are committed to making this Center thrive. Goodness, Claire, you're codirector of the Center. You've spent your entire professional career here. And you, Max, I know you. You wouldn't be doing this if you didn't share our passion for the Center's mission."

Melissa waited for each of them to nod their agreement.

"And you'll look great together on tape. You're both tall and slim. Claire, I nearly creamed when you wrapped your long legs around Max's tight butt as he suckled your boob. You looked sweet when you kissed his bald head and ran your fingers over it."

"I don't do sweet," Claire huffed, refusing to look at Max. "And I love both you and Harry, and I think you both love me."

Melissa drew in a deep breath and flashed an eyebrow. "You each owe me a lot. I'll take your lack of comment as agreement."

Claire was vaguely aware of Max shifting on the bed. He probably wanted to be somewhere else about as much as she did, but neither of them could avoid Melissa's withering schoolmarm glare. So why was Max so indebted to Melissa? Claire scowled. Like her aunt before her, Melissa didn't seem at all reluctant about calling in her debts.

"So this is what we are going to do," Melissa chirped happily.

"We?" Claire glowered at Max as they each responded in unison.

"The two of you," Melissa said, pointing at them, "will take some time to get to know each other. I," she added, pointing at herself, "will check in on your progress. When I or the two of you believe you are ready, we will do this scene over." She arched an eyebrow. "Until then, we're not erasing a thing. You might want to take showers and set up your schedules."

She turned away, then pivoted back around to face them. "Remember, I think you each have given me this advice at one time or another—be open to surprise. You don't have to love each other to be able to perform convincingly in front of the camera—but liking each other will help. Bye. Good luck with your homework."

"Now look what you've done," Max groused, sliding off the bed. "If you had cooperated, Melissa might've been satisfied, and we could've gone on with our lives—alone and happy."

Claire tugged at her robe sash. "It took two of us to screw this up." She scowled at the door Melissa had just exited and whooshed out air. "Come to my office after you've showered. Maybe we can work something out. Melissa's not going to be satisfied until we do. She can be such a shrew."

"That's a good one, you calling her a shrew." Max held up his hand before she could retort. "All right. That wasn't help-ful, I know." He frowned, looking somewhat sheepish. "I do owe Melissa a lot. I would've shriveled up into nothing if I hadn't renewed my sense of purpose. She encouraged me and helped me keep my confidence in my aging body. But now I owe her."

Claire nodded knowingly. "She does have a knack for do-ing that." A wisp of a smile split her lips. "Maybe if you and I can work out a truce of sorts — then we could team up to pay Melissa back for treating us like children."

Max chuckled as he headed toward the hall door and the Center bathrooms. "That could be fun." He turned and winked conspiratorially. "Aren't children supposed to have fun?"

"Someday those two are going to tire of your matchmaking efforts."

Melissa stuck her tongue out at her husband, then inter-laced her fingers with his as they strolled down the hall to her office.

"Harry, you and I would probably not be married if it hadn't been for Claire's interference, if you recall."

"How could I ever forget?" Harry stood aside to let her en-ter the office. "She went too far on that shoot at the Catskill mansion — dressing you in the same gown your aunt wore the last time she and I performed on camera. And then you had on the same jewel." He shook his head and shrugged. "Oh, hell. You may be right." He gave her a lecherous smile. "It would be a damn shame if we had missed out on each other."

She nodded. "So you see, I'm not doing anything Claire hasn't done."

"What about Max?" Harry continued. "Isn't he sort of an innocent bystander in all of this? Like the reluctant professor who only got involved because his wife twisted his arm?"

"Maybe at first, but he's committed to the cause, even if he only helps us out occasionally," she said, sitting on the couch. "But we can't let him slip away again. You even said he was in danger of fading away after his wife died. It was you who wanted to get him involved with us again. Wasn't that one of the reasons you sent me out to meet him not long after I joined the Center? I know you and Claire wanted to do a tape with an older man and a younger woman, but there must've been any number of men who would've been willing to help out."

"Particularly if they knew you were the young woman," he quipped. "No, you're right. The Center was Agnes's passion first, but she was able, in time, to draw Max into working with her on camera. They added a lot to our efforts to appeal to an older audience. But that doesn't really explain your penchant for getting Claire and Max together."

Melissa stared down at her hands lying in her lap as Harry sat down beside her. She gave him an impish grin. "Maybe I have a soft spot in my heart for them. I've enjoyed Max since I first met him. He surpasses every fantasy I've ever had about English professors."

"You have a soft spot in your heart for everyone," Harry huffed. "So how many fantasies did you have about English professors? And have they all been fulfilled?"

"Max is a very considerate, tender man," Melissa said, ignoring his jibe. "You wouldn't have put us together on the set if you hadn't thought so yourself."

"That was before we were married."

"I have no desire to work with Max again," she interjected, in case her husband misunderstood.

"But you would if it was important for the work of the Center?"

Melissa scowled at Harry. "Of course I would. That's different. But you're the only man I need."

"I know, I know. I'm not even sure why I'm pressing you, and I appreciate the fact that you're willing to work with Max. He is a dear friend of mine. I would trust him unquestionably."

"He holds a very special place for both of us," she said, squeezing Harry's fingers tight.

"How's that?"

"He's the only other man I've allowed in my ass, and he's the only man we've worked with together, if you recall." She batted her eyelashes at him.

"You do have a superb memory. I'll never forget that time either. I was afraid old Max was going to have a heart attack while pumping into your butt." Harry chuckled softly. "But then you clamped down so hard on my cock, I forgot about everything except fucking your vagina as rapidly as I could."

Melissa felt her nipples harden. "Ah, you do have a memory for detail. Maybe someday we'll want to revise the Center's materials on three-ways."

"Maybe. But I thought we gave up working in front of the camera when we got married."

"Me, too," she replied.

"Then nothing is cast in stone?"

"Exactly."

"I've noticed Simone has been sniffing around you from the moment we hired her."

Melissa ignored her husband's probing smile. "She's *your* research assistant."

"And a good one, too. Even better than I'd hoped. She has quite a head on her shoulders for thinking through complex analysis, and she's an excellent interviewer."

"Her smile lights up a room," Melissa admitted. "You know she wants to work more on camera."

"She's talked to me about that. I think she's a natural performer. That may be a talent that helps her with going out and interviewing folks, too." Harry squeezed Melissa's thigh. "Her dark skin would contrast very nicely with yours on camera. With Simone, you may have found your match for enthusiasm."

"Umm." Melissa tried not to show too much interest.

"You know I'm okay with you working on set from time to time?" Harry asked.

"I know that. I just haven't decided yet." She gave him a half- smile. "Simone does seem eager — maybe too eager. Perhaps she can put that good head on her shoulders to other uses." Melissa placed her hand on Harry's inner thigh and nudged his semihard arousal. "I bet my favorite cock has wondered about that possibility more than once. Simone does dress to seduce."

Harry coughed, then returned her hand to her lap. "So, what else do you have in mind for Max and Claire?"

"I'm not sure, but I do think they need to spend time together outside the Center. Maybe we should send them on a trip."

"You are a devious woman. But you're right, certainly no more devious than Claire."

"And no more than my aunt was when she was alive."

"That's true. And your heart is usually in the right place."

"Usually?" Melissa smirked.

Harry looked down his long nose at her. "Usually."

"I know!" Melissa gave Harry a brilliant smile. "You and I were planning to represent the Center at that conference retreat on sexuality and aging at Monterey next week. We'll send Claire and Max instead."

"But . . . I was looking forward to us getting away." Harry shook his head. "Hell, you've got your mind made up. We'll send them. I doubt they'll be as happy about this change in plans as you are. But sure, Ms. Matchmaker, why not?"

"You're kidding." Max sat with one leg crossed over the other on Claire's office couch. He'd no sooner rapped on the door and entered than Melissa had followed, looking as if she'd won the lottery.

Melissa glanced back and forth between him and Claire, who remained safely sitting behind her desk with her mouth half-open and her eyes snapping.

"We know all we need to know about aging and sex." Max kept his voice smooth and steady. "We're not strangers to either. We hardly need to attend a conference to learn more."

"I'm quite aware of that," Melissa puffed. "Not that either of you is old, but isn't that the point of the series we're trying to get off the ground? You're never too old for sex or intimacy. Who better to send to represent the Center? Harry and I can't speak from the same experience base. It's not that I expect you to learn more. I want the two of you to share what we are doing here at the Center. You will be advocates. And" — Melissa glanced briefly at her feet — "you might find some time to get to know each other a bit more."

"That's what this is all about, young lady." Claire's voice rose.

Max gave her credit for keeping her seat.

"Since when have you become a puppeteer?" Claire asked.

"You have more experience with that than I do," Melissa responded evenly. "But you both are committed to this project. If we can't get some decent work out of the two of you fairly soon, we'll have to either scrub the project or find re-placements. People want more information on aging and sex-uality."

Melissa blew a strand of hair away from her lips, then raked her hands through her dark tresses. "When I go out to talk to community groups, that topic is right up there with safe sex practices and fighting AIDS. You might be surprised how many older women come up to me after a presentation at a church to quiz me about safe sex at their age. We know that in some states, with huge retirement populations, vene-real disease and even AIDS is a significant problem, and per-haps even a greater fear." Looking more than a little frus-trated, she folded her arms and shook her head. "Harry has often told me we wouldn't have a community education arm of the Center or an interest in aging and sexuality if it hadn't been for Agnes Wilson's strong advocacy and success at gen-erating some necessary financial support."

Max gulped. He knew his cheeks were burning, and his eyes misted. Melissa had no compunction about hitting below the belt. He tried to breathe. He knew how important this mis-sion of the Center was for Melissa and had been for Agnes. Hell, for him and Claire, too.

Melissa exhaled, almost closing her eyes. "We've invested a lot of time and resources into this project—but maybe you two are ready to give up."

"Son of a bitch." Max looked at Claire and tried not to plead. "Agnes would never forgive us if we gave up."

Claire's shoulders slumped. She wet her lips and shook her head, then glared at Melissa and looked back at Max help-lessly.

They'd been trapped. Did Melissa have any idea how many buttons she'd just pushed? Max knew Claire saw Agnes as the glue that held him and her together. Did Melissa really think he'd been thrilled Claire had tutored his wife? Did she even know? The two women hadn't worked often on camera together, but he knew the two scenes they'd done for a tape demonstrating the use of strap-ons were electric. Max swallowed. The ecstasy on Agnes's face had been wrenching as she toyed with Claire, then relentlessly pummeled her until Claire, laughing and thrashing, rode wave after wave of what seemed like an endless orgasm. He'd nearly worn out that tape—and his arm. That tape had become his torture, his self-flagellation for letting another woman do for his wife what he hadn't been able to do.

Claire glanced at him, and he nodded.

"We'll go," Claire said softly. "But don't get confused about the two of us, Missy. We are doing this for the Center. That's all." A small devilish smile crossed Claire's lips. "And just for the record, you have a long way to go before you match your aunt's and my skills at conniving."

Melissa shrugged her shoulders. Max gave her credit for keeping her mouth shut once she'd won.

"And," Claire said, pointing her fingers, "this little switch in plans will cost the Center some extra dollars."

"What do you mean?"

"Max and I will require separate rooms."

Max laughed, then nodded his agreement. "Absolutely, if you want me to come back a sane man, then separate rooms are a necessity."

"I'll see what I can arrange at such late notice." Melissa grinned, bowed from the waist and waved goodbye. The door shut quietly behind her.

Claire stretched her neck, avoiding Max's gaze.

He could get up and help her with her muscle tension, but he wasn't about to do that. She could stew in her own juices. She'd been a thorn in his side for years—and it didn't look like he'd be rid of her anytime soon. He glanced at the door. Why couldn't Melissa stick to her own business? He loved that young woman a lot. Hell, she'd thrown him a lifeline. But she had no idea what she was asking of him.

He'd finally overcome his natural survival instincts to agree to having sex with Claire on camera for the good of the Center and for the cause that he and Agnes had so vigorously shared. But Melissa wanted him and Claire to share an intimacy like she shared with Harry. That was impossible. He and Claire had treaded far too much water over the years for that to happen.

"Well, are you going to say something?"

Max furrowed his brow at Claire, who ran her fingers through her shoulder-length blond hair. He'd rarely seen Claire show any vulnerability. This was one of those rare moments. Perhaps he should treasure it by seeing how long it would last. But then he'd never been good at torturing insects when he was a kid. "Guess we'll go learn about aging and sexuality. Wonder if there'll be any other attendees our age. Maybe they'll be like Melissa—talking about something they don't know."

"There's a lot that girl doesn't know." Claire smiled sadly. "Some days she reminds me more and more of her aunt. So glib. So daring. So adventurous. And so completely convinced she knows what's best for others."

"Phoebe was all of that." Max drew in a deep breath, then let it out slowly. "So, did Phoebe approve of you volunteering to be Agnes's coach?"

Claire sat up straight and gave him a strange stare. "My, you are getting bolder with age. How many years have you wanted to ask that question?"

He shrugged. "Are you going to answer?"

"Why not?" Claire rubbed her arm. "No, Phoebe did not approve. And I didn't volunteer."

Max scowled, then turned his head to the side.

"Not really," Claire insisted. "Your wife could be very

insistent."

He nodded. "I'll give you that much."

Claire exhaled and sighed. "You must know that Agnes believed the Center was the last resort for saving your marriage."

He grunted noncommittally. "Did that mean you had to take her on as lover?"

"Agnes didn't know what to do—she'd struggled with empty nest issues too long. You and she had drifted apart." She hesitated. "The bedroom, apparently, had never been at the center of your life together."

"I wish I knew half of what I know now when we first met. She was a delightful woman."

"Agnes was a fifty-year-old woman when she came to the Center, but she was determined. Innocent, but very committed to saving her marriage. She assumed if she could bring excitement to you and purpose to her life, then you both had a chance."

"And she found that in your arms?"

"Of course not." Claire pursed her lips. "You must know that's not true. Through her work here at the Center, she found her passion. She found a purpose beyond her family—even beyond herself. Is that so bad?"

Max shook his head. "At the time, I didn't realize she wanted more."

"But you did before she died." Claire glanced toward the door as if escape might be her desire.

Maybe he should leave. He started to rise from the couch. Claire shook her head. "You asked. I'm not finished."

Max settled back down on the cushions.

"Agnes wanted to work for the Center. She was more than willing to volunteer. We found her some filing tasks, but that didn't satisfy her for long. I wanted her to learn how to run a camera, but she wasn't interested. She wanted to work in front of the camera because she wanted viewers to know that older folks wanted active sex lives too."

"But she didn't have one."

"That was a problem. She really didn't know enough to produce more than a ten or fifteen-minute tape." Claire crossed her arms and stared at him. "I wonder why?"

He tried not to blush.

"So I became her coach. She never tried to hide that fact from you or anyone else. She never was with another man. She didn't want to betray you."

"Another man seemed hardly necessary, given your wide array of sex toys and strap-ons."

"I won't deny it. We got along quite fine, and I enjoyed being with Agnes. I believe she enjoyed being with me, but there was still something missing for her."

Max refused to break the silence.

"You." Claire nodded. "So we worked on how she might entice you into sex play—to being more open to exploring new ways of being together. You probably won't like hearing this, but I literally often role-played you, so Agnes could hone her sexual skills."

"So all of that was to do me a favor? Bullshit!"

"I said we enjoyed each other, but Agnes wanted you, too. It's ironic. Given that Melissa is trying to throw us together, that's also what Agnes wanted. She'd suggested a three-way with you several times. I resisted. And from what I heard, so did you."

"You better believe it. Agnes was enough woman for me, and I certainly didn't need her sex coach."

"Maybe I've said too much. I didn't intend to stir up the past."

"No," Max backpedaled. "I didn't mean to get huffy. I wanted to know. Melissa has no idea what she's brewing with her little intrigues."

"You're right about that." Claire paused. "So, do we go to Monterey?"

"I'll give you an answer, but I want you to answer another question first."

"Shoot."

"Why did you complain about me pinching you when we were taping on the set earlier today?"

Claire blushed from her chin to her high cheekbones.

"I thought so. You were on the verge of climaxing,"

"No." Claire shook her head, looking trapped. "Okay. I didn't want you to make me come."

"And I was?"

Claire stroked her throat and nodded.

"Why not?"

Claire didn't avoid eye contact, but her fingers trembled slightly.

When she spoke, he had to lean close to make out her raspy whisper.

"I don't know."

CHAPTER TWO

"More energy, ladies," Melissa prompted from beside a cameraman.

Claire smiled — Inez Ramirez lay stretched out atop Simone Stone's darker body. The women quickened their tongues in each other's pussy. Everyone wanted to please Melissa, even if she seldom worked in front of the camera.

"That's better," Melissa encouraged. "Stay with it. Don't stay on close-up too long," she reminded the cameraman. "Tasteful and educational are our goals. We're not doing porn."

Claire nodded her agreement. This tape on women loving women would market well. She knew it. Marketing for the Center had been her primary responsibility for years, and Melissa had a knack for staying in touch with audiences with her voice-overs and directorial skills. But then, she was an artist.

"Now, Inez, I want you to demonstrate how to stimulate a woman's clitoris. Work on Simone and see if you can bring her to climax with just the clitoris."

"You know that's not an *if*," Claire said, keeping her voice low so as not to disturb the performers. "You, more than any of us."

Melissa didn't flinch at the reminder that she and Inez had been lovers before Melissa hooked up with Harry. They remained best friends, and Inez's skill with computer technology helped all of them ride the digital revolution. Claire grinned widely at Inez as she stroked Simone's swollen clit between forefinger and thumb. Inez remained highly skilled in most things digital.

Simone's moans started in tandem with soft pants which quickly built into cascading chirps. She raised her head, arched her pelvis, then rocked against Inez's tongue. The Center's most recent hire, their first full-time African American, was proving to be a tremendous find. Simone's enthusiasm for sex was quite astounding if tapped properly. She vocalized more than any other performer currently on staff.

Harry and Melissa had chosen well. Simone seemed more than willing to adapt to the rather demanding mix of assignments given to beginning assistants at the Center. They were typically involved in library research, graphics development for Center catalogues, and performing in front of cameras. Simone spent most of her time working with Harry on Center research efforts. But she clearly relished the opportunity to work on camera.

Simone's delightful chirps were building into howls. Her face contorted. She dug her fingernails into Inez's back. "Just a little more," Simone managed between gasps.

Claire tried to keep her breathing steady as she watched the performance near its crescendo. After all these years, she'd never grown tired of supporting the new hires. Some needed more encouragement than others. Some were tentative. Some might have preferred the library work to this. Simone yelped.

Claire grinned. She had no doubt about which aspect of her job Simone preferred.

"Come for us, Simone," Melissa said from the sidelines, caught up in her cheerleading role.

Claire smacked her lips as Simone screamed.

"Yes." Inez looked up and grinned triumphantly, continuing to stroke Simone's clit, then dipping her head to gather some of Simone's flow. Simone's eyes rolled back, and her body heaved repeatedly, yielding more liquid reward for Inez.

Claire gulped. Her days in front of the camera were very limited. She hadn't planned on working with Simone. However, after what she'd just witnessed, she might have to reconsider.

"That's a take," Melissa announced, stepping toward the bed where the exhausted women lay. "Exceptional work, girls. Really."

Melissa sat on the edge of the bed, rubbing Simone's forehead. Simone nodded, apparently welcoming this mothering touch. Melissa could cajole, but she was not reluctant to give praise when it had been earned. Simone and Inez had definitely earned it.

"Beautiful," Melissa continued. "We can only imagine how many women and men will be encouraged and affirmed by this tape. Even guys will learn how to better love a woman orally."

Inez and Simone moved to sit beside Melissa. Melissa took each woman by the hand, then leaned over and kissed Inez's cheek.

"You were tremendous, as always."

"Thank you," Inez said. "It was a little slow going, but we got into it."

"And you," Melissa said, turning to Simone to kiss her cheek. "You really came on fire. You two were inspiring to watch."

Simone nodded her head and moved slightly, bringing her lips to bear on Melissa's lips rather than her cheek. Claire tried not to laugh when Melissa's eyes rounded. Simone's remained shut.

Melissa didn't break away immediately. Rather, she deepened the kiss. She placed a hand behind Simone's head, sealing their embrace. It was a tender kiss—nothing overly provocative. Searching rather than probing.

Melissa gently broke the seal of their lips. "My," she said softly, "I hadn't expected that. You caught me by surprise."

"Sorry," Simone said, not looking very contrite. "I was curious what the boss tasted like."

"I see," Melissa said, rising to her feet. "Curiosity can sometimes get people into trouble."

"I hope not this time," Simone grumbled, now looking a little more worried.

"No, not this time. You are a good kisser. So why don't you two go get showered and take the rest of the afternoon off? You've earned it."

"Great!" Inez said.

"Thanks," Simone murmured. Standing, she gave Melissa a tentative stare. Her dark nipples stood erect like pinpoints. "Will you ever work with me?"

Melissa shook her head.

Simone's eyes filled with disappointment.

"It's not you. I rarely work on camera since I married, and for the most part, I only work with Harry."

"But it's not impossible," Simone said.

Melissa chuckled, then hugged the young woman quickly and stepped back. "If there's any truth that I've learned, it is that nothing is impossible. If I change my mind, you will be one of the first to know. Now run along."

Melissa stood in place and watched as the two women headed for the showers. When she turned around, she seemed surprised Claire was still there.

Melissa shook her head and hugged herself but was unsuccessful at hiding her own taut nipples showing through a pale yellow blouse. "So, what do you make of that?"

Claire shrugged. "Simone's enamored with you. You're one of her bosses. You're off limits—at least sort of. She's probably the only one on staff who hasn't worked with you."

"But all of that can be said of you, too. Has she hit on you?"

"Maybe she has something against older women."

"Maybe." Melissa headed for the exit, and Claire followed. "Simone is an excellent talent, but we can't have her dictating Center policy."

"Or who she's working with?"

"Right." Melissa shook her head, apparently trying not to smile. "Have you ever been with a more expressive woman?"

"Not unless it was one of those occasions I can't remember."

"Oh, by the way." Melissa stopped in the hallway leading to her office. "I have your Monterey rooms worked out."

"Great. Separate?"

"Of course. Because of the late notice, I had to take two adjoining suites. I hope that'll work."

"Must be a little pricey."

Melissa only smiled.

"It'll work," Claire said. "As long as the adjoining door locks."

She followed Melissa into her office and again appreciated the many chalk and acrylic drawings of nudes decorating the office walls. A few of the models were engaged in various acts of lovemaking. They'd only been marketing Melissa's sensuous artwork for less than a year, and it was increasingly being sought through the Center's distribution network.

"The conference looks like academic dull," Claire complained. "Did you see some of the titles of the papers being presented? *Stress Relief through Sex, Orgasmic Rates for Women Across the Life Cycle, Rising to the Siren's Call After Seventy.* Who attends this shindig? We're practitioners, not academics."

"Max is—or was—an academic."

"I think he studied English, not sex. Poor choice on his part, but be that as it may, why is it important for the Center to be represented at all?"

Melissa sat in her desk chair, projecting her prim and proper air. "We are educators, Claire. You know that better than I do. It's the purpose of this place. We need to have a presence at these kinds of conferences if we want to be taken seriously about educating older folks about sex. Harry is thinking about expanding the research arm of the Center in this direction."

"Then send Harry."

"But that will take time and more money," Melissa demurred sweetly. "And as our chief fundraiser, it makes a lot of sense for you to nose around and find out who is funding what."

"We could get most of that info cheaper by having Inez do a web search."

Melissa shook her head. "Contacts. This business still thrives on contacts. Besides, the afternoon workshops don't appear so heavily couched in academic jargon."

Claire nodded. "I did notice that, but the program also makes clear that those workshops prohibit any actual sexual contact. What good is a workshop if you can't practice what you preach?"

"I'm sure you'll enjoy Monterey. Besides, there will be plenty of time for you and Max to explore . . ."

"Yeah, well don't get your hopes up, girl. I've got a lot to do to get ready to be away from the office for a week. Maybe by the time we're back, you will have decided what to do with Simone."

Melissa winced. "She'll be working with Harry on more research projects in the future. We selected Simone, in part, because she has some fairly strong research experience."

"I don't doubt that," Claire quipped. "She'd look quite fetching sandwiched between you and Harry."

"Right. Go. Get out. Before I throw something at you. Now!"

"Bye." Claire laughed over her shoulder and waved her hand at a very perplexed-looking Melissa. It was nice to see the usually self-assured brunette looking a little tattered around the edges.

Self-assurance? Claire blinked and leaned against the hallway wall. She'd prided herself most of her life on being cool and self-assured. So why was she vacillating between dreading the Monterey trip with Max and brimming over with giddiness about it?

She lurched away from the wall, then stalked toward her office. She was not giddy, had never been giddy, and would never be giddy. Impossible!

A little wary, Max risked a glance at Claire, who sat cross-legged opposite him on the floor of the small breakout room, their knees nearly touching.

"This is at least better than sitting on hard chairs listening to speakers drone on and on," Claire whispered, "turning sex into something drier than desert sand."

Max smiled and nodded at her. She had been very antsy throughout the morning lectures. Perhaps the afternoon workshop held more promise for her—now it was his turn to be skittish.

He'd hoped to team up with someone else as his partner, but Melissa had failed to inform them that they were registered as a team throughout the afternoon workshops because they were replacing another team—her and Harry. This workshop was something those two had signed up to participate in together. Actually, he'd glanced around at the few women who had not already come to the gathering as part of a pair and thanked his lucky stars he was sitting across from Claire and not one of them. At least Claire was a known commodity. Sort of.

He shook his head at her. They were supposed to be studying each other in silence. She must've been a pain in the ass for any teacher from the time she started kindergarten.

He knew she held it against him that he'd been an English professor and still taught part-time. While it wasn't his intent, that difference in perceived status seemed to make her feel inferior. Sometimes she'd strike out at him in unpredictable ways. Didn't she know he'd always resented her superior sexual talents? After all, it was she who had turned Agnes on to exploring her passion, not him.

He studied Claire's terse lips. The woman didn't smile enough. For one so much into passion, why didn't she smile more? Her gray eyes smoldered. What was she really feeling? Would she ever tell him? Hell, would he ever tell her, really? She had looked quite harsh back when she wore her straw blond hair very short. Fortunately, she'd recently let it grow enough to wear it in a small ponytail like she was now. That was an improvement. He caught himself wondering what she'd look like with long flowing hair. It seemed almost impossible to determine.

Did she color her hair? Most likely. She must be near sixty. He was sixty-two, and Agnes had been a year younger than he. He thought she was a little older than Claire.

He focused on Claire's aristocratic nose and high cheekbones. Were those the features that had first attracted Agnes?

Why had he been so insistent on not talking about Claire with his wife? Now he wished he knew more about what had drawn Agnes to Claire. He'd reluctantly agreed to volunteer with the Center, but he'd drawn the line when it came to working with Claire. Agnes had tried her best to coax him into a three-way with her, but he'd refused. And here he was, examining Claire as if she were a specimen under a microscope. He should've asked Agnes more questions before she'd died.

"Now if you're comfortable enough with your partner," the workshop leader said, breaking into Max's concentration, "I want you each to strip to the waist. Nothing provoking. Just get bare to the waist."

"Shit," Max mumbled between clenched teeth.

"It's not exactly like we haven't seen each other naked," Claire chastised, undoing the buttons of her blouse. "With any luck, we'll be able to rotate partners. I see a couple of young hunks I wouldn't mind checking out."

"I bet," Max said, removing his shirt.

"Good," the leader said. "Using your eyes only, I want you to study your partner. Pay attention to the lines, shadows, and folds of flesh. How often have we been taught to abhor folds of flesh, but they are part of aging no matter how well we take care of our bodies. Appreciate the lines, the shadows, the folds. Again, no talking, and absolutely no touching. I'll give you five minutes or so for this exercise before moving on."

Max nodded, trying to do his part. He'd been a teacher for too long not to try to follow instructions. He focused on Claire's neck. He thought he could faintly see her pulse. Her neck was long and elegant, fitting her lanky body. Her breasts sagged a little, probably with age, but they remained nicely rounded. Her pink nipples stood very alert, as if they too were watching closely.

Those brown spots a couple inches below her right breast—were they tiny moles? Why hadn't he noticed them before? He considered himself to be quite observant.

His eyes lowered to her elongated belly button. He'd never paid much attention to navels, maybe because professors were too often accused of navel gazing. Claire's, however, was distinctive. Her waist narrowed remarkably for a woman of her age. If he doubted that, he could merely glance around the room. There were others equally trim, but they were hardly the norm, and most of them were younger. Claire had

26

taken good care of herself over the years. Maybe that was a byproduct of her work.

Peeking above the line of her skirt were a few visible pale hairs that only served to draw closer attention to her crotch. Had Claire ever looked sexier completely nude? He'd seen her naked often enough, and he'd made a point of studying her tapes, particularly some of those she'd made with his wife. He might not like her, but he couldn't deny Claire was one hell of a sexy woman—probably at any age.

He glanced up as the cofacilitator walked by where they sat. The redhead couldn't be any older than Melissa. What the hell did she know about aging? At least the male instructor was closer to his age. So were they a team outside of workshops?

"Okay," the young woman said to the group. "Very good. I think you know what we're going to ask of you next." She nodded, then smiled brightly. "That's right. Please remove the rest of your clothing and return to a comfortable sitting position to study your partner. Only this time, we want you to tell your partner what you are seeing. Be specific. We're not looking for generalities." She stopped. "Oh, please, guys, if you have an erection, don't try to hide it. There's no need for shame, but we don't want you or your partners to touch.

"Ladies, if you get wet during this exercise, again, please no shame. Our bodies often respond as if they have minds of their own. And that's okay. If they don't get turned on by looking at or listening to your partner, that's okay too. Actually, since we don't allow touching, your bodies might be a little less disappointed if they don't turn on."

After settling back down on the floor, Max watched Claire arrange herself. Was she getting into this, or was she trying to provoke him? Instead of sitting cross-legged like she had been, she leaned back on her elbows, left one leg on the floor and raised the knee of the other until her foot was flat on the floor. She'd provided a more than adequate view of her partially separated pussy lips.

"I want the partner facing the wall to begin by telling his or her partner what he or she sees," Rebecca instructed. "Words like pretty and handsome don't cut it. Too general. Be specific. You may begin."

Claire waited. A wisp of a smile crossed her lips. Did she have any idea how distressing this exercise was? She lowered her focus to his crotch, then arched her eyebrows. "So, talk to me," she whispered. "Am I responsible for that?"

He ignored his stiff cock and her goading as best he could. He wet his lips, and words began to form. "Your nipples are as taut as I feel. Let's see." He let his gaze rove over her entire length. "Your thighs exude strength. Your calves are tight like those of a runner. You must work out. I hadn't thought of the discipline it must take to maintain your body that way." He paused. "Your mouth looks like it wants to break out into a smile, but you control it so much it takes on a tight, nearly pained look."

She blew him a kiss, then peered down toward her crotch, challenging him.

Max swallowed. "Yes, I'm getting there. Your pussy is distinctive. That thin line of pale blond curls provides an elegant touch, like the rest of you." He frowned. It might not have been wise to let her know he found her elegant. "Your labia are open slightly, as if inviting attention. Let's see. Yes, I thought so. Your pinkish color is deepening, because you're getting damp down there." He cracked a smile. "Now isn't that interesting. Those lips are getting puffy even as I speak. You're not as unaffected by all of this as you might want us to believe. Am I making you cream?"

This time she did smile—a little. She opened, then closed her thighs slowly as if winking at him.

"Whoa," he muttered. "Your asshole is even puckering and

widening."

"Enough," Rebecca said to the ten entranced couples. "Let your partner speak."

He nodded at Claire.

"You're right," she rasped. "I am wet. I can't remember ever being this wet without taking care of matters one way or another."

He frowned at her.

"I know," she said. "I'm supposed to be talking about you. How did you ever get to be such a Boy Scout? Do you always do what people tell you to do?"

He held his tongue.

"All right. I'll get with the program." She furrowed her brow. "I never paid a lot of attention to your bald head until now. It's smoother than I remembered. I've thought of a couple uses for it I've never tried."

He arched his eyebrows. Maybe they should do a tape on sexy old bald guys. That would surely be a hit.

"Your Roman nose is distinctive. I expect that's one thing we share—strong noses. Anyway. You have a kind mouth. Maybe too kind. Oops. I'm sure I'm not supposed to be editorializing."

Claire sat up straight, then crossed her legs. He hadn't noticed earlier that her clitoris was peeking out from its hood. So she really was turned on. Good.

"Your chin is strong, maybe balancing the kind-looking mouth. Shoulders and chest, while certainly not massive, are strong and still show well-developed pecs. A nice mat of dark hair could attract fingers.

"So . . ." She lowered her eyes. "Belly is not as flat it probably was when you were younger, but neither do you carry much of a paunch. Your hairy legs are the right size to carry that tight butt of yours. Hardly any flab there."

"And now," she focused her gaze on his crotch. "You sure

I didn't cause him to harden that way?"

He shrugged his shoulders. He saw no way to deny the obvious.

"He's quite respectable for a man of any age. Firm, well used." She chuckled. "Your cock is a blend of softness and hardness just like your face." She shook her head. "I have no idea what to make of that. Your balls hang like they've seen better days." She pursed her lips. "Too bad I can't cradle them in my palm. I doubt there is any other gesture a woman can give a man that requires more trust than cradling his balls. That never fails to give me a sense of power. On occasion," her chin dropped slightly, "I find cradling a man's balls to be humbling."

She looked back up at him with sparkling eyes. "Have I ever cradled your balls?"

He moved his chin from side to side.

"I didn't think so."

"Okay, that's enough," Rebecca said, breaking into the exercise. "We are out of time, and I expect many of you have found this to be an intense exercise." She smiled boldly. "We have purposely set aside a two-hour break between this workshop and dinner in case any couple, or anyone for that matter, desires to take care of any needs before eating. The evening meal will be served in Banquet Room A. See you then."

Max glanced around at other nervous couples scurrying to get their clothes back on. No one had seemed particularly bothered by the general sight of nakedness until they were told the exercise was finished.

"They sure do like to leave us hanging." Claire gave him a curious look. "Are you headed back to your suite?"

He shook his head. He wanted to be more in control of himself before going back. "Think I'll settle for some whiskey."

Was that a flash of disappointment sweeping across her

face?

Claire shrugged. "Mind if I tag along? I'm too keyed up to go back and stare at four walls."

"No problem. Though I'm not sure I want to talk much about the day. I've had aging and sexuality up to my ears."

Claire's lips crinkled into a smile. "I forgot to tell you that you have the cutest ears."

"What? How's that?"

She smacked her lips, then shrugged. "Don't know. They just are. Let's go get a drink."

"I haven't seen a sunset like this for years."

Max stood with Claire at the edge of the Pacific Ocean, watching the fiery red ball settle gently over the aqua blue water.

Tears came to his eyes as he was flooded with memories of sharing sunsets on the Midwest prairie with Agnes.

"It's nearly beyond description," Claire breathed. "It's like one of Melissa's paintings coming to life."

Red and orange streaks crisscrossed the sky long after the sun had disappeared. Max inhaled the heavy ocean air. He'd missed the open spaces and air promising new life. He'd have to get out of the New York metro more often, maybe to eastern Long Island or up to the Mohawk Valley. He'd considered buying property in the Adirondacks. Maybe it wasn't too late. It wasn't as if he didn't have the money, and it would be something to leave his daughter and granddaughter.

"Do sunsets always make you so pensive?"

Max quickly remembered he wasn't alone on the beach. "Sorry," he stammered. "It probably sounds strange, but watching the sun set is an experience Agnes and I shared over and over again. No two sunsets were ever the same. Similar, but never the same. She'd get enrapt with them. I guess it was sort of catching."

"I thought as much," Claire said softly, looking out across the water. "She shared stories about your camping trips and seashore vacations. Only I recall her saying that it was you who had turned her on to sunsets. You grew up in the Midwest, right?"

He nodded. "Nebraska. If you're looking, you can see some incredible sunsets on the prairie. Unfortunately, many folks who live there never actually pay attention to the sun rising or setting."

"That's probably true of so much in life." Claire slipped off her sandals and tiptoed into the water's edge. "Cold!" she shrieked, half-laughing and stepping back and forth into the water. "Take off your sneakers and join me. Being a Manhattan girl, I seldom saw memorable sunsets, but I've witnessed my share of sunrises over the ocean, and I've always been refueled by the feel of water."

He didn't speak, instead bending to untie his shoes. Claire did have a magnetic quality about her when she wasn't so intent on keeping her guard up.

She smiled easily. "I was on my high school and college swim teams. When I really get down, I probably spend too much time soaking in my Jacuzzi. I come out looking like an old, dried prune."

"I find that hard to imagine," Max said, stepping into a small wave. The shock of the cold water sent chills up his back.

"Can we walk a little?" Claire grabbed his hand as if it was the most natural thing to do.

They carried their shoes and strolled across the wet, firm sand. Only the sounds of gulls calling and the light slapping of the waves filled their ears.

Strangely, her fingers armed his. Did his warm hers? Why did he even wonder? He'd only shared sunsets with one other woman.

They must've walked a half-mile or so before Claire halted and turned to him with cloudy eyes. "Maybe we'd better go back," she whispered. "Thanks for walking with me. After so many hours in meetings, this has been very calming and re-freshing."

She hesitated. "Agnes was right. One of your qualities she praised over and over was that you are a gentleman—a gentle man. I haven't experienced many gentle men." She shook her head. "Thanks for walking with me."

Max grabbed her chin and stared intently into her eyes. "I hope gentle isn't being equated with weak. I can stand my ground when I have to." He grimaced, then dropped his hand. Why was it necessary to explain anything to her?

Claire broke the ensuing tension with laughter. "Don't get your back up. Agnes also described you as quite stubborn, willful, and single-minded."

"Sounds like the two of you talked a lot about me."

"We did," Claire said, looking amused. "How could I roleplay you if I knew nothing about you?"

He sputtered, but before he could respond, Claire stuck her arm in the crook of his and guided them back toward their hotel. He probably should've said more, but he didn't. Walking barefoot with Claire on the beach induced a mellow mood that he didn't want to disturb. She was full of surprises. It had never occurred to him she might be comfortable with silence and nature.

Later that night, Claire lay in the king-sized bed in her suite trying not to focus too hard on the day's events. She couldn't help reviewing the day, hour by hour. She didn't have to take much time to dispense with the morning sessions and lunch. Boring! Max had apparently taken those in stride, but then he was an academic. The afternoon was much more fascinating, if not intriguing. As she'd implied to Max, she couldn't recall ever being so turned on without doing something about it—and she was still on edge. Why had gazing at Max so intently while trying to remain relaxed under his equally intense appraisal become more demanding than anything they'd tried to do in front of cameras?

Was it simply stopping to look without going anywhere in particular? She heaved against the pillow she was clutching to her breasts. Did every man and woman try to fuck without looking at each other?

It wasn't like she wasn't aware of the principles behind the research. Variations of Tantra had been around for ages. She'd first encountered them in college, but it was easy to lose the discipline to practice them.

Max looked like he'd been somewhat disturbed by the afternoon. He'd never volunteered any comment about the exercises over drinks or dinner.

Their stroll along the beach at sunset was the loveliest experience of the day. They hadn't said a lot—though it was clear they'd each been awed by the red ball slowing dropping into the ocean. That was not a sight they had in New York City. She wouldn't give up her life in New York City for all of California, but this was turning into a rather pleasant retreat. *Thank you, Melissa.*

They'd both laughed when she'd tried tossing a stick in the water and nearly lost her balance. Max had caught her, and for a moment, she'd thought he might kiss her. Maybe that was merely her imagination.

Their goodnight was rather awkward.

She half-expected him to knock on their adjoining door and help her over the edge she'd been clinging to since she'd caressed his cock with her eyes. She smacked her lips. Was he lying in his bed waiting for her to rap on the door?

Claire shook her head. Not tonight. She didn't want to appear too eager. Her loins tightened with desire. She could use his help, but she'd get by without him, at least for the night.

She was way beyond finesse. She lowered one hand to her pussy, then dipped two fingers into her moist heat. She strummed her clitoris with the fingers of the other hand.

"Ah," she moaned softly.

She bucked her hips riding her fingers toward completion. She pounded the bed with her feet and bit back cries of ecstasy, not wanting Max to hear anything in the next room. Finally she slowed her fingers and rode the waves, visualizing the small waves of the Pacific Ocean crashing over Max's feet and hers.

CHAPTER THREE

"Didn't you sleep well?" Claire sipped her orange juice and grinned at Max, who didn't appear ready to greet the day—let alone the sunrise that had occurred a couple of hours earlier.

"Not really." Max glanced at a couple at a nearby table, then back at her. "And you?"

"Like a baby. Last night's walk on the beach did wonders for me. I'm recharged and ready to go. You look like you may've left your batteries back in the suite."

"Something like that." He yawned, massaging his thigh. "I have to get out and walk more. Walking in sand takes more out of me than on level ground."

"Exercise is important at any age, but particularly as we get older. I'm surprised you don't exercise regularly. How do you stay in such good shape?"

Max shrugged and gulped some coffee. "I suppose I eat reasonably well. I fall in and out of exercise routines. It's not that I don't ever try. It's that I don't get out as often as I should. And you?"

"I'm fairly consistent," she replied, trying not to appear too smug. "I have a ski-type machine, and I work with light weights."

"That explains a lot." He arched an eyebrow. "And of course there is your work and lifestyle. Sex can be quite energetic."

Claire put down her fork, dabbed her lips with a napkin, then gave him the sternest glare she had in her repertoire.

"Let's get something straight, Max. I don't respond well to innuendo. For your information, my reputation far exceeds reality — my choice. Oh, I've had very promiscuous phases in my life, and I'm not in the least bit ashamed of them. But there wasn't a woman after Agnes until Melissa showed up at the Center. Her resemblance to Phoebe was uncanny and un-hinged me for a while." She clasped her hands together. "It was in her studio, and she gave me back a part of me that I'd let go unattended for too long. That was also when she first suggested that I start working on camera again and that I pick up on this theme of aging and sexuality."

Claire felt her cheeks burning. "That was when she sug-gested I might want to work with you." She cleared her throat. "It's been a long time since I've been with a man."

"Except me?" Max croaked.

"Yes," she said, softly, "if you want to count that aborted effort."

He scowled and ran his palm over his bald head. "So you're telling me you seldom have sex."

"That's not what I'm saying." She smiled brilliantly. "I am an expert at self-pleasure. My sex toy collection probably ri-vals many stores. I should own stock in a battery company. Quite the contrary, sex is part of my daily routine."

"Routine," he blurted out. "Sex isn't routine."

She narrowed her eyes at him. "Do you jerk off?"

"Claire!" His exasperation led him to glance around quickly before answering. "Of course I do. That's different."

"The hell it is," she responded evenly. "I've seldom found a lover as able to bring me off as I am."

Max didn't miss a beat. "Agnes was one of those who did."

Claire sighed heavily. Would she and Max ever have a con-versation about anything without Agnes entering the picture? "Yes, after a lot of coaching on my part and effort on hers, she got to where she could read my body with the discerning touch of a connoisseur."

"I see." Max looked down at his plate of cold scrambled eggs. "Guess I didn't measure up the other day."

Claire chuckled. "Ah, the male ego. One effort hardly makes for a proper baseline." She chewed her lower lip. "But I stopped you because you *did* have me on the verge."

"That's right. You never did explain that."

Claire pushed back her chair from the small table. "Nor do I have to. Take your time. I'll sign for breakfast on the way out. If I have to sit through an entire morning of lectures, I'm going to need to take a power walk first. And it doesn't appear you are up for that."

He shook his head.

Claire sashayed out of the restaurant.

Max had never known a woman who exuded more pride and confidence. He drank his coffee and grimaced. Like the eggs, it had turned cold. Where was their waitress when he needed her?

He went back over part of their conversation as he stared at the seat Claire had vacated. Had she been truthful about not living up to her reputation in recent years? He'd bought into the scuttlebutt that her lifestyle throbbed with every kinky thing from paddles to chains to whips. Why had she allowed those stories to persist if they weren't true?

Melissa must've caused a meltdown for Claire, as she had for him. Was Melissa the glue that was binding them together, or was it Agnes?

Discerning connoisseur. Agnes?

Had he really been Claire's only man in years? He should've been more attentive. Maybe that explained why she'd broken off instead of climaxing. He must've rushed her.

He glowered at the waitress refilling his coffee cup. She

had no idea what she was interrupting.

"Thanks," he mumbled, then returned to his thoughts.

Why should it matter to him if he'd rushed her or not? They'd only been making a tape. But somehow, he should've been more sensitive to her mood changes when she began writhing beneath him. That was one of the advantages of age. He didn't have to be afraid of rushing himself.

Next time, he'd stay focused and try being more discerning. He pursed his lips. If there was a next time.

Max stood and felt a sudden ache in his calves. Damn, he really did have to take exercise more seriously. If he wound up working with Claire, he'd want to be more fit and ready.

He chuckled. Fit and ready. Wasn't that a term horse racing handicappers used to describe a horse they expected to pop a good race?

Claire glanced around the workshop circle. There were no absences from the previous day. Apparently, the workshop hadn't required too much of any participants. Max sat cross-legged on pillows next to her. He seemed a little more relaxed than the day before. So what would their leaders want from them today?

"Good afternoon," Rebecca began. "I'm pleased to see you all have returned. The first thing we are going to do is remove our clothes. Everything we do today and tomorrow will be done in the nude."

Rebecca began unbuttoning her own blouse and everyone followed her lead. "We don't ask you to undress to unduly arouse you."

Claire wet her lips at the sight of the young woman's perky breasts. Intentional or not, those boobs were damn arousing.

Rebecca continued as she stepped out of her skirt. "We do want each of you to become comfortable with your own nudity as well as with that of others."

Smiling, Claire pulled off her panties and admired Rebecca's shorn pussy. Very nice. A tasty morsel no doubt, but she didn't think their leader was about to share.

"Now then," Rebecca said, standing comfortably within the circle, "Ed and I have divided you into groups of four. We want you to use this time to talk with each other about sex and aging. Fears, hopes, and so on. We'll provide a list of possible starter questions and topics. We've assigned couples to groups with the intent of having an older couple matched with a younger couple. So get in your groups and we'll see how this goes. Ed and I will move among the groups to provide assistance if needed. Remember, there are no taboo topics. If we can be comfortable with each other's nudity, we certainly should be able to talk about things that matter."

Claire smiled encouragement at a young woman and man as they rather self-consciously settled on pillows across from her and Max. The young man introduced himself as David and shook their hands.

"My name is Claire, and this is Max. We're pleased to have you join us," Claire said, hoping to set their group at ease.

"Oh, I'm Gretchen," the slightly rotund young woman said, pointing at her oversized breasts. "Oh," she sputtered, realizing her mistake, "I'm not wearing my nametag. Sorry."

She did a slight curtsy to the man next to her, then appeared to try to shrink out of sight.

"It's okay," Claire said. "I'm sure we'll all be a bit more comfortable in a few minutes. Do we want to try these questions Rebecca and Ed put together?"

"Sure," David said.

Gretchen bobbed her assent.

"Okay." Claire glanced at the card with the questions and frowned. "The first one has to do with fear. What do you fear most about growing older—in terms of your sexuality?"

"That we won't be able to have sex," David and Gretchen said almost in unison.

Claire smiled. At least she didn't have to explain the birds and bees to them. Had she ever been as innocent as they appeared? She glanced at Max, who looked quite undecided about the couple. They might as well have been from outer space. "Max, did you feel that way when you were their age?"

He blinked at her and finally said, "Oh."

Was that the proverbial light bulb turning on?

"I guess I forgot. Sure—there was a time when I thought people over forty didn't have sex. And then fifty. And then sixty."

"And now?"

Max smiled at her, then at the young couple. "I can attest to the fact that people over sixty do indeed have sex and can enjoy it very much."

Claire thought she saw tension oozing from their little cluster. Perhaps it was important to start with that question. It wasn't where she would've started, but Max would've kicked her if she'd jumped into the middle of the prepared list.

"Do you want me to ask the next question, or do you have something you'd like to ask?" she asked, glancing from David to Gretchen.

Gretchen smiled. She looked much more attractive when she smiled. Yes, she probably did have potential in bed.

"I don't think about it a lot," she began. "When I do think about getting older and having sex, I'm afraid I'll sort of dry up and not be interested or interesting. I guess that hasn't happened to you?"

Claire chuckled. "Not exactly. Lubes have become much more important as the years go by. They help my natural lubrication. As far as interest is concerned, I imagine that's related to sex continuing to be satisfying, but also to having an open mind. Being open to trying to new things—positions, toys, and so on."

"Toys?" Gretchen's brow furrowed. "Oh, you mean a vibrator? I have one of those. I use it occasionally when David's out of town for a week or so."

"You might want to try using it together," Max interjected. He turned to David. "You'd be surprised how a simple vibrator can help a couple consider new possibilities."

David nodded absently as if he was more focused on forming a question than on listening. Finally he blushed and blurted out, "What about you, man? Don't you have a difficult time getting it up at your age?"

Max's laughter rumbled from his belly. Claire peeked at him.

She wasn't certain she'd heard him laugh like that before.

"It may take a little more effort." He glanced quickly at Claire. "If you have an understanding woman, she'll find a number of ways to help you get hard and stay hard." He smiled. "Oral sex used to be a luxury. Anymore it's often a necessity. That's not all bad."

"Hadn't thought of that," David said, glancing at Gretchen.

"One advantage is," Max continued, "I can generally last much longer, so my partner can come several times without any danger that I'll ejaculate prematurely."

"Wow," Gretchen said. She looked quickly at David with rounded eyes, then settled back down.

"Do you still come?" David asked.

"Usually. Sometimes I don't. That used to frustrate me more than it does now. There's always another time." Again, Max looked at Claire as if questioning how far he should go. She nodded her encouragement. "Sometimes, I come in a woman's vagina. Sometimes I need more help. Sometimes my partner will jerk me off in her mouth. Sometimes I'll jerk off over her breasts or ass." He grimaced. "Probably the most disappointing thing is that I don't produce as much semen as I used to."

He shrugged. "If anything, orgasms are more intense now than ever before. They require more focus — more attention on the part of both partners." He gave the couple a quirky smile. "You might be surprised how magical a woman's finger in a guy's ass stroking his prostate gland can be while she's blowing him. That seldom fails to yield results."

"What?" Gretchen gasped. She closed her mouth and looked furtively around the room.

"Perhaps we don't need to spend more time on techniques," Claire said, smiling thoughtfully at Max.

Had he been about to go into a discussion of how the anal canal is a tighter fit than the vagina? Max was a teacher, but she had much more experience teaching about sex. An instructor didn't want to go too far outside their students' experience too quickly. From the look of shock on Gretchen's face, she clearly hadn't considered the asshole as an erogenous zone. On the other hand, David's eyes glazed over while Max tried to answer his question.

"Do you have any fears, Claire?" Gretchen squeaked.

"Of course I do. My greatest fear is probably the one you alluded to earlier — interest. It's certainly not a factor yet, but I do worry sometimes about losing interest. Sex has been so much a part of my life, I can't imagine being without it. Be it with a man, or with a woman, or with my toys."

"Oh." Gretchen blushed. "I've only been with a girl once. I didn't like it."

"I don't suppose it's for everybody. That's okay."

"Maybe we should begin to think about sharing toys," Gretchen said to David.

He gave her a warm smile. "We probably can't start too early." He glanced over at Max. "The years do go by quickly."

Max nodded. "Each year seems quicker than the last. And life has a way of throwing you enough curves. Enjoy as you go."

Agnes. Was he thinking about Agnes again? To Claire's surprise, Gretchen began to laugh.

"I'm sorry," the young woman said. "You reminded me of something my Irish grandmother told me. Enjoy the journey. Be open to surprise. And the journey ain't over until you stop breathing."

"A wise woman," Max acknowledged. "So how old was your grandmother when she died?"

"Oh, she isn't dead. She's still breathing. Grandma Shannon is sixty-eight. She's gone through three husbands, and she's definitely still breathing."

"Sixty-eight!" Max rolled his eyes and shook his head.

Claire chuckled softly. So there was wisdom being passed both ways from generation to generation.

Max was still shaking his head as he and Claire entered the lounge. Cripes, he might as well have been giving advice to his granddaughter. He frowned. Not that he didn't want Roseanne and her beau to learn the information he'd shared with David and Gretchen, but maybe it was better that they hear it from somebody else. He hoped someone would tell his own granddaughter that sex didn't have to end at forty.

He nodded at Claire, who stood grinning beside him. She seemed to enjoy the workshop very much. "Whiskey?"

"Sure," Claire said quickly. "I bet David and Gretchen are going to use the two-hour break before dinner more creatively, but whiskey sounds fine."

"They'll be lucky if they make it back in time for dinner."

"You were good with them," she said, taking him by the hand and leading them toward the bar.

He squeezed her fingers lightly. Since when had it become natural to hold her hand?

As soon as they reached the bar, he ordered two whiskeys over the rocks.

When their drinks arrived, he lifted the glass to his lips, welcoming the burning sensation washing down his throat. Perhaps a little less eager, Claire sipped her whiskey.

Claire reached behind her and undid her ponytail. Her hair fell to her shoulders. He liked her with her hair down—she looked younger. More girlish.

"You certainly had David and Gretchen enrapt." Claire lifted her glass in a toast. "I'm glad to hear Agnes was as good a student as I thought she was."

"Apparently, she had an excellent coach. I don't deny I was a beneficiary."

"If that still gnaws at you," Claire snapped. She paused, then continued in a softer tone, "I'm afraid I can't do anything about that. She was a willing student. I was a willing teacher. That's in the past. You're going to have to get over it."

"I'm working on it," he grumbled.

"So, do you think Melissa is getting out of this trip what she hoped for when she sent us out here?"

He shrugged, not eager to follow Claire's line of thinking. "You're making contacts with potential funders and potential outlets for the Center's materials. I'm trying to explain what the Center is about when people ask. I'm actually rather surprised how many people are already aware of the Center's work."

His drinking partner thinned her lips and glared hard at him. "Yes, all you say is true, and you know that's not what I was asking. You can be quite evasive when you want to be."

"You're not the first person to make that observation," Max retorted.

"No, I'm sure I'm not." She took a large swallow of whiskey and closed her eyes.

When she opened them, he knew he had no escape.

"So, are we going to be able to work together when we get back?"

He tried not to shrug his shoulders—no need to further irritate her. "Do you want to?"

"You can be impossible." She blew air through pursed lips. "Having been here the last couple days and listening to people—even some of those dry speakers. Professors should be required to take classes on communication. Anyway, after listening to many of these women and men tell their stories, I'm going back even more pumped about the Center producing materials for baby boomers. It's not that we haven't paid some attention to older couples' questions and needs, but we can do much more. And I want to be part of that."

"I see." He ran the back of his hand across his mouth. She wasn't about to let this drop. "You could always find another older man."

"I could do that." She spent a long moment studying the bartender and the bottles under the bar mirror. "But I'd prefer not to. I've liked some of what I've seen and heard from you since we left New York. Melissa may be right. Simply getting to know each other better might help us stay in sync when we work together in the future."

Max took a swallow of his second whiskey. He was drinking too fast. "Doesn't mean we have to like or love each other, I suppose."

"Of course not!" She actually looked offended. "It's not that I don't find you more likeable than I expected, but I don't see what that has to do with our working together."

"Right." Claire sure had a knack for getting under his skin. He wasn't sure he'd ever be quite so glib about having sex, even on camera. "So, are you going to beat me over the head the next time you're nearing an orgasm?"

She thinned her lips and shook her head. "I'll manage. I haven't let a man bring me off in years."

"Because that puts you temporarily out of control?"

"Maybe."

"I guess I'm willing to try." He ducked from her glower. "I suppose Melissa will think it's a waste of money if we don't at least give it a go."

Claire stood abruptly to leave. He made no move to leave with her. He wasn't nearly ready.

She leaned close to his ear. "I'm underwhelmed by your eagerness to work with me. Working together might require some practice. I'll leave the adjoining door between our suites unlocked. If you want to practice later tonight, you know where to find me. Bye," she whispered before rimming his earlobe with the tip of her tongue.

She didn't wait for a reply — not that he had any to give her.

Instead, he waved at the waitress.

"You ready for your check?" a young scantily clad woman asked.

"No." Max shook his head. "Two more whiskeys, please."

He kept his brain on hold until his drinks arrived. After taking a gulp, he let himself settle in for a long evening. He hadn't spent an evening drinking for a very long time. It appeared he was ready to make up for lost time.

Damn woman! Practice — shit! Did she think he was going to try out for the part? She was the one who'd broken it off on camera the previous week. He knew he'd brought her close to a robust orgasm. Her panting had turned ragged, and she'd dug her nails into his back. He remembered her inner muscles tightening around his shaft. She'd been so damn close.

But then she'd refused. Refused him. She'd pushed him away like an unwanted afterthought. He recalled her shaking as she fumed at him, then at Melissa. Then he thought she was incensed — now he knew she'd been afraid. He'd watched her lose control with Agnes on more than one tape. Why the hell not with him?

47

Max scowled at one empty glass and another full one sitting before him. The empty one looked lonely. He brought the full glass to his lips.

Practice. Did she want to practice faking orgasms? He squeezed his fingers into fists. That wouldn't happen. He wouldn't let that happen. Agnes had done that for years. He wouldn't let Claire get by with faking.

He blinked. Was that a new realization? Had he ever acknowledged that Agnes had been stroking his ego even though she'd seldom actually climaxed? He'd come to that realization in part because Agnes's orgasms were radically different after she'd been at the Center for a few months — after she'd been with Claire. Only then did she squeal and scream announcing her orgasms. Only after her involvement with Claire did Agnes cream. Only after Claire did Agnes develop a voracious sexual appetite. Thank God, that appetite had still included him.

It wasn't as if he'd never asked Agnes how their lovemaking was for her before she began volunteering at the Center, but she'd always said *fine.* And he'd left it at that. They'd managed to have a daughter. Beyond those times of trying to get pregnant, they'd seldom talked about sex. It was simply something they did. Weekly, then monthly. Until it hadn't mattered whether they did it or not.

He squeezed his eyes shut. It must've mattered some. Agnes had sought out the Center and its resources. And he did respond to her renewed sexual enthusiasm and seemingly outlandish ideas.

But why hadn't it occurred to him that Agnes was faking orgasms all those years? What the hell else had she been faking?

Damn. He shuddered. He wished Melissa had come along with them to Monterey. She might have some answers for him. While she never knew Agnes, she did understand what made women tick. And he could talk with her.

Damn if he'd let any woman fake orgasms with him anymore.

Practice!

He emptied the last whiskey glass, dropped more than enough money on the table, and lumbered toward the exit. Practice!

By the time he found his suite, he was convinced someone had moved it on him. It must've been that conniving, elegant, sexy Claire woman. He finally got the damn keycard to produce a green light. He pushed the door open and stumbled into the bedroom.

Practice. He fell on the bed and peered over at the door separating his suite from hers. She wanted to practice. Didn't that just beat all? He'd give her practice. In a minute.

He closed his eyes and sank into the mattress. "No faking," he mumbled.

He'd allowed one woman to puff him up with her fakery for years.

Never again.

Claire would come for him willingly and loudly or he'd sure as hell die trying. He grunted into the pillow, then shuddered. He was going to be late for practice. Would Coach make him do laps?

CHAPTER FOUR

Claire found herself walking faster than usual down the hallway to the afternoon workshop. She hadn't seen anything of Max since leaving the bar. She'd been so pissed at him for not knocking on her door that she'd purposely skipped the morning sessions.

Max hadn't shown up for breakfast, either. She hated to admit it, but her anger had turned to fear. Had he gotten drunk and fallen into the ocean? Had a heart attack? She quickened her pace. Almost anything could've happened.

She'd actually decided she could work with him without having to hold back. That should at least please Melissa. Nor would it be a huge burden for her, but if Melissa expected any more than that she would be greatly disappointed.

If she were younger, Max might actually have some possibilities. But she wasn't, and she'd lived by herself for so long now she figured if she tried a live-in lover, one of them would wind up committing murder—which wasn't far from her mind at the moment. The bastard had given her enough grief. Where the hell was he?

She opened the door to the workshop area. Her anger quadrupled in spades. There he was, sitting on a pillow with his head in his hands. *Isn't that just great!*

Here she'd been frightened out of her skin, and he'd been oblivious to the world. Hung over. She hoped it was a raging, insufferable hangover.

"You okay?" she asked, taking her seat on a pillow next to his.

Max looked up at her, and she cringed from the pain in his eyes.

"I'll live a while longer, I guess."

"Hard to tell. You really want to do this workshop? We could skip it."

"No need. This is the last one. Wouldn't want to miss whatever our delightful tour guides have planned for us today."

Claire rose to her feet. "I'll get us some coffee."

"Thanks," he muttered. "I've been drinking coffee and eating salt all morning. It's helping some."

"I'll have to take your word on that."

Claire walked across the room to the coffee urns and poured coffee from the caffeinated pot. She set the cups down to lick her burnt fingers. Damn, she hated paper cups. A lavish hotel should be able to afford to hire staff to wash extra cups.

"Here you go," she said, sitting back down beside Max.

He looked grateful, if not slightly remorseful. "Thanks."

"Welcome again, group," Ed said, drawing the couples' attention. "This will be our last time together. We hope we have given you some exercises you may take home with you to try at your leisure with your partner or partners. For this last session, we will first remove our clothing. Nudity has a way of making us all equal, don't you think?"

Claire nodded but wasn't totally convinced as she looked from Max's raging hard on to Ed's flaccid penis dangling between his legs as if it had no care in the world. She was pleased to know Max's bout with whiskey hadn't destroyed him entirely.

"This afternoon we want you to share stories with your partner. We too seldom talk to our lovers about our sex lives, especially about past partners. And yet, what we bring to any current relationship is certainly shaped by past relationships. So part of the purpose of this task is to get us talking about sex and to share our life stories.

"Another way of doing this when you return home is to write down your stories, then share them with your lover. A problem with writing your stories of course is that you may take the opportunity to edit." Ed shook his head. "It's important not to edit. Let the words flow. Let them claim their power. Let them become you. Also, it's our experience that to the extent possible, your stories carry more power if you can tell them in the present tense."

Ed walked around the circle eyeing each person with genuine interest.

"You each probably have numerous stories, and each story is valid and valuable. To start us off today, I suggest that we go back to our first encounters with a sexual partner and share that story with the person sitting across from you. We seldom forget first encounters." Ed heaved a sigh. "We realize that not all sexual encounters are positive. We do suggest for this exercise that you select one that you feel at least somewhat positive about.

"Even with that caveat, someone as they tell their story may experience a rush of negative memories. If that happens, please raise a hand—or the listener may raise a hand—and Rebecca or I will join your group. We are here to support you. So with that cautionary note, do not be afraid. Let your stories flow.

"One of us will tell you when to begin to wrap up your story so your partner can have an opportunity to share. We will begin with the individuals who are facing into the room."

Claire faced Max with her back to the wall. She gazed at him thoughtfully while trying to come up with something to share. It was probably just as well that she would go first. He still looked quite blitzed.

"You got your ears on?" she teased.

"I can hear pretty good." He gave her a lopsided smile.

"The ringing has subsided. I'm doing quite fine. Go ahead."

"Guess I'll share my first real sexual encounter. It happened my freshman year of college," Claire began.

"College?"

"Don't look so shocked. I was regarded as a bright goody-two-shoes in high school. I dated a little. A few kisses. A little rubbing of my breasts. No guy got inside my clothing."

"No one got out of the batter's box?"

"Exactly. I didn't even do much self-exploration. I'd been told from the time I was a little girl not to touch myself. Until college."

"Sorry to interrupt," Ed called out. "But I'm not hearing many present tense stories. Give it a try. It can make a difference."

Claire rolled her eyes. "I'll try," she said to Max. "I'll entitle this story *Encounter with the Same Kind — Phoebe.*

"I am asleep. I am dreaming. Hot breath—not mine—fills my nostrils. Something brushes against my cheek. Something warm and wet slides across my lips. My eyes pop wide open. A scream builds in my throat. Phoebe clamps a hand over my mouth. *Shh,* she says, on her hands and knees straddling me. She is clad only in a t-shirt. I am wearing a t-shirt and panties. *You are so beautiful. I want to kiss you.* She kisses my forehead, my cheeks, my nose, my eyes.

"Her eagerness confuses me and emboldens me. My body has never been so alive. My skin warms. I raise my arms to wrap them around her. Instead, I let them fall back to the bed. She nibbles at the corner of my mouth; I turn so I can nibble at hers. She needs no more encouragement. Her lips bruise mine with intense feelings I never knew existed. All the time, she is moaning and groaning my name.

"Her tongue separates my lips and gently probes my mouth. My eyelids close and open. My hands become fists, pounding the bed. She moves a hand under my shirt to cup a breast. She pecks at my nose. *Hi,* she says. *Are you surprised?'*

"I nod at my roommate.

"Why do you think I parade before you naked as often as I can? I want you. I want you to want me."

"I lie perfectly still beneath her, but I cannot ignore the sharp tingles moving from the breast she still cradles across my abs to my loins.

"Do you want me? she asks with a catch in her throat.

"Don't stop kissing me, I manage to say.

"I won't. She giggles. *Ever.*

"Her lips cover mine, and her tongue is again in my mouth. This time, when she caresses my tongue, I respond. My tongue comes to life—playing tag, chasing her tongue as it retreats into her mouth. I lose track of everything but our tongues until I realize Phoebe is rolling my nipple between her fingers. She swallows my scream. I settle into the mattress, waiting for my body to dissolve.

Shh, she cautions. She places a finger into my mouth, I clamp down on it. She raises my t-shirt, then lowers her head until she is washing my breasts with her tongue.

"My head is spinning. I suck her finger as if it provides mother's milk.

"Phoebe laughs softly, then taps her tongue against a nipple before taking the breast in her mouth. I am climbing a mountain of strange emotion. Fear, pleasure, desire. I fear what I am doing is wrong. I fear she will stop. I bask in the adoration she is showering on my breast. I desire more. What, I'm not sure. But I want more. My hips begin to rise and fall of their own volition. I renew my sucking of her finger, trying not to whimper too loudly. To my horror, Phoebe's mouth leaves my breast to the cool night air. She pecks at the corner of my mouth and shifts to kneel by my side. I can see her broad victorious smile in the soft moonlight spilling through the dorm window.

"I can help, she whispers. Do you want more?'

"Help me, I say.

"She nods and gives me two more fingers to suck on while she returns her oral attention to my breast. I tense, then relax. The warmth of her mouth reheats me.

"She slides a hand down across my belly. My pelvis tilts toward her as if welcoming a secret invader. She cups my panty-clad mound, and I bear into the pressure of her hand. Goodness. She fondles and caresses. Foreign sensations build under her palm. Her slowness frustrates me, but I am not completely certain why. Languidly, she lifts her mouth from my breast. *Nice.*

"*Please. Don't tease me.*

"*I want you to come for me.*

"I nod. I want to come for you. Help me.

"Without saying a word, she drops her mouth to my breast. Her fingers deftly work their way under my panties. She doesn't bother with removing them. Instead, she slides a finger up and down my cleft.

"*So wet,* she murmurs against my breast.

"Her finger separates my pussy folds, then widens my portal. My butt lifts off the bed, and I am enthralled by her finger entering me. She waits, as if letting me catch my breath. I doubt that is possible.

"I bite down hard on her fingers in my mouth, and the one in my vagina begins that age-old in-and-out journey. She's sawing me in half. My entire loins fill like a water balloon ready to burst. Her finger becomes more insistent, more demanding. My hips begin to churn in response. My head twists back and forth, but Phoebe never withdraws her fingers from my mouth.

"Her finger curls deeper.

"*Ah,* I groan. Tears form in my eyes. Goodness!

"I am flowing. It is as if her finger penetrated the membrane of my internal balloon. I explode, not fully aware. I shatter into a zillion points of light. My body overheats, chills, and shivers as I drain the heat from my roommate's body. Phoebe, the conqueror, the seducer, the lover — my first lover. At that moment, I am certain there will never be another lover. My soul mate found me and I — I did not run away.

"Gradually, Phoebe drops my breast and withdraws from my vagina and my mouth. Trying not to feel abandoned, I crack an eye open to see her beaming at me.

"She blows me a kiss.

"*That looked grand.*

"I nod, unable to find any words.

"*I'd like to taste you, if that's all right. It a shame to let all your juices go to waste.*

"Again, I nod my consent. How could I deny her? At that point, I would've followed her to the moon.

"Phoebe kneels between my legs. She lifts my still-humming hips enough to tug my panties down.

"We won't be needing these for the rest of the night.

"That was the last time I wore panties to bed.

"Curious, I lean forward on my elbows to watch. She smiles, then keeps her focus locked on my eyes as she dips her tongue into my pussy. As if I had done this in another lifetime, I arch my back and spread my hips wide to welcome her tongue."

"That's about it, folks," Rebecca said quietly. "Better wrap up your story so your partner will have a chance to share."

"That's about it," Claire said. "That was only the beginning of a very long night. I'm not sure I've ever felt more in love than on that night."

She waited patiently for Max to take over.

At last he cleared his throat. "That was special. I'm glad you shared it with me. My story isn't nearly as good as yours."

"I doubt there are good and bad stories — just stories. So tell me," she said, hoping her eagerness to hear his story wasn't too evident.

"It probably won't surprise you that my story involves Agnes."

Claire shook her head.

"She was the only woman I was with until she died. Our first real time occurred after we were engaged. I was twenty, and she was nineteen." He chuckled. "Too young to know much about anything. Neither one of us knew a damn thing about sex other than it was something we'd been told not to do until we were married. I sometimes wondered what would've happened to us if we'd been four or five years younger. Claire, you grew up during the sexual revolution. We were a few years ahead of it. I expect those few years might explain a lot."

"Your story," Claire prompted.

"Right. It happened on a Sunday afternoon at the apartment we'd rented. We were cleaning it up in preparation for moving in. Our wedding was less than a month off.

"During our dating, we'd progressed through the various stages of foreplay. She'd jerk me off and I'd play with her pussy. I don't think either of us knew anything about female orgasms, so we never stayed with it long enough for that to happen. Maybe it wouldn't have anyway."

The corners of Claire's mouth turned down sadly.

"Of course, neither of us had a clue about oral sex. Looking back on it, I sometimes think we both grew up under a rock. There were crude jokes about oral sex, but I doubt it occurred to either of us that such crudity actually referred to some very pleasurable possibilities.

"Anyway, on this fateful Sunday afternoon, we kissed longingly and had shared our *I love you's.*"

"Present tense?" Claire whispered.

He nodded. "You'd think for an English professor this exercise would be easier. Okay. I'm fondling Agnes's breasts, and I shower them with kisses. I suck on them and squeeze a finger into her tight pussy. Agnes grits her teeth. I'm not sure whether that's a good sign. I assume it isn't, so I reclaim my finger.

"Agnes gives me a strange look, then shifts across the living room carpet until she is able to wrap both hands around my cock. In very short order, I am ready to spout. Wanting to prolong matters a little, I grab her wrists and she stops.

"She shrugs and lies down beside me. Neither of us speaks for minutes. Breaking the heavy silence, Agnes rises on one elbow and stares at me mischievously. It's that playful look which I don't see often enough that continues to entice me. Her blue eyes mist a bit, and she blurts out *You want to do it, don't you?*

"*What?* I reply as if I don't know what she's talking about.

"You want to put your thing in me, don't you? You've wanted to for months.

"She points at my very stiff cock.

"Well, sure, I stammer. I've dreamed of having sex with you. Haven't you?

"Maybe it will release some pressure, she confesses. We are going to be married in a few weeks. Go ahead. Do it. Just don't get me pregnant. She rolls onto her back and her hands curl into fists at her sides.

"I'm not about to pass up this opportunity, but I'm not certain whether her willingness to do it is to release pressure in her, in me, or in both of us. It does, however, feel like we're in a pressure cooker. But this is not a good moment to explore emotions; not that there is a good moment.

"I do not wait for her to change her mind, but swiftly pry her legs farther apart to give me room to kneel between them. Her eyes are squeezed tight. How to proceed is clearly left to me.

"I fumble around in her folds while trying to breathe until I find the appropriate target. I press my claim on her pussy by bringing the head of my cock to its entrance. I move slowly.

Looking back on it, maybe not as slowly as I thought then.

"I'm halfway in before I have to stop. Her scalding heat amazes me. I quiver and push onward. She yelps as I seat myself. I am falling deeper into boiling liquid. I close my eyes, then reopen them quickly. Agnes is lying there with tears streaming down her cheeks and clenched fists at her sides. Her jaw is rigid.

"*Do it,* she demands without opening her eyes.

"For my part, I am thrilled and awed. I am in. I am inside a real, throbbing pussy! No fantasy. No dream. No imagination. This is the real thing. My cock already pulses with urgency. There is not one brake anywhere in my body. Hurriedly, I plunge in and out of Agnes, four, five, six times, and then I shout, *Oh shit!*

"I pull out, ejaculating all over her belly.

"I am gasping for air. I continue pumping into my fist until I'm done.

"Agnes opens her eyes. *That's it?*

"Collapsing by her side, I groan and give her an embarrassed nod.

"*At least you waited until you were out of me.*

"Agnes struggles to her feet and heads for the bathroom. When she returns, she is cleaned up and wearing her blouse and shorts.

"*I hope you liked that, Max. There won't be any more of that kind of horsing around until our wedding night.*

"My cock, my entire body droops. I knew it hadn't been great, but it wasn't that bad."

"Okay," Ed interjected. "We're running out of time. You better wrap up your stories."

Max shrugged his shoulders. "That was about it, anyway. Another two weeks passed before I began to wonder why I hadn't encountered that resistance, that intact hymen I had heard about. Agnes was not into horseback riding. I wondered if there was more about her than she told me. She was my first. Was I her first?"

Ed and Rebecca walked to the center of the circle.

"You seemed so intent on sharing your stories that we didn't save enough time to really wrap up like we typically do," Rebecca offered. "But I do hope you will continue sharing your stories. We've enjoyed you. We hope you've enjoyed the experience. See you at dinner. Two hours."

Max stood and held out his hand to help Claire to her feet. Claire smiled. He *could* be gallant. She tried not to show any sadness at his story, but it sure explained a lot about him, and especially about Agnes.

He escorted her into the hallway. "Whiskey?" she asked.

He shook his head. "I've had enough whiskey to last a few days." He gave her a lusty look. "Let's go practice."

"My, that was romantic," she quipped, hurrying down the hallway matching Max stride for stride.

He stopped abruptly. "I didn't think you were looking for romance."

"I'm not," Claire quickly backpedaled. They resumed walking. "But"—she flashed her eyebrow—"I am a woman, and I don't want to be taken for granted. You could've said, Claire, would you like to go back to our suite and practice having sex?"

"Ah." Max stopped them midstride. He turned and cradled her chin between strong fingers. "Claire, would you like to go back to our suite and practice having sex with me?"

Claire pursed her lips thoughtfully, then grinned. "Yes, I believe I am ready to practice having sex with you."

Claire walked to the door adjoining their suites, unlocked it, then peeked back over her shoulder at her reluctant paramour. "Why don't you take a shower in your bathroom, and I'll take one in mine? Don't forget the mouthwash."

Max dipped his chin and grinned. "Sorry about that. Hope

I didn't asphyxiate you sitting so close in the workshop."

"I managed. But I do prefer to kiss a fresh-smelling mouth. There should be robes in the closet. There are in mine." She paused. "When did you eat last?"

"I'm all right. I had a candy bar and soda before going to the workshop."

"That'll help a lot," she said sarcastically. "I don't want you fainting and pinning me to the mattress. I'll open a bottle of wine and set out some cheese and crackers."

His eyebrows shot up. "My, you are prepared."

"Yeah, well you're a little late. I was prepared last night."

He shook his head and glanced toward his suite. "Better late than never."

"We'll see." He shuffled toward his shower. Once he'd disappeared, she strolled into her suite, humming softly. She was more than a little surprised at how her body tingled anticipating their practice session. But then she'd heard so much talk about sex the past few days she'd begun to worry it was only an abstraction.

Wanting to be ready before he returned, Claire didn't spend long in the shower and was careful not to get her hair wet. She brushed her teeth and gargled mouthwash. His breath had been rather intense when he was telling his story.

She smiled at her reflection in the mirror. She couldn't help thinking of Max recounting his first time with Agnes. Claire shuddered. Thank God she'd been born a few years later than them. Of course, she hadn't realized how much of a desert her first nineteen years had been until Phoebe ushered her into the sexual revolution. And thank God Phoebe knew what she was doing.

Claire touched up her lipstick. At first, she'd been skeptical of Agnes's naiveté when the woman showed up at the Center. But the redhead had not been putting on an act. She'd really been a fifty-year-old novice. What a shame for her and for

Max to have subsisted for so many years without having much of a clue how to love each other.

Claire slipped on the plush terrycloth robe provided by the hotel and opened the small refrigerator. She was slicing an assortment of cheeses when she heard Max pad into the room. "You want to open the wine?"

"Sure." He took the bottle and corkscrew from her, uncorked the bottle, and poured wine into two glasses.

After handing her a glass, he lifted his in salute and grinned confidently. "To practice."

"To practice," she replied, pleased that Max had apparently found his stride in the shower. His reluctance to practice seemed to have vanished. She hid a smile. "Why don't we sit on the couch so you can munch on some crackers and cheese? I really do want you to have something in your stomach before we begin in earnest."

He nodded his assent. "I can think of something I'd rather munch on," he said softly, sitting down beside her.

"In due time," she said, patting his thigh. "Remember, one of the advantages of age is we don't have to rush because of galloping hormones."

He chuckled around a cracker and sipped his wine. "Just so you know. My hormones are already trotting."

She tipped her head back and laughed. "Just so you know, mine are trotting also."

"Good."

Maybe there was something to the age factor. She couldn't recall ever being this relaxed before a first sexual encounter with a man. She refused to acknowledge that fiasco at the Center as their first time.

Max set down his wineglass and peered at her. His eyes gleamed and sparkled. "I think I have enough energy to manage a kiss."

She held his gaze, then tipped her chin in invitation. He

leaned over and nibbled at the corner of her mouth. Only their lips touched. They explored slowly. Max etched her upper lip with his tongue. She rimmed his lower lip with hers. He tilted his head slightly, then slanted his lips across hers.

Claire willed her hands to stay in her lap. This already surpassed her expectations. *Let him lead.* She didn't have to lead all the time. Their eyes hadn't closed, as if they didn't want to miss a thing. Claire warmed, realizing this really was their first kiss. They'd skipped this step entirely at the Center. What fools they'd been—he was a delicious kisser. Who would've guessed?

Max broke the kiss and leaned away from her. "You have such soft lips."

Claire smiled and waited.

He reached for her robe. "May I?"

She swallowed and nodded. "You'd better."

He parted her robe only far enough to cradle a breast. She arched slightly into his palm. He caressed it with his thumb. He circled her nipple, careful not to touch it. Her skin heated each time he touched her. With his focus locked on her as if intent on savoring her tiniest response, he covered her nipple with his thumb and pressed inward.

He might as well have pressed some internal starter switch. She mewled her pleasure, encouraging him, wanting more, determined not to hold anything back this time.

He smiled and dipped his head until his mouth covered her breast. Her hands moved as if being released from jail. She rubbed his bald head and playfully planted a wet kiss on it.

His tongue swirled around her nipple, teasing, tantalizing. His teeth nipped at the sensitive peak. He tugged on it. *Cripes.* He was coaxing her to the edge already.

She lifted his chin. He looked like a small boy awaiting his punishment. "That was lovely," she whispered. "But are you certain you don't need more to eat? We still have plenty of fruit."

"Positive," he said hoarsely. "I've developed quite a hunger for you."

She nodded. "Then let's move to the bed. This couch is getting a little cramped."

Grinning broadly, Max rose to his feet and bowed deeply. "At your service, madam. Lead the way."

Claire stood and shrugged off her robe. She was pleased to see his eyes widen as he took in her nakedness. He doffed his robe, and they both smiled at his half-stiff cock.

She led him by the hand to the bed. After pulling back the covers, she patted the bed, and he sat.

"I could use a little more nibbling myself," she said, dropping to her knees.

She encircled a hand around his semihard cock, then quickly took him into her mouth. She'd forgotten how much she loved the feel of a cock growing hard in her mouth and throat. Peeking up at the sight of pure delight on Max's face, she chuckled to herself. And so many women thought they had no power.

Slowly, she began bobbing up and down while Max's fingers combed her hair. She knew he wasn't in any danger of coming. That gave her freedom to explore his full length. She twisted her fingers around its base, then pressed its crown into her puffed out cheek. She took all of him until she could kiss his belly. Gingerly, she hefted his substantial testicles. He'd given up holding her and had leaned back on the bed, propping himself up on his palms. She winked at him, and he gave her a look of awe.

He held out a hand to her. "Why don't you join me on the bed? I want to pleasure you, too."

Reluctantly, she dropped him from her mouth. "Doing that for you gives me a lot of pleasure, too."

"You don't have to stop what you were doing. But I want

to taste you too."

"That can be arranged," she said, crawling onto the bed.

Max helped her straddle his chest until he must've been eye to eye with her pussy. On her hands and knees above him, Claire relished the feel of his hands kneading her buttocks. Deliberately, she wagged her butt without lowering her loins. Max ran a thumb along one side of her pussy lips, and she nearly came unglued. So much for deliberate.

"You win." She chuckled, settling against his solid frame.

Immediately his chin, mouth, and nose glided up and down her folds.

"Ah," she moaned, "welcome to my table. No silverware needed. No napkin provided."

With Max occupied, Claire curled her fingers around his cock. To her delight, he'd softened some. She plopped him into her mouth, not at all displeased that she had to start over.

Only this time was different. Max seemed determined to have his cake and eat it too. She gasped as his tongue slithered down her crevice. He separated her pussy lips and wiggled his tongue side to side as he worked it to the top of her outer lips, then slowly back down.

Somewhere along his life journey he'd learned how to use his tongue. She smiled around his cock. Had she had an indirect hand in his learning? Had Agnes been her proxy, preparing him for this moment? Preparing him for her? This was what Agnes had longed for, but she'd wanted to be present, too.

She squeezed her eyes tight trying to blot out Agnes's image. She didn't want to think about her now.

His tongue eased into her slit, drawing her attention sharply back to the present. She shifted her weight back toward him. He clasped her butt in both hands, then began to work his tongue in her as if it were a drill.

Claire arched her back and wailed softly. How had he

brought her to this point so quickly? She shook her head. Some questions shouldn't be asked. *Enjoy, girl. Just enjoy.*

To her dismay, he withdrew his tongue. "You won't offend me if you want to do your clit."

He pushed two fingers in her, only to quickly replace them with his tongue. She dropped him from her mouth, suddenly unable to concentrate on anything but her mounting climax. She nodded to no one in particular, rested her head on Max's belly, and reached beneath her to stroke her clitoris.

She rode a wave which she recognized as only the beginning. Her shoulders shook. She clenched her teeth, pushing back against him. He swiveled his head from side to side, then up and down. She couldn't keep track of his tongue. Then his tongue pushed hard into her sex and waggled. His lips were inside of hers—no way could he penetrate farther.

Her groans grew into a chorus. Her fingers strummed her clit as if it were a banjo string. She tried to find the right beat— it was just out of reach.

But Max wasn't finished. His wet finger rimmed her anus. "Good God!" she screamed, pressing back and impaling herself on his finger. "I'm coming. Don't stop fucking me. Pussy. Ass. Sweet Jesus."

Claire crashed against his body. She resisted the urge to soar off into her own space to nurture her orgasm. She blinked, trying to breathe, wanting desperately to stay where she was for this first time with Max. He lapped at her juices. She practically purred in response, glad that she hadn't missed this—thanking Melissa for being so insistent.

With effort, she withdrew the hand pinned beneath her weight. Max gently retrieved his finger from her ass but didn't stop feasting on her pussy, swallowing her juices until her flow ceased.

At last he left her and settled back on a pillow. His hands continued to caress her bottom as if he couldn't will them to stop.

They lay still for what must've been minutes, until she shifted her weight off him. She moved to kneel between his legs, then grinned. "Quite acceptable for a first-time practice." She wrapped her fingers around his semihard shaft to let him know she hadn't forgotten him.

"You taste better than anything I could ever imagine." Max gave her a half-smile. "I'm glad I didn't overstuff with cheese and crackers."

Claire nodded, idly working her fingers up and down his rod. His cock responded quite nicely. She bent down and kissed it briefly.

"Do you mind?" she began. "My pussy is quite tuckered at the moment. Is it okay if I finish you in my mouth?" She batted her eyelashes at Max. "I'm afraid I didn't get nearly enough nourishment before we began this practice session."

She hesitated slightly. "And it looks like we're going to need many more practice sessions to get this just right for taping. So we don't have to get it all done at once."

"Be my guest," Max said. "He's been half-mast and full mast so many times, I'm sure he'd love any attention you might give him."

"I hoped as much," Claire murmured, reaching under a pillow to pull out a bottle of lube.

"My, you were prepared."

"I take pride in being prepared for most any contingency I can imagine. Now, I do recall you blowing that young Gretchen away by saying something *like a knowledgeable woman's finger in your asshole massaging your prostate gland never fails.*"

He wet his lips.

Kneeling between his raised knees, Claire winked at him before bending over to spread lube around his anus. She waggled her tongue playfully as he studied her intently. She slowly pressed a finger inward. His groans pleased her. When she met the initial barrier, she waited, then lowered her head to reclaim his cock.

She kept one eye focused on Max, gauging his response as his cock enlarged rapidly. He swallowed slowly as he waited for her next move. She smiled when his anal opening expanded and her finger slid easily inside, then searched for his prostate gland.

"Ah," he moaned. "You're on it. Oh, yeah."

She'd discovered what she was looking for. She stroked his butt until she found a satisfactory rhythm. His howls made it clear there was no need to tarry. She bobbed up and down his entire cock—first slowly, then faster.

His thighs tightened and his bottom squeezed against her finger. "I'm almost there."

Was that a warning or praise? Maybe both. She kept her mouth and finger moving in sync. She thought she felt him expanding in her mouth. It would take practice to know for sure when he was about to come, but he couldn't last much longer. She knew he wasn't trying to hold back. This just took a little more effort than it might've when he was younger.

His fingernails dug into her shoulder. "Holy shit, you got him. Don't slow."

Slow? That was the furthest thing from her mind. She quickened her pace until she must've appeared as a blur to him.

"Yes!" he hollered.

Yes! His hot ejaculate spurted against the roof of her mouth. She swallowed, then swallowed again. Hasn't he complained of diminished semen? What must he have been like as a young man?

Claire stilled her finger, then ever so gently withdrew it. She didn't cease pumping his cock down her throat until it had grown quite soft. She laid her head on his thigh and gazed back at him, his cock still resting in her mouth.

Max looked like he wanted to cry.

His adoration scared the hell out of her. She was very pleased she'd satisfied him, and he had no doubt he'd satisfied her. But she didn't want—or need—adoration. She closed her eyes and drifted off to sleep, still sucking gently on his soft cock.

In the ornate room was a throne fit for royalty. A woman sat on it. It was a redhead. Was that Agnes? Claire tried to peer closer, but the image refused to sharpen.

She shuddered, then tried again. The woman had blond hair. What the . . . That wasn't Agnes. Whose throne was it? She heard steps from behind her. She turned to peer at the source. A bald-headed man had entered the great chamber.

Claire awoke to the tantalizing touch of fingers massaging her shoulders. She cracked an eye open.

"You're going to get very stiff lying there like that," Max cautioned. "Why don't you slide up here where I can hold you?"

She blinked, then slid up next to him. It couldn't hurt to be held, at least for a little while.

He kissed her neck. Her breasts nestled against his chest as his hands continued caressing her back. Her eyelids became heavy. Vaguely, she thought they might not make it to the conference's final banquet.

She smiled against his cheek. They had enough to eat between them.

CHAPTER FIVE

Letting the noise from the jet engines overtake the sounds of nearby passengers, Max closed his eyelids, basking in the bliss of the past twenty-four hours. He turned his head slightly to sniff Claire's hair.

As he expected, she'd claimed the window seat, leaving the aisle for him. He was grateful Harry had bequeathed them the original first-class reservations. The plane had hardly reached its flying altitude when Claire had yawned, murmuring something about needing to catch up on sleep. She'd settled back in her seat and dozed.

That didn't bother him. He didn't need to talk anymore. He welcomed an opportunity for reflection. Only minutes after she'd nodded off, Claire had curled up and laid her head on his shoulder. She'd intertwined her fingers with his, then brought his hand to rest on her bare thigh. She'd hardly twitched a muscle in the last ten minutes.

Max grinned, wondering what the stewardess made of them. Did she think they were an older couple celebrating an anniversary? Was she envious of the warmth she assumed they'd been able to maintain over the decades? Certainly, she'd recognized them as lovers.

But looks could be deceiving and often were. If the stewardess asked, he didn't think he could adequately explain the unique relationship he and Claire were forming. They might not have exactly been adversaries before, but almost. Wary combatants, possibly.

Then Melissa had sprinkled her magical dust on them—

sending them off to California to get things right. Max chuckled softly. They probably hadn't gotten everything right between them yet, but they'd certainly moved beyond fighting.

Claire amazed him. She'd been a delightfully considerate lover. He'd expected her to be interested only in her own pleasure. Quite the contrary, he'd felt guilty at times over how much attention she'd paid to his pleasure. Looking back on it, he doubted either one of them had left her suite unsatisfied. Sated and aching, perhaps, but not unsatisfied.

In the old days, they might've made love all night. That was no longer practical, if it ever had been. They'd awakened before dawn. There'd been little shyness between them as they each did what they had to in the bathroom before returning to the bed.

Then they'd stretched out side-by-side, facing each other, cuddling and kissing for quite a while, until Claire reached between them to stroke his cock to full hardness. She'd smiled softly as she'd draped a leg over him and guided his cock into her sex. They'd rocked back and forth, varying their speed and depth.

Claire came several times. He loved to watch her face when she embraced her orgasms — sometimes she was noisy, sometimes quiet, but always expressive. He didn't think she'd ever faked an orgasm. She probably wouldn't know how.

She hadn't seemed particularly surprised or bothered that he didn't ejaculate. Perhaps she'd taken all he had the night before. It was clear to both of them that he'd climaxed — he just hadn't ejaculated again.

"Maybe next time," she'd whispered in his ear before kissing him again.

They'd gone downstairs for a late breakfast and had spent the remainder of their time taking a last stroll on the beach and packing.

So the stewardess shouldn't be chastised if she mistakenly

considered the two of them lovers. They'd behaved surprisingly comfortably, like old-time lovers. There wasn't a constant need to make love or to explain, as was often the case with younger lovers. It was enough to curl up against each other and touch.

Claire's fingers squeezed his. How would she react to him when they got back to the city? When they were back at the Center?

They'd have to be careful. It was one thing for the stewardess to walk away with a wrong impression. It would be quite different if Melissa did.

The coming days were going to be tough enough without Melissa getting her hopes up about them. He grinned. Would Melissa understand their need for additional practice? He and Claire had agreed that practice should continue. They had hardly begun to explore all the possibilities that might be revealed on a DVD.

They hadn't talked about where or when they'd practice. That could be awkward. Would she insist their practice sessions take place at the Center? He enjoyed being at the Center, but practicing only there seemed a little too clinical. And thus far, their practice hadn't seemed clinical at all.

Would Claire invite him to her place? Should he invite her to his? He winced. He'd never made love with anyone in his bed other than Agnes.

Maybe it was time to buy a new bed.

Sitting around the small table with Claire, Max and Inez, Melissa nearly had to sit on her hands to contain herself. Claire and Max might be well past fifty, but they were behaving like young twenty- or thirty-year-old lovers. She couldn't be more delighted. She peeked at Inez next to her—she, too, had a smile splitting her face. Melissa had invited Inez because it was Inez who did most of the Center's web work, including conducting consumer surveys. Her work had provided a major impetus for moving into creating videos for individuals and couples over forty.

So why were Claire and Max both in denial? And what was this demand that they required more time for practice before working in front of a camera?

She could live with that. She wondered if they could. She rubbed her neck and realized she'd better focus on what Claire was saying. The Center's codirector was certainly trying to appear and sound professional.

"So you see," Claire said, continuing to chatter about the Monterey workshops, "we might want to consider doing a video on couples sharing stories. This could be for couples of any age."

Inez gave Claire a perplexed look. "How is that different from sharing fantasies?"

"It's more personal," Max said, clearing his throat. "I believe sharing stories about real events deepens a bond more than fantasies do." He grinned. "Not that I'd want to give up on fantasies."

Melissa entered a note on her electronic memo pad. "Sounds like something to consider. Maybe the two of you could work on how we could best transfer this kind of storytelling to the set. Our audience isn't going to want to hear stories. They will want to see them acted out. What else did you come back with?"

"I picked up three possible funding sources," Claire pointed out with pride. "Two foundations and one private donor."

"What did you have to do to get the private donor interested?" Melissa always had a hard time with how freely Claire worked with private donors. As far as she knew, Claire had never had an ongoing relationship with any of them, but the woman was hardly hesitant about distributing samples of her work.

She and Claire differed in that matter. Claire could share her body, particularly with women, as easily as shaking hands. But having an ongoing relationship with a woman or a man was quite another matter. Did Max have any idea what he was getting into and how far he'd already progressed?

In the old days, Claire had been referred to as the Center's *Ice Queen*. Not anymore. Melissa knew she'd had more than a small role in cracking Claire's exterior, but it looked like Max was chipping away at it with his own fine-tuned skill. *Never underestimate a man with a Ph.D.* She'd underestimated Harry initially.

Melissa covered her mouth to hide a grin. Maybe her intuition about Max and Claire was right after all. If so, Harry would be shocked. Given the pivotal role Claire had played in getting her and Harry together, if Claire and Max actually stuck, then maybe they should do a video on matchmaking. She peeked at Inez. At least they could do a fantasy piece on the topic.

"Speaking of fantasies," Claire said, switching the subject, "how are things working out with Simone? Is she still fantasizing about you?"

Melissa groaned. "Worse. She's coming on to Harry, too."

"Many of our viewers," Claire chirped, smiling too broadly, "are interested in three-ways. Isn't that right, Inez?"

"That's what the survey data says," Inez said, her eyes sparkling at Melissa.

Melissa warmed, certain that Inez was remembering their first three-way with Harry. That tape had received rave customer reviews.

"Two guys and a girl or two girls and one guy," Inez continued. "They want them both."

Claire tried to conceal a grin. "Of course, I guess you could fire Simone?"

"She's very talented." Melissa rolled her eyes. "Not only with her body, but equally important, with her mind. She's really contributing nicely to the Center's research efforts to tap sexual interests and practices of non-white cultures. Harry thinks she should go back to graduate school."

"Wow!"

Melissa wet her lips and sighed. "She could still work here part-time."

"So you haven't vetoed a three-way?"

"We haven't said yes, either." She shrugged her shoulders, well aware she wasn't very convincing. "We won't do it just because Simone is fantasizing about it." She glanced hesitantly at Inez. "But we do wonder if it might contribute significantly to our work on three-way sex."

Inez's grin widened. "No doubt."

Claire blew her a kiss. "Poor girl, she's wearing you down. From what I've seen, I doubt Inez would tell you it would be a bust with Simone."

"She's good." Inez nodded. "I've worked with her several times now. She's very professional, brings enthusiasm to her role, and can be incredibly creative. I never know quite what to expect from her, but I can always be sure she'll hold up her end of things. I think she loves to work in front of the camera. She likes to be watched, yet she's quite willing to share the scene. I'll work with her as often as I can."

"Everything you say comes through clear on tape." Claire reached over and squeezed Inez's elbow. "Not that a super partner doesn't bring the best out of Simone." She glanced quickly back at Melissa. "I don't know what's holding you back. I'd have a hard time turning that girl down."

"Maybe." Melissa chuckled to herself, wondering how many girls Claire had turned down in her lifetime. "You and Max may each have the opportunity to work with her."

Melissa grinned as Claire and Max sat straighter. Claire smacked her lips.

Max looked disbelieving. "Why?" Max asked.

"We want to do a tape highlighting younger women and older men and another with younger women and older women."

"Why not younger guys and older women?" Claire asked, sharply.

"We should do that, too. And of course with Simone, as well as with Inez, we present inter-racial diversity, which is important." The backlog of possible work started to boggle her mind.

They needed more follow-up fantasy videos. She'd been surprised to learn that fantasies remained among their best sellers. Customers reported using them as part of foreplay. Some turned the tapes off during lovemaking while others let the tapes run, imagining they were part of an orgy. Still others said they left the tape running to pretend they themselves were being watched. Melissa made a mental note to discuss a single video devoted to voyeurism—watching and being watched—at another time.

"How about men?" Claire asked. "We shouldn't have just women of color."

"Harry's working on it. He's interviewing a couple candidates next week." Melissa chuckled. "Simone tried to get her boyfriend to come in. Apparently, she hadn't told him about her change of jobs. When she asked him, he split."

"Guess she's finding out this kind of work isn't for everyone," Claire responded. "Sounds like she chose her work over her boyfriend. Simone does seem quite committed to the mission of the Center." Claire smirked. "Or at least to getting into your panties."

"I hardly think working with me on camera once or twice would merit dumping a lover."

The corner of Claire's mouth turned up. "Depends on the lover, I suppose."

Melissa steepled her fingers. "So, how long do you think you two will need to practice before working on camera?"

Max and Claire shrugged their shoulders in unison.

Melissa chuckled. "Let me know when you're ready. In the meantime, we all have plenty to do." She glanced at Inez. "Can you stay a couple minutes? I have another idea to discuss with you."

"Sure," Inez said as Max and Claire rose to make their retreat.

When the office door closed behind Max and Claire, Inez started to giggle, and Melissa quickly joined in.

"Can you believe it?" Inez stammered through laughs. "The two of them are getting it on outside the Center. Amazing. Who would've ever thought they'd be a pair?"

"Me," Melissa confessed, covering her mouth. "But I doubt they see that yet." She beamed. "But they are, aren't they?"

"He looked quite protective of Claire. And she never once berated him. I thought after the way she railed at him on set that first time, there wouldn't be a second time." Inez's mouth curved into a smile. "But I guess they're busy smoothing out their rough edges. Anything for the good of the Center."

"If that's what it takes to convince them to spend time together, so be it. Now then." Melissa hesitated before forging ahead. "Some new toys have come in we need to test for our customers."

Inez arched an eyebrow.

"We? You mean me and Simone."

Melissa shook her head. "You and me."

"We've only been together twice since you married. I thought you didn't want to work on camera anymore." Inez tilted her head to the side. "This has to do with Simone, doesn't it?"

"I don't want her to think she's any more special than any of the rest of us. We've been together many times, Inez." Melissa gave Inez a half-smile. "And I have missed working with you. But you're right, I don't want Simone to think her position is any more important here than anyone else's—or less important, for that matter."

Inez broke into a grin. "Sounds like you've decided to work with her."

"Secretly?"

Inez nodded.

"I've been envious of the two of you." She swallowed. "But I haven't actually decided. Harry and I are still sorting out the pluses and minus." She shrugged, not knowing what else to say. "Anyway, a couple of double dildoes arrived that I thought we might test out together on camera."

"Sounds like fun. And you expect Simone to watch?"

"It won't be a closed set."

Inez giggled.

"I'll be delighted to work with you again." She reached out and interlaced her fingers with Melissa's, then brought their joined hands to her lips. "I've always known you could be devious, even in your cheerleading ways. You know if Simone watches us testing those toys, she's going to be after you like a laser beam. She won't be satisfied until she has her face buried in your pussy."

Melissa felt her cheeks heat up. "I think you're right." She wet her lips. "I hope so."

"Do you always eat like a bird?"

Claire didn't crack a smile. She used her fork to separate another flake of her tuna niçoise. Deliberately, she snagged a small bite and lifted it to her mouth. She glanced around the early dinner crowd and chewed thoroughly, wondering briefly how many patrons were meeting for business and how many were meeting with other thoughts on their minds. She smiled at two women at a nearby table holding hands while sharing a flambeed flan.

Claire looked back at Max. "If you approve of this body as much as you claim, then you'd better appreciate how I eat. I'm not telling you what to eat."

"I'm sorry," he quickly said. "I wasn't putting you down. It's just that I've never known anyone so disciplined about eating."

"I enjoy my food. I just avoid sugars and saturated fats as much as possible."

"You rarely eat dessert."

"Perhaps I prefer a different sort of dessert." She slid her bare foot up the inside of his leg.

"Damn." Max coughed, then glanced quickly around the small restaurant.

Claire smiled. It wasn't exactly like anyone was paying attention, and with the long white tablecloths nearly touching the floor, no one could see what she was doing. What would Max do if she slipped under the table to give him some head? She chuckled. He might not survive, and she didn't need that on her conscience.

"What's so funny?" Max asked suspiciously.

"Just pondering dessert. I guess I can wait until later. We haven't practiced for more than forty-eight hours. I assume you're ready."

"I've been ready since the plane landed. So where are we going to practice?"

"I noticed you didn't say your place or mine." She reached behind her, retying her ponytail. "I've given that a lot of thought. The Center is too damn sterile. Sex in front of a camera is one thing. Spontaneous sex there is another, but planned practice"—she scrunched her mouth—"feels rather sterile, too. I don't want to go to a hotel. I've had enough hotels for a while."

Claire studied his neutral features carefully. He wasn't about to bail her out on this one. "Oh, okay. You can come over to my place."

His face immediately lit up in a broad smile.

"But I don't want you to get the wrong idea. You are not sleeping over." She scowled—they'd fallen asleep so easily after making love in Monterey. "And if we should fall asleep after having sex and not wake up till the morning, you didn't sleep over. We just fell asleep," she added lamely.

"Somehow, I may have missed something in the translation, but I'm fine with practicing at your place."

"I didn't think you'd complain. And I don't care how often we might inadvertently fall asleep, you will not move any clothes into my condo. Understood?"

"Understood," he responded dryly. "You seem to be making a lot out of practice sessions."

"I'd rather be clear upfront. Remember, I plan for all contingencies."

"Right. You must live up to your name—Clairvoyant."

She couldn't hold back a chuckle. "I don't recall anyone ever making that connection. So how long do you think it will take Simone to get into Melissa's panties?"

"Not long, I'd predict," Max responded. "I wonder if Melissa knew how often she was wetting her lips when she talked about Simone."

"So you noticed, too."

"Uh, huh. I expect we both know that's a sure sign Melissa is turning on to the idea of hooking up with the Center's newest hire."

"You sure do pay attention to women." She purposely wet her lips. "I like that. Why don't we pay the bill and get out of here? I think I'd like you paying a little more attention to me.

I wouldn't want to dry up from lack of practice."

He winked at her, then brought her hand to his lips. "There is definitely something to that old adage *use it or lose it.*"

"Can you move your thumb about half an inch to the right and a half-inch up?"

Max complied with Claire's request, then ground his thumb into her well-oiled shoulder blade.

"God, that's heavenly," she moaned. "You're an artist at massage." She rotated her neck, then arched her back against his pressure.

Max smiled. He straddled her naked form comfortably, keeping most of his weight off of her. His limp cock lay against the small of her back. There was no need for him to be ready until needed.

Max leaned over and kissed Claire's nape, then nibbled on her ear. He'd oiled her entire backside. He was touched by how she was surrendering to his fingers. He'd rarely seen her so unguarded. "You're not going to fall asleep before practice begins, are you?"

Claire sighed. "I'm trying not to. But it is tempting."

He wiggled his soft cock against her back.

"But then he's even more tempting."

He lifted her ponytail. "May I untie it?"

"Of course."

Max unknotted the tie, then ran his fingers through her loose hair. "Your hair is so silky. I like it long. I know you recently grew it out some – did you ever wear it even longer? He felt her chuckling beneath him.

"In my college days, it fell about halfway down my back. During my Woodstock period, it fell below my ass."

"Jesus," he murmured. "You must've been a beauty then – of course, you still are."

"That was a very smooth save, Max," Claire said, twisting

under him until she faced him. Thankfully, she was smiling. "So, are you going to oil my front?"

He nodded, then squirted oil across her chest and belly and began to rub it into her pores. He wasn't trying to be erotic, but then, when skin touched skin, how could one not be?

Claire closed her eyes as Max liberally applied oil across her breasts.

"That's nice. I used to tease my lovers with my long hair. I could hide from them behind a wave of hair. You might be surprised how sensual hair can be when it's wrapped around a cock."

He tried not to focus on her words too much. He splayed a hand under each breast, then worked his way down her abs until his palms rested on her pelvis.

"Cripes!" She moaned. "Are you toying with me?"

"Not at all." He squirted oil on her thighs, legs and calves. After fitting his fingers and thumbs over her hips, he dragged them the length of her lower torso. Her butt rose up off the bed in response, causing him to smile. He knelt back and peeked at her face. Her eyes were wide open.

"Didn't you forget something?"

He shook his head, then grinned before bending at the waist to draw a thumb up either side of her pussy.

"Oh wow! I guess you didn't forget."

"Patience," he murmured, scraping a finger the length of her clit, which had swollen considerably. "You want to come now?"

Claire bit her lip. "A little one might be nice."

"Thought it might. Though I doubt a little one is in your repertoire."

He held her gaze as he ran a thumb and finger along the length of her clit. She gasped. With his eyes, he commanded her to come while he stroked her clit leisurely over and over.

"Damn, you're jerking me off." She twisted her head to the

side, breaking their eye contact. "Never . . ." she mumbled. "Where did you learn . . ."

Her hips bucked against him, but he did nothing to help her find her release. He didn't have to. He knew it and she knew it.

He didn't stop methodically stroking her clitoris until she slapped his hand and rolled away from him. He waited, pleased that he'd surprised her.

Two or three minutes passed before she turned back to face him. Still flushed, she sighed. "You're more inventive than I expected. Now, it's your turn."

In short order, he was on his stomach sucking in air as she squirted oil across his shoulders and over his back. She massaged the oil in evenly—it was indeed his turn not to doze. Oil began dripping down the crease of his bottom, bringing him completely alert.

"Have I told you you've got a nice tight ass?" Claire dragged a finger up and down the crease between his buttocks.

"I believe you have." He felt her finger rim his anus. He groaned. Her lips brushed across his buttocks.

"Later, maybe," she whispered. "On your knees, please."

He moved to get on his hands and knees.

"Knees only."

Max did as Claire requested, raising his bottom in the air. He sighed when she cradled his balls and slid oily hands along the length of his cock. He smiled. *Inventive* and *creative* described her quite aptly. She'd probably always keep him guessing.

Her palm suddenly smacked his butt, hard.

"Damn!" He jerked. "What the hell?"

It wasn't that she'd hurt him, but she sure as hell had surprised him.

"Aren't you aroused by being spanked?" she asked

teasingly.

"Aroused?"

"That's right. It does wonders for me. The purpose is not to injure or act out in anger, but to arouse, to love. And," she admitted, "to tease. And you were a naughty boy bringing me off by only fondling my clit. Would you like me to show you what I mean?"

He closed his eyes and groaned. It was clear this had a lot to do with trust. He nodded. "Go ahead."

"I'll just use my hand this time."

He nodded. He saw no need yet to tell her there wouldn't be a next time.

"The technique is to be rhythmic. Again, there is no desire to cause pain, only to stimulate."

Her hand connected with his butt again. Then again. And again. Each smack seemed quite measured. He couldn't ignore the fact that his cock was getting harder than it had in recent memory. "Now we'll try the other cheek," she said, slapping his opposite cheek. "Is this okay for you? Not too hard?"

He smacked his lips, then shook his head. "You could probably be a little firmer, if you want to."

Her laughter warmed his ears. "You are a quick study."

She smacked his cheek harder, planted a quick kiss on it, then smacked it again. Her fingers coiled around his cock and slithered up its length.

Was she going to jerk him off?

"Roll onto your back, please."

He turned over, breathing easier. At least in this position, he could see what she was up to.

She clutched his cock and grinned triumphantly.

"I would really like you to spank me, too, but I think we should take advantage of this massive hard cock. Don't you?"

He nodded, then stared at himself in her hands. He

blinked. Were his eyes playing tricks on him? He'd swear he'd grown an inch. Surely that wasn't because she'd surprised him with the spanking.

She moved into position to straddle him and beamed at him. "I'm going to take him for a ride, if you don't mind."

"Be my guest. You seem to have the keys."

As soon as the tip of his cock penetrated her heat, he closed his eyelids, then blinked them open quickly to watch his cock disappear farther into her interior.

She slowly dropped to his hips and squirmed, settling him in place. "He fills me very nicely. Here we go." She rocked up and down on her knees very slowly. She pulled on her nipples. Without stopping, she asked, "Do you like what you see?"

"You're a beautiful sight."

"This is so much fun." Claire grinned. "I may not give you your cock back."

"He's found a happy home."

She nodded. "Let's see what we can manage here. Tuck up under me a little more. That's right." She leaned back a bit, reached behind him, and smiled broadly. "Yes, I can reach your asshole."

Claire didn't really have to tell him that. He gritted his teeth as she pushed a finger partway in. He doubted she'd be able to reach all the way, but that might not be necessary. His cock was throbbing with anticipation. His hips began to buck, wanting to take over.

"Let me," Claire said. "You'll dislodge me from your ass."

He relaxed.

Her features tensed and she leaned farther back, changing the angle of her pussy's grip on his cock. Then she began laughing. "There," she said, sliding her finger all the way into his ass.

"Christ," he muttered as she stroked his prostate gland.

"He's getting bigger still," she said, sounding more than a little awed. "He's swelling."

He'd never had a woman do a play-by-play like this before.

"Come for me, Max," she pleaded. "You're almost there." He nodded. His chin fell to his chest. She never slowed.

"Holy shit, you've got him!" he howled, feeling the beginning of his eruption somewhere between her finger and her pussy. "Don't stop." He shuddered and quaked. His heart pounded in his chest.

She never let up until he waved at her and shook his head. He wasn't able to form a single word. She stilled immediately. He gave her credit for recognizing the thin line between pleasure and pain. She withdrew her finger from his bottom and leaned over, then covered his eyelids and cheeks with kisses.

He wasn't aware that tears had slid down his cheeks, but he wasn't going to apologize for them, and he didn't think she'd want him to. This was the first time he'd come inside her. That was worth a few tears—and any other form of celebration they might think of.

When she raised her head, he saw that her eyes, too, were misty. She kissed his lips, dropped him from her pussy and gave him a wobbly smile. "That was incredibly special."

"Thank you," he mumbled. "You were spectacular."

"Nonsense. It took both of us." Her voice trembled. "It always does. It always will." She kissed his neck, then settled on his chest.

Max loved the crush of her warm breasts. He raked his fingers through her hair and let her doze. For a woman only interested in the short term, she sure used the word *always* a lot. He wasn't sure what he thought about that. He might have to think about it later. For now, he couldn't imagine anything more he wanted to do than hold Claire.

He closed his eyes and grinned. It looked like they were going to *inadvertently* fall asleep. He didn't have the strength left to get down to her garage, climb into his car, and drive back up the river to Hastings on Hudson. He wiggled a little to settle in more comfortably. He stroked her smooth back lightly. Yes, sleeping over or not, this was much better than driving back to his place.

CHAPTER SIX

"You sure believe in vitamins."

Claire glanced up to see Max frowning from across the kitchen island while she counted out her morning pills. "I believe in what works for me. I take it you don't have a vitamin and supplement regimen."

He shook his head. "Can't say I know much about them. I don't like pills."

She shrugged. "I'm not thrilled with pills either, but I do have faith in these. They help with everything from aching joints to improving my sexual lubrication."

"Oh."

She loved catching Max in one of his embarrassed moments. Obviously, he wasn't accustomed to discussing female problems. "I do believe you've benefited from my attention to lubrication."

He nodded, then glanced around her kitchen. His gaze settled on an old black-and-white photo of her and Phoebe standing next to their bicycles. "So do you still bike ride?"

She laughed softly. "Not as much as I'd like. It takes a fair amount of effort to get to the bike trails. And New York City drivers and pedestrians aren't noted for keeping an eye out for cyclists. How about you? Do you ride?"

"I used to. I have miles and miles of bike trails nearby. It's something I should probably get back into. I can't think of an easier way to get back in shape."

"You don't seem to be badly out of shape." She gave him a curious look. "So, do I have anything to do with this renewed desire of yours to get into shape?"

He grinned and sipped the coffee she'd made. "You bet. This video Melissa wants us to work on isn't going to be made in a day."

Claire nodded her agreement. "And if I know Melissa, she's not going to be satisfied with just marketing a single DVD targeted at seniors. We'll have to be prepared to work on more than one." She cleared her throat. "Speaking of Melissa, I don't want her interfering in my personal life."

Max sat straighter. "Meaning us?"

"Exactly."

"Melissa does seem to suffer from romantic fantasy."

"Maybe that's because she couldn't have fantasized about her own life a year or two ago. Be that as it may . . ." Claire stood and carried their dishes to the sink. "I don't want her fantasizing about us. Neither of us is. So why should she?"

Max remained silent.

"I think, in order to keep our personal lives separate, we should come up with something to do to begin a video session. Her imagination might not get the best of her if she sees us actually working with the camera on."

"You may have a point." Max folded his arms across his chest. "What about practice? Does this mean you don't want to practice anymore?"

Claire gave him a half-smile, then walked over to stand behind him. She kissed his bald head slowly, then more urgently.

He relaxed back against her breasts.

She slid a hand down his chest until she could squeeze his soft arousal through his trousers. "Does this answer your question?"

"I hope so. Perhaps you could be a little clearer."

She chuckled against his ear and unzipped her smock, then held a breast in each hand and slid them across his bald pate.

"Incredible," he moaned.

She tucked her breasts back under the smock and zipped it up. "There's not enough time now," she said, walking around the island. "But we haven't begun to practice everything we need to. I haven't seriously considered how to love that bald head of yours. You haven't spanked me. There is so much more we can do that may help our viewers." She winked at him. "You haven't even been in my ass yet—well," she smirked, "with your cock. Have you ever had a woman fuck your ass? Really fuck it."

Shades of red worked up his neck to the top of his head as he considered what she meant by that question. If he couldn't figure that out, she wasn't about to explain it. He managed to waggle his chin from side to side.

"The way you respond to my finger, I believe you would enjoy my strap-on."

"Would you like to practice at my place?"

Claire tipped her head back and laughed, but immediately sobered. Max made her laugh a lot. "Sure," she said at last. "I would like to see where you live."

"We might try some bike riding. We can't spend all our time in bed."

Somehow, bike riding sounded more intimate than she was ready for, but she didn't want to cause the hopeful smile that had formed on Max's lips to disappear. "I guess we could rent a bike. It would take a lot to get my bike out to your place."

"I could get a bike rack."

"For your convertible?"

"Why not? It'll work. Why don't you plan on spending the weekend at my house?"

He must've witnessed the consternation coursing through her body.

"If you want to come back at any time, trust me, I'll bring

you back."

She nodded. "There's an excellent train system. I think I'd like that. But, Max, don't get the wrong impression. We are only practicing."

"Absolutely."

"I do think I have to relent on one aspect of this practice agreement."

"What's that?"

"Each of us should feel free to bring along a duffel bag with a change of clothes and necessary toiletries." She stuck her tongue out at him. "Your clothes do smell a little ripe this morning."

"Sorry."

"Don't be. It was my misjudgment. Now, if you don't mind, I have to get ready for work. I still have a day job. Are you dropping by the Center today?"

"No, I have a lot of errands to catch up on." He gave her an odd look. "And with you coming for the weekend, I want to make a few improvements around the place."

"Don't go overboard on my account."

"Claire, I know I shouldn't ask." Max stood as if prepared to run. "But did Agnes sleep in your bed?"

Claire crossed her arms under her breasts. "I was hoping you wouldn't ask, but I won't lie to you," she said, perhaps too sharply. "Yes, several times. We watched the reflections of us making love in my bedroom mirrors just as you and I did this morning. Does that bother you?"

He shook his head. "Surprisingly, no. It's actually a relief to know. Maybe a little comforting, knowing you shared that kind of intimacy."

"Do you think Agnes is always going to be in the middle of our practice?"

Max slid off the stool to stand before her. "I admit Agnes was in the middle at first. I think she's taken a seat on the sidelines now." His mouth crinkled into a small smile. "Is it okay if she watches?"

Claire smiled back at him, knowing he was making a huge effort to be honest with her. "I like to be watched. And I expect Agnes has paid the price of admission to both of us."

Max took her roughly into his arms. His hands roved over her back and grabbed her butt. "Damn, you are something else," he said, grinding her crotch against his.

She hadn't seen this urgent, demanding side of him. She wished she didn't have an appointment to get to. Max turned them around until her butt rested against the island. Had he taken her silence to mean she had time for him?

He didn't ask, nor did he bother with unzipping her smock. He slid his hands up her bare thighs, pushing the smock upward. Her breathing quickened. His face broke into a broad smile when he discovered she wore no panties. Had he expected otherwise?

He cupped her mound with unaccustomed urgency. She gasped for breath as he wedged a finger between her folds to probe her sex. He locked his focus on her eyes, then sawed his finger back and forth, challenging her to say *no*. A second finger curled into her. She whimpered. Maybe she did have time for a little one. Did Max have a plan, or was he operating on pure adrenaline and lust? She suspected the latter. His spontaneity propelled her to another plateau. Was he going to lay her back on the island and have her as a second breakfast?

Her eyes widened at the sight of him fumbling with his belt. His trousers fell down around his legs. He pushed his briefs down. His nostrils flared. Without even stepping out of his trousers, he grabbed his hard cock and guided it to her entrance. He stalled partway in, then grunted and shook his head. His hips rotated back and finally drove forward, impaling her to the hilt.

Her little scream only added fuel to his fire. Claire tried to squirm to get a better fit, but Max wasn't waiting for her or himself. She leaned back into the island and managed to spread her legs farther apart. His eyes remained open, but she doubted he saw her through his glaze.

"Don't deny me," he commanded.

She shook her head wildly. "Take me. Have your way with me. Fuck me!"

A giggle lodged in her throat as he threw back his head and pounded into her over and over. She placed a hand over his heart. It was thudding rapidly. To her amazement, she sensed his cock thickening. She'd taken care of him earlier upstairs. Hadn't she?

She found enough support from the island to wrap her legs around his butt. His hands moved to support her. His pace did not slow.

"Hurry," she said, encouraging him. "Fill me, Max. Don't leave me empty. Fuck me, Max. Go for it!"

His mouth fell ajar. His eyes widened. He howled her name until she felt him spilling into her. She hugged him tight to keep them both from falling. He huffed and puffed, gasping for air. It took a while, but she eventually felt his heartbeat slowing on her breast. She patted his butt, then lowered her feet to the floor.

"Where did all of that come from?" she whispered.

He shook his head. "Hope I didn't hurt you."

"Never. You can take me like a wild man any time." She chuckled. "Too bad we don't have that recorded."

Without pulling out of her, Max leaned back to peck at her nose.

Was that pride in his eyes?

"You might be better than a daily vitamin for me. I haven't come this frequently for some time." Max glanced at the clock, then unceremoniously withdrew his cock.

Claire immediately felt bereft.

"I've made you late," he said apologetically.

"No," she said, smoothing out her smock. "You've made my day. And for your information, we never did it on the island."

"Huh?"

"Agnes and I."

His mouth curved into a smile. "Good."

"You may want to recover a little more before you head back, but I really do need to get to work. I don't want to have to explain to Melissa why I'm late."

"Just tell her we were practicing."

Claire gave him a quirky smile. "Somehow that didn't feel like practice."

She quickly left the kitchen before he had a chance to recover. On her way out of the condo, Claire remembered she wouldn't be able to talk to Melissa right away. Melissa had other plans. She grinned, then scrunched her shoulders waiting for a taxi.

Melissa never wanted to be interrupted before a taping. She cherished the time for centering.

Claire smiled broadly at the doorman holding the taxi door for her. This was a morning she didn't want to miss. She settled back into the seat and touched up her lipstick.

Melissa hadn't worked with Inez for nearly a year. Testing toys was how the two of them started when Melissa first came onboard at the Center. Claire had invited the two of them to demonstrate and test vibrators as a way of familiarizing Melissa with the demands of working before a camera. She'd been a quick learner, and she and Inez had begun working together often after that. It had been the two of them who'd eventually forced Harry to finally set aside the Center's long-standing non-fraternization policy regarding outside sexual contact among staff members.

Glowing from her tryst with Max and the anticipation of

watching Melissa and Inez, Claire did her best to mentally encourage the traffic to move faster. She grinned at nothing.

Simone was going to be smoked if she came by for the morning's taping session. Melissa had told Claire she'd made a special point of inviting Simone. Unless the set was going to be closed for some reason, staff often showed up to support one another, even if they weren't onstage. Claire didn't doubt Melissa's intent for a moment. She was putting Simone in her place.

Claire put together the fare for the cabbie. Melissa was also probably showing off a little, strutting her stuff. Simone had never seen Melissa work in the flesh—maybe on tape, but not in the raw. Melissa was probably making clear to everyone at the Center except Simone that she was about ready to take on their newest staff member. Claire set her lips. She hoped she wasn't going to be out sick when that day occurred, or at the dentist, or some other place. She definitely wanted to watch those two kittens tangle.

Watching those two go at it for the first time should be worth the price of a Super Bowl ticket. That wouldn't happen today. This morning's work was only a prelude. By the time Melissa and Inez were finished, Simone might explode with desire.

Soon, Simone would get her wish. She'd have birthday and Christmas rolled up into one and most likely Fourth of July to boot. Simone might still have her doubts, but Melissa was preparing her for a feast she'd never forget. Melissa was a virtuoso at hosting a feast of the senses.

Feeling a little more nervous on camera than she'd expected, Melissa held the mike steady in one hand, then smiled.

"Hi," she said to the viewing audience. She glanced quickly at Inez on the stool next to her in a matching white robe, then back to the camera. "As you can see, Inez and I are ready to introduce you to another form of play that you might want to try with your partner or partners."

She held up a slender eighteen-inch-long object, then laughed as it flopped in her hand.

"This is commonly called a double dong. Its name does little to describe the kind of pleasure two people can derive from it." She tilted her head to the side and flexed the object into a u-shape. "Actually, one person can come up with a number of ways to enjoy this toy alone." She winked at Inez. "Hard is not always better.

"So, Inez, how are you doing this morning?" she asked coquettishly. "Are you ready for some play?"

"I am." Inez beamed at her. "We haven't worked together for nearly a year, so I'm quite excited at being together again."

"Neither one of us works in front of the camera very much anymore." Melissa pouted at the camera. "Our loss. Our other responsibilities at the Center keep us both very busy. But part of the message of this session is—take a break from your routines now and then to play a little. We don't expect you to incorporate a double dong in your sexual lives on a regular basis, but sometimes, even sex becomes too serious. Lighten up—don't count orgasms—you don't even have to climax to enjoy sex—be playful." She winked at the camera. "Of course, an orgasm now and then adds a little spice.

"Okay, when you next see us, we will be out of these robes and all the appropriate orifices will be well lubed. We hope you enjoy the tape, and even more importantly, we hope you enjoy your own play."

Slouched back on several pillows, Melissa eyed Inez propped up against the pillows opposite her. They faced each other with Melissa's legs draped over Inez's, their loins almost touching. Melissa grinned — Inez's vulva was already open for play. "You ready to begin?"

Inez wet her lips. "Whenever you are."

Melissa turned to look at the camera. "Hi again. As you can see, Inez and I are in place and ready to play. You should know that off-camera, we've both used plenty of lube, and we've each used a vibrator to hone that edge that makes playing with the double dong more pleasurable.

"So, here we go. This is a very flexible dong. Some are quite stiff." Melissa wet first one end of the dong with her mouth, then the other. "Some are fatter than this one. This dong is large enough to give pleasure and small enough to fit most anywhere." She arched an eyebrow, then handed one end to Inez. "You may want to try several different shapes and sizes to find out what you like best. Some have rough surfaces. Some are shaped like the head of a cock." She shrugged. "Personally, while I enjoy this, I'm not about to mistake a dong for a real cock."

"Enough talking," Inez said, widening her legs and rubbing her end of the dong up and down her slit.

"You're right." Melissa giggled. "More action and less talk."

She dragged her end of the dong along her pussy and wiggled it from side to side. One of the cameramen had moved to hover above them, enabling the viewer to have a close-up view as well as the wide-angle shots available from the other camera. Later, they'd merge the tapes with more voice-overs when necessary.

Melissa nodded at Inez, then tilted her pelvis as she pushed the dong into her vagina. Inez mirrored her action. Melissa appreciated the view of the flexible toy disappearing inside Inez. Inez's eyes rolled as she took more of it, then began rocking against it with one hand on the dong to keep it from bending.

Melissa did the same. She bucked against the object and smiled at Inez. They glided the dong in and out of their bodies with alternate strokes. Melissa reached her free hand out to Inez, who grabbed it with her free hand. They pulled each other up until they sat facing each other. They switched hands so each was controlling the strokes of the dong going in and out of the other.

Smiling, Melissa puffed air from her mouth. This was the part she liked best — each partner had to read the wants and desires of the other partner. Inez's panting turned to whimpers. Melissa increased the pace of the dong. She knew Inez well. Those whimpers would turn into wails, then Inez would crash.

"Almost," Inez managed. Her hand stopped moving as she concentrated on the buildup within her body.

"Enjoy." Melissa skimmed her free hand across Inez's clit.

Inez broke into laugher and her wails filled the set as she climaxed. She reached out to hug Melissa, ignoring the dong entirely.

Melissa kissed her eyelids, her nose. Their mouths collided with tongues searching, tasting. Melissa relished Inez's familiar taste, a taste she'd not experienced for far too long.

After Inez stopped shuddering, Melissa pulled away and spoke to the camera. "As you can see, serious orgasms can result from play. Guys, you don't have to be left out of double dong play. We'll demonstrate one possibility in a minute, but actually, you might want to try what you just witnessed. This particular dong is designed for vaginal and anal play. Some guys like to share a dong with their female partner." She arched an eyebrow at the camera. "You might both be in a position to jerk the guy off. That can be fun. I guarantee it."

"Next." Melissa grinned at the camera after she'd placed a

couple of pillows under her lower back. "Yes, we took a little break, but we're ready to go again. Inez is going to demonstrate how to use a flexible double dong to pleasure her partner. Again, guys, you should be able to easily imagine yourselves playing Inez's role. Go ahead, Inez."

Inez scooted into position, kneeling down beside her. She slid one end of the dong between Melissa's pussy folds. Melissa flexed her pelvis encouraging Inez, and Inez didn't disappoint.

"Ah," Melissa moaned as the end of the dong passed into her.

She shuddered, then clamped down on it.

Inez paused, then wet the other end of the dong.

Melissa swallowed and shot a quick smile at the camera. She blinked. She'd totally forgotten Simone Stone. But there the girl stood beside the cameraman, as if she were directing the angle of the shots. Simone's dark nipples clearly strained against the fabric of her white blouse. When their gazes connected, Simone blew her a kiss.

Melissa turned her head back to watch Inez just as the other end of the dong banged against the crease of her buttocks. She couldn't contain a flinch when the toy pressed against her anus.

Inez hesitated. "You okay?"

"I'm fine. Take it slow and easy."

Inez nodded, then began to feed the object into Melissa's butt.

Melissa swallowed and held up her hand for Inez to wait. Looking toward the camera, Melissa said, "As with any anal play, we want to go slow until your partner opens for you."

Melissa blinked when she noticed Simone standing near the cameraman giving her an obscene gesture. Then she nearly giggled — that was hardly an obscene gesture. Simone was rotating her finger as if she were opening her ass for her. *Son of a bitch.*

Nodding again at Inez, Melissa grinned. "I'm ready."

The dong pushed inward until Melissa was full. "Nice," she murmured.

She brought her knees to her chest and hugged them, giving Inez free access and the audience a view to see that they weren't faking anything and that she wasn't in pain.

"You may want to practice before being this vigorous. Okay," she said to Inez. "Take me to heaven."

Soon, Melissa lost track of whether her vagina was fuller than her asshole. Inez had both ends working their magic. Melissa couldn't breathe fast enough. Her heart beat too rapidly. Inez was methodical with the dong, fucking her steadily without changing pace. It was the rhythmic thrust first in one orifice, then the other that had driven her to the edge, until she couldn't tell what was happening other than she was on the verge of imploding.

Melissa clutched her knees tighter, her head lolling from side to side. The camera blurred. Simone blurred. Inez blurred.

"Good God, I'm soaring!" she cried out. "Stop. Let me go. So good. So free."

Vaguely, she became aware of the dong slipping first from her ass, then from her pussy. She remembered what they were doing and struggled to focus on the camera. She gave the camera a lopsided grin, then made out Simone giving her a high five sign. Still kneeling beside her, Inez grinned broadly.

Melissa wet her lips to speak. How had they gotten so dry? She blinked, then sighed. "As I said," she barely managed to whisper, "play can produce some serious orgasms. I've got to rest. See you later."

She gave the camera what had become her signature wave of the fingers and rolled away from it to curl into a ball. Everyone would have to wait—even the Simones of the world. She had the aftershocks of a splendid orgasm to savor.

Later that afternoon, Claire stepped into Melissa's office grinning and shaking her head. "Woman, you have not lost your touch." She took a seat on the couch without waiting to be invited. "We need to get you in front of the camera more often. Your voice-overs are always good, but never better than when you are actually on set telling the viewer what's happening for you. You draw us all into the scene like we're no longer observing."

"Umm, glad you liked the performance." Melissa smiled easily. Her body still radiated a pleasant afterglow from the morning's work session. "Hope the viewers will enjoy it half as much as I did."

"I was surprised," Claire flashed an eyebrow, "that Simone didn't jump in and try joining you two."

"She did seem enthralled. So are you and Max ready to go on set?" A giggle escaped Melissa's lips. "Or do we have to wait for perfection?"

"That's the other reason I came by." Claire crossed her long legs at the knee and smoothed out her skirt. "We're ready. Well, at least as ready as we'll probably ever be."

"That's excellent news. The sooner we get started on shooting with you and Max, the sooner we can consider other possibilities."

"Other possibilities?"

Melissa shrugged nonchalantly. "I doubt we'll be able to handle all the potential topics for aging couples in one tape. Besides, the Center makes more money if we spread themes over multiple tapes. Series bring back customers. And as you know, that's what's financially best for us."

"I do the books. I'm well aware of that, but I'm not sure Max is," Claire hedged. "Maybe he's only committed to one tape. After all, he only works for us part-time. Maybe we won't be that good in front of the camera. Screwing in front of the camera isn't the same as screwing in your own bed."

"I'm sure you two will do fine. Each of you has contributed to other tapes with different partners. I'm looking forward to seeing and editing your work." Melissa batted her eyelashes. "I'll wager you'll be able to get Max to commit to more than one release."

"Don't count on it. Max has a mind of his own. When he doesn't want to do something, he doesn't." Claire swallowed, then looked suddenly vulnerable. "And when he does want something, he goes after it."

Melissa withheld a grin. She'd love to know what that slight hitch in Claire's voice was about, but decided it was best not to pry — too much.

"So you and Max are progressing well?"

Claire stood and stretched. "I'll let you know what we want to do for the initial taping so you can work on your intro and voice-overs."

"Thanks," Melissa said, coming around to hug Claire. So Claire wasn't going to answer her question. "Thanks for taking some risks for the Center."

Claire nodded, her eyes narrowing. "Some risks may be too great."

"Are you okay?" Melissa squeezed Claire's shoulder. "You seem a little stiff this afternoon."

Claire gave her an indecipherable glare. "Mind your own business, girl."

"Oh." Melissa smirked. "I'd forgotten how much of a wallop Max can pack."

"Bye." Claire opened the door, then grinned over her shoulder. "This ought to keep you out of my hair for a while. Come on in, Simone. I was just leaving."

Melissa groaned inwardly as the ever-bubbly Simone slipped by Claire and entered. After her morning, she didn't have the energy to banter with Simone. How much longer could she fence with her before either firing her or caving in to her own desire?

"Have a seat, Simone." Melissa watched cautiously as Simone sat down across from her on the couch, then tugged on her short skirt. Given the smirk on Simone's face, Melissa doubted the girl wore panties. That hardly set her apart here at the Center. "Simone, did you have something on your mind?"

Simone didn't answer right away. Instead, she rose to her feet to examine the sketches of nudes hanging on the office walls.

The young woman's shining appreciation for her art made Melissa soar.

"You created all of these, didn't you?"

"Yes."

"You have a lot of talent. You demonstrated a lot of that this morning with Inez." Simone kept her gaze focused on the sketches and paintings. "I didn't know you could be such a tease." Simone chuckled softly. "Maybe even as much as me."

Melissa blinked, trying to keep track of Simone's words.

"They're very provocative," Simone murmured. "Very sensual. My nipples harden just looking at them. I can't decide which I like best, the charcoals or the acrylics. How do you select your models? I recognize Inez, Claire, and of course, Harry. Inez told me you have a graduate degree in art. So tastefully sensual. I'm envious. Did they all work here at the Center?"

Melissa walked over to join Simone in front of one of her favorites of Claire sitting on an easy chair in her old Brooklyn apartment—before Melissa moved in with Harry.

"I'm glad you like them. That's a lot of questions. Not all the models worked here. Some go back to my graduate work."

"Do you still draw? I know some of your work is sold

through the Center, and you exhibit at the gallery around the corner."

"I don't make enough time for art." Melissa folded her arms across her chest. "There's never quite enough time. Do you have a favorite?"

Simone's grin split her face.

"I like the one with the guy dressed in a tux fucking the woman in the evening gown from behind. Guess they were in a rush."

"Looks like," Melissa agreed.

"And the one with the woman loving the woman in the wedding dress is absolutely precious. Artsy and poignant. You should do more work with partners. Most of these sketches are only of a single female or male model.

"I really love this one of Claire with the double dildo." Simone wet her lips. "I love having one end of a dildo in my pussy and the other in my ass, don't you? Like you did this morning with Inez." Simone kept her focus on the sketch. "I would've done that for you, if you asked me. You've captured the pure joy in Claire's eyes along with the strain of her pinched mouth. Pleasure and pain. Very nice."

"I'm glad you like it," Melissa muttered, wondering if her office could get any hotter.

"But," Simone said, pouting delightfully, "that's not my favorite."

Melissa scowled questioningly at Simone.

Simone gave her a devilish smile. "It's not up here."

"What?"

"How long do I have to work here before you draw me? Everyone else on staff is on your wall. When are you going to do me? Or"—Simone's face contorted into an exaggerated pout—"am I not good enough for you?"

Melissa nodded, perusing the sketches. Was Simone talking about art, or sex, or both? She was wrong. Not everyone who'd worked for the Center had a place on her walls.

The thought of sketching Simone had crossed her mind. She peeked out of the corner of her eye at Simone, patiently waiting for a response. Could the young woman's nipples get any larger?

Melissa couldn't decide if she was thinking more about her art or more about having sex with her aspiring model. She fully acknowledged that she hadn't always been able to keep the two separate.

Had Inez and Claire been giving Simone advice? There probably was no better way for Simone to worm her way into Melissa's heart—or into her panties—than appealing to her artistry.

She'd neglected her craft too much the last several months.

She seldom worked in her home studio, and while the Center had constructed a small studio for her, she hadn't gotten into much of a routine of using it. There were always other pressing matters. Maybe it was time to get back to her art. She never felt freer than when she was in those crazy moments of hurriedly trying to capture a certain look and mood of a model, then later coming back to fill in the details. There was little in life that gave her a greater high.

Melissa smiled thoughtfully at the sketch of Claire. That was another time when she'd blended art and sex, a delightfully delicious time. She'd always told Harry that art inspired sex and sex inspired art.

Harry—what would his advice be if he were here? She could hear his deep whisper: Go for it. You've been neglecting your art. She needs your affirmation. Enjoy her. Let her inspire your art.

She turned and nodded at Simone.

A smile crept across Simone's face even before Melissa could speak.

"Think about some poses you might like to try, and I will,

too."

Simone bobbed her head up and down, her frizzed curls bouncing. Her dark brown eyes sparkled with a happiness Melissa had seldom witnessed on her.

"I will. I am so pleased. I've never modeled. I hope I won't disappoint you."

"You'll do fine." Melissa smiled softly, brushing a finger across her cheek. "I don't ask people to pose rigidly for hours on end. We'll talk about it more . . ." She checked her electronic notepad. "How about tomorrow at two? You know where my studio is?"

"Yes. That works for me. Thank you so very much," Simone said, rising on her toes, then leaning in to graze Melissa's lips.

Simone's eyelids slowly closed as Melissa deepened the kiss. She inhaled Simone's scent, getting a sudden rush. Their breasts crushed together.

With her eyes closed, Melissa licked Simone's lips. Simone's tongue played with hers. Lost in the moment, Melissa cupped Simone's butt, then drove her tongue into her mouth. Simone's fingers dug into Melissa's bottom. When Melissa felt her skirt being rolled up and Simone's hands sliding inside her panties to cradle her bare buttocks, she twisted away.

"Tomorrow," she stammered, ignoring the pained surprise in Simone's eyes.

Simone nodded warily, catching her breath.

"I can wait. You won't be sorry," Simone whispered. "I promise. Until tomorrow."

Watching Simone swing her butt wildly as she made her way out the door, Melissa exhaled sharply and reached under her skirt to rearrange her sticky panties. Another split-second and tomorrow would've been an afterthought.

She'd have to write a fantasy that would do adequate

justice to Simone's seductive ways—if that was possible. She'd better start preparing Harry for her to continue working in front of the camera. Hopefully, he'd decide to work with them.

CHAPTER SEVEN

M ax stood back to admire the changes he'd made in his bedroom. He'd gone out and bought an antique four-poster bed. He'd given a lot of thought to getting rid of the old bed, but not much to its replacement.

When he saw the four-poster in the store, it immediately reminded him of the fantasy that Claire had set up in the Cats-kills when he, Inez, Harry, and Melissa had brought to life a Manet painting. It was Melissa's idea, but Claire had made all of the necessary arrangements, including setting and cloth-ing. She had been at her most devious that day, and at the top of her game. For some reason, he'd associated her ever since as fitting nicely into that historic period.

He had no doubt she'd be enthralled with the four-poster bed, and he knew she'd look fantastic on it. He surveyed his work with the mirrors with satisfaction. Those had required more thought and effort than the bed, but he had covered all the angles. He'd never watched himself while making love until two nights earlier. Even given his work with the Center, he'd never realized how much of a voyeur he actually was.

He exhaled before bending over to begin his new stretch-ing routine. He'd purchased some light weights and a glider. A new bike sat in his garage. He'd tried it out and was pleased that bike riding skills immediately resurfaced. He tried to touch his toes. Not quite. That would be a measure of his suc-cess.

He was determined to tone his body as best he could. He had to build up his strength and stamina if he expected to fuck

Claire like he had in her kitchen — and he fully expected to do it often.

He'd lost control, unusual for him. Was it the image she'd conjured up in his mind of her and Agnes making love in her bed? His desire in the moment to overpower her for spanking him? His need to show her he was as strong as her?

He shook his head. Even a shrink wouldn't figure that out.

And why didn't really matter. Claire had shown no signs of withdrawing from him. She must know he'd do nothing to hurt her. All her babbling had only thrown flames on his burning inferno.

He might not come again in a week. His loins still quivered when he replayed that scene in his mind. He planned on doing a web search on vitamins and supplements for guys. He wasn't going to leave any more to chance than he had to.

He'd hardly been able to think of anything else but Claire since he left her condo. He did manage to conduct a seminar on Chaucer, wondering how many of the coeds were aware that his mind wandered to a particular woman as they read and reread excerpts. If they were at all aware, they probably thought he was recalling experiences of his youth rather than anticipating the future. He'd refrained from phoning Claire, but then she hadn't called him, either. He'd pick her up Friday after work as they'd agreed.

Had she thought about him at all since she walked out of the kitchen leaving him with his pants down and a very limp, but very satisfied cock?

Claire breathed deeply as she took in the scene in Melissa's office studio.

Melissa worked feverishly at her easel sketching Simone, who was posed in front of a mirror. As usual, Melissa had come up with an artsy way of depicting the human form.

Simone stood in the center of the small studio wearing only a panty, which had been drawn down to show the hairline leading to her dark pussy but still kept her cleft hidden. Her left hand rested on at the base of her throat so that with her wrist separated her rather small breasts. With her head turned on an angle, she gazed mysteriously out of the corner of her eye at Melissa. Her puffy lips parted in anticipation.

Claire sucked in a breath. That was a turn-on, but the artsy part of the pose was cast in the mirror image. From a frontal view, Simone's right arm simply appeared to be resting on the small of her back. In the mirror however, the viewer could see that her hand and wrist had slipped inside the bikini panty. Although her fingers remained hidden, it appeared Simone was playing with herself. Or at least that was a plausible suspicion. Jesus. Who had come up with that pose? Was she preparing herself for a lover? Or had she been caught by the observer seeking her own satisfaction? Would she invite the observer to help? The pose would yield a wide array of interpretations—which, no doubt, was Melissa's intent.

Claire tiptoed over to peer at the sketch.

"You're doing great. Exceptional, really. Simone, you're going to love this sketch. It captures your raw sensuality perfectly. Any sharp observer will walk away wondering if you are preparing yourself for a lover, or if you are slowly bringing yourself off."

"I've just about got this one roughed out. There." Melissa took a step back and viewed her work, glowing with satisfaction. "That'll do it until I have time to get back to it later. You can relax a bit, Simone. Do you want to take a break before we do the second pose with Claire?"

Simone shook her head, eyeing Claire cautiously.

Claire hadn't thought the woman had a shy bone in her body until now.

"No offense, ma'am," Simone said, casting Melissa a

pleading look.

Claire felt like she'd aged ten years in the amount of time it took Simone to draw a breath.

"But I don't understand why I can't pose with Inez. I've never even worked with Claire."

"Contrast," Melissa said, attaching a new canvas to her easel. "I told you before. This will be a black-and-white sketch. Inez's skin tone, while not as dark as yours, is too similar. Claire's alabaster skin, on the other hand, will provide an excellent contrast." Melissa paused, then frowned at Simone. "You are still willing to work with me on this?"

Simone's eyes rounded, but she nodded her head, assenting to Melissa's judgment.

Claire chuckled and gave Simone credit for not pouting. So she had a few prejudices against older women. Nonplussed, Claire welcomed a challenge. "Let me see if I can help you get comfortable." Claire doffed her blouse and bra.

Simone's eyes blazed as she stared at Claire's breasts.

Claire felt her nipples stretch erect. At least they seemed to pass inspection. "Not too bad," she murmured, hefting her boobs, "for a woman pushing sixty."

Simone shook her head frantically but remained silent. Perhaps unaware of what she was doing, she pulled on her own nipples. They were nice — very nice, Claire admitted — but they weren't going to lengthen as much as her own. She'd only known a few women whose nipples were that responsive.

"From what I understand, Melissa wants us kissing, wearing only panties." Claire stretched, then glanced over at Melissa. "Is that right, Melissa?"

"Yes."

"Melissa can pose us exactly the way she wants us later," she said, focusing on Simone, "but why don't we experiment a little?" Simone stood her ground when Claire reached out and brushed the back of her hand against her cheek, then ran a fingernail the length of her breast and tapped on a very alert nipple.

"I've admired you on set, but your nipples are even thicker and darker than I remember."

"My titties are too small," Simone huffed. "Yours are just right." She reached out to cradle a full breast.

"Nice," Claire purred, covering Simone's dark hand with hers. "That's more like it. Your fingers are electric, but for your information, I've seen all shapes and sizes of boobs. Just like cocks, there is none too small or too big. They are just right, if given the proper attention."

Without saying another word, she dipped her head and drew Simone's entire breast into her mouth. She suckled as if it was the most luscious boob she'd ever known.

"Good God," Simone exclaimed, interlacing her fingers in Claire's hair. "You are good. I didn't know. I'm sorry I doubted . . ."

Claire clamped her teeth around a nipple and bit lightly, delighting in Simone's soft whimpers. She raised her head, then brushed her lips along the curve of Simone's mouth. "I have had a fair amount of practice nibbling on boobs."

"You can practice with me any time."

"That's good," Melissa interjected. "We want to do a tape highlighting younger women loving older women. Maybe you'd like to work with Claire on that."

"Absolutely." Simone's eyebrows shot up. "Wow! Are you willing to work with me on camera?"

Claire turned to glare at Melissa, but she did leave her arm around Simone. It wasn't like Melissa was springing a new idea on her, but she hadn't decided if she wanted to work with Simone. Simone rubbed her hip against hers. Claire grinned at Simone, then blew her a kiss.

"How can I turn down such eager enthusiasm?"

"Fantastic!"

"I will also want you to work with Max," Melissa added. "As part of our younger women, older men tape."

Claire couldn't believe the face Simone made. She abruptly stepped away from her.

Simone looked furtively from her to Melissa. "He's too old."

Claire chuckled. "Max is only a few years older than I am."

"No matter," Simone folded her arms across her belly. "He must stink."

"Where do you get such crazy ideas?" Claire asked, more shrilly than she liked. "He does not stink. I can tell you that's a fact. So can Melissa."

Melissa nodded. "Max has worked with our entire female staff. You will not find a more considerate lover in our entire stable." Melissa scowled. "Simone, you may have to decide whether you're part of this Center family or not. I assume your reticence has nothing to do with Max being white."

Claire didn't move or speak—neither did Melissa.

Simone cringed. "Of course it has nothing to do with him being white. It's just that," she looked wildly around, "he's bald. He has white hair. I don't want to get into faking orgasms. I don't do porn."

Claire couldn't determine who laughed harder, her or Melissa. "I can assure you," she said, "if you ever have to fake orgasms with a man, that man will not be Max Wilson."

"I agree," Melissa said between laughs. "Though it's hard to believe I said something almost like that when Harry first suggested I work with Max. You might want to be certain you've built up your energy before joining Max. Older men do last longer."

"Really?" Simone's brow furrowed in disbelief.

Claire joined Melissa in a nod.

"This family thing." Simone sighed. "If I don't work with

Max, I don't work with Claire or with you?"

"I haven't decided whether we will work together," Melissa pointed out in a tone that lacked conviction, "but definitely not if you choose to reject Max."

"I see." Simone's lips curved into a small smile. "It might be worth seeing for myself how long your Max can last. Okay." She turned to Melissa. "Can we continue? I'll do whatever you want."

"Good. I'll get you two set up in the poses we talked about," Melissa said, walking around her easel to where Simone and Claire stood. "We won't worry about the mirror this time. We hardly need a prop when we have the two of you.

"Let me see. Turn and face each other with Simone on the left and Claire on the right. Simone, tilt your head back a little like this, and Claire, tilt yours a little forward like this, as if you are the pursuer. Now, just ever so lightly, touch your lips together. Let me step back and take a peek."

"Excellent. This is going to be super. Deepen the kiss a fraction, then scrunch in closer so your boobs are just touching. Too bad Simone is my height, or we could have your nipples touching."

Claire smiled against Simone's lips as the shorter woman rose on her toes to slide her nipples across Claire's. Keeping her eyes open, Claire teased her partner by darting her tongue between her lips.

"Hey, you two. Don't get ahead of me," Melissa scolded.

"Super idea, Simone. I know you won't be able to stand up on your toes for long, but now and then will give me a feel for it. A nice touch.

"Now then, I don't expect you to hold the kiss for a long period, either. You can move back and forth by taking little breaks. Just don't step out of the embrace. The final touch," she said with glee. "You each have an arm around your partner's back for support. Move your lower body slightly away from your partner like this." Melissa turned Simone slightly so the observer would have a three-quarter view of her mound.

"Ladies, I'm sure you're going to like this last gesture. I want you to slip your free hand into your partner's panties."

Claire's breathing slowed as Melissa took Simone's right hand and tucked it into her panties. Simone's eyes filled with mirth as she furled her fingers over Claire's vulva.

Melissa winked at Claire when she interlaced her own fingers with Claire's, then slid them together down Simone's panties. Probably Simone hadn't seen Melissa's wink. For that matter, Simone had closed her eyes and broken off their kiss to rest her head against Claire's shoulder. Simone whimpered and moaned — no doubt entranced with ten fingers caressing her pussy. She widened her hips and tilted her pelvis, clearly seeking more.

Melissa lingered extra long before retrieving her hand.

Simone's eyes popped wide open, looking abandoned.

"My, you weren't kidding," Melissa teased. "You are wet."

Melissa returned to the easel and made a display of licking her fingers and wiping them on a nearby towel before picking up charcoal.

"Okay. Pose, please."

Claire tucked her fingers up against Simone's mound and resumed their kiss. Melissa was right, Simone was soaking wet. Likewise, Simone's fingers curled over her mound, and one finger already delved into the crease of her pussy lips. How fast could Melissa sketch?

"Don't get too far ahead of me, ladies," Melissa cautioned. "This is going to take a while."

Minutes dragged by. Claire breathed through her nose as best she could. She and Simone would break the seal of their lips every minute or so, but neither of them showed any sign of wanting to give up their hold on the other woman's pussy.

After what must've been at least fifteen minutes of standing and rocking back and forth on the balls of her feet, Claire turned her head to look at Melissa, who was sketching furiously with her tongue between her teeth.

"How much longer?"

Melissa shook her head. "We're getting there."

"We're pretty hot over here. You must be hot as hell with all those clothes on while working so rapidly." She eased a finger into Simone's pussy.

Simone moaned on cue, then pushed her finger inside Claire.

Claire turned to Melissa. "It is getting hotter over here. At least take some clothes off so we won't feel like exhibitionists."

Melissa paused and gave her a half-smile. "Since when have you worried about being an exhibitionist? If I take some clothes off, are you two going to get back into position?"

Both women nodded, but neither one moved until Melissa's glorious round breasts stood free and bare before them. Claire smiled — was Melissa remembering another time when she'd been sketching Claire nude in the easy chair at her old apartment? That day she'd also cajoled the artist into shedding her clothes while drawing, a prelude to experiencing Melissa's talented tongue for the first time.

Claire wedged her finger a little deeper into Simone, who sighed and swiveled her head back and forth. With any luck, Simone would be equally fortunate before the afternoon was done. "That's better," Claire said, seeking Simone's mouth. They held the pose for couple minutes, then Claire broke the kiss and winked at Simone. They both looked toward Melissa expectantly.

Melissa didn't disappoint. Without hesitation, she moved around the easel and stepped out of her skirt. She wasn't wearing panties. Ah, she had prepared for a long sitting.

"I thought so," Simone murmured. "Or at least I hoped so."

"May I join you?" Melissa asked with a broad smile.

"What about the sketch?" Claire asked.

"I finished all I need for now. I was waiting for your invitation."

Claire backed away from Simone and flexed her fingers before licking them. "So how do we proceed?"

"The carpet is as good as anywhere, but this is Simone's show." Melissa nodded toward her. "She's probably given this a lot of thought."

Simone looked hesitantly at Claire. "I hope you aren't offended, but I've been dying to taste Melissa."

"Somehow, we've all noticed," Claire demurred. "You go ahead, I'll figure out a place for myself. I'm pretty good at improv."

Melissa stretched out on the carpet, spread her thighs and held out her hands, inviting Simone to join her. The dark-skinned beauty dropped quickly to kneel between Melissa's thighs. Her gaze roved over Melissa's body.

Claire didn't know if Simone was saying a prayer of adoration or if she simply wanted to memorize the view.

"Thought you'd want to do more than look," Melissa prompted with a half-smile. She cupped a breast. "This is for you, if you want. I have very sensitive breasts."

Simone nodded and leaned over to lick her way from Melissa's belly button to the proffered breast. Then she laved the breast and blew on the raised nipple before taking it into her mouth. Melissa arched her back, offering Simone more. Simone suckled until Melissa's cheeks were quite red with passion.

It was Melissa who curled her fingers over Simone's shoulders, pulling her lower. Little moans came from Simone as she worked her tongue from breast to navel. Now that she had

Melissa where she wanted, Simone did not appear to be in a rush. She was savoring her opportunity.

Melissa rolled her eyes wildly at Claire, then laced her fingers in Simone's curls, guiding her lower still.

Simone backed down Melissa's torso until she again knelt comfortably between Melissa's thighs, then bent down to part Melissa's pussy and wiggle her tongue along the glistening folds.

Claire swallowed hard—Simone's raised butt was waggling in time with her tongue.

Simone raised her head, smiling widely at Melissa. "I can't believe I'm doing this."

Melissa giggled, tilting her pelvis. "Believe me, you are. I hope one little taste didn't quench your thirst."

"Hardly," Simone whispered.

Once Claire was fairly certain Simone was settled in place, she scooched across the carpet to kneel behind her. Simone's moans became high-pitched as Claire kneaded her tight bottom. She marveled at the contrast of her long pale fingers sliding down the crevice of Simone's darker ass. Melissa did have an eye for contrast. Claire smiled. Simone wiggled her butt from side to side in encouragement as she continued burrowing into Melissa.

For her part, Melissa appeared rather taken with her younger supplicant. She twined her fingers in Simone's dark, curly hair as if protecting herself from any sudden change of mind on Simone's part.

"What a tight, inviting booty." Claire chuckled, before planting a kiss on one butt cheek, then on the other. She rested her cheek on Simone's butt and toyed with her wet pussy, easing two fingers between its folds. Simone grunted, then wedged herself back against Claire's twisting fingers.

Claire had lost track of Melissa but heard her fists pounding the floor.

Perhaps surprised by Melissa's outburst, Simone ceased tonguing.

"Don't you dare stop, Simone!" Melissa screamed. "If you want to work with me, don't you dare stop."

Claire laughed as Simone renewed her efforts by humming against Melissa's pussy folds. Melissa moaned softly, obviously desperately wanting more. The humming sounds became less distinct, and given Melissa's renewed banging on the floor, Simone must've reenergized her tongue.

"My clit," Melissa yelped. "Don't forget my clit."

Claire heard Simone's muffled chuckle, then saw her elbow crook, suggesting that she was taking Melissa's demands seriously. For her part, Claire sawed her fingers in and out of Simone's pink pussy.

Just as Melissa's wails peaked and Simone's groan intensified, Claire rimmed Simone's anus with her tongue. The young woman went berserk, jerking this way and that way. It was difficult to determine whether she wanted more or less. Until proven otherwise, Claire assumed Simone was demanding more.

Melissa lay finished, panting for breath, clearly not about to complain that Simone had concentrated on her own pleasure.

And Claire wasn't about to deny anyone pleasure. She quickened the cadence of her fingers deep inside Simone's pussy, then pushed her tongue into the young woman's ass, quickly matching the rhythm of her tongue with that of her fingers.

Simone's squeal turned to sudden wails. She pressed her bottom tighter against Claire's mouth.

"What are you doing to me? I'm shattering. Oh my God!" she screamed, reaching around to pull on her butt cheeks, widening them, giving Claire even more access. "More."

Claire didn't disappoint. She plowed her tongue in as far

as she could.

"My nipples. Oh. Oh. Oh."

Claire realized that Melissa must have revived enough to be pinching Simone's nipples. Melissa scooted forward enough to clamp her lips on Simone's mouth, swallowing their protégé's screams.

There was no more sound, but Simone's knees wobbled.

Claire held her up by wrapping an arm around her thighs. Simone broke the seal of Melissa's lips to render a curdling scream before crashing on top of her newest lover. Melissa wrapped her arms around Simone, cooing to her as if she were a baby.

Claire crawled forward until she could fold an arm around both women. Simone's frame still shook under her arm.

Simone heaved a huge sigh, then turned her head to face both of them. "Wow!" she mumbled. "I must be in heaven."

Kissing her forehead, Melissa whispered, "It was good for us, too. You okay, Claire?"

"I'm fine," she said, getting to her knees. "You two take a little longer to recover. I think I know someone who will be more than pleased to finish me off. Max is picking me up after work. I'm going to spend the weekend with him."

"Now you tell me," Melissa complained, looking like she hardly had the strength to protest. "When you know I don't have a brain or the energy to quiz you."

"I thought it was pretty good timing, too." Claire leaned down and kissed first Melissa, then Simone. "Don't do anything I wouldn't do."

Melissa rolled her eyes but made no move to relax her hold on Simone.

Still looking rather glazed, Simone said, "I'll never make unfounded judgments based on a person's age again."

"Well that's something, I suppose." Claire stepped into her skirt. She stuffed the panties from her scene in her pocket, wondering what Max would say if he found them there. She quickly buttoned her blouse. "Too bad I can't draw. You two would make quite the picture lying there like that. Well, I've got to run. I've got a bike to ride. And maybe a man."

"Claire," Melissa said, hesitantly.

"Yes?"

"My camera is on the shelf beside you. Would you take a couple pictures of the two of us? I don't often work from photos." She smiled down at Simone and brushed some curls off her forehead. "But I may have to make an exception for this little adventure. I assume you'd like a drawing of us. I won't keep the photos."

"I'd be thrilled," Simone said, pecking at Melissa's nipple. "Will you hang us on the wall?"

"Hey, no more. Not yet. You must recover faster than me. If I can do justice to us, we'll be on the wall." Melissa looked at Claire for help.

Claire laughed. "I'm taking three pictures, then I'm out of here. You'll have to figure out how to extricate yourself. Or I could send in Harry to help."

"No, please don't," Melissa said. "This isn't going to shock him, but I do need to do a little more prep work before he joins us."

"Ah," Claire said, snapping the third shot. "Never underestimate the importance of preparation. Keep that in mind, Simone."

Simone nodded her head. "I may not know much about aging." She grinned at Melissa. "But I do know something about preparation."

"Yes," Claire quipped. "I guess you have been preparing for this moment since you were hired here."

"Longer than that. Since I first saw Melissa's artwork hanging in the small gallery around the corner. I knew then that I had to have her draw me, and that I needed to taste her."

Claire chuckled and shook her head. "And I thought I was the queen of conniving." She glanced at Melissa. "No harm done. Looks like we're all quite satisfied."

Melissa snaked her tongue out at her. "Maybe I should team up with Simone for advice the next time I want to do some serious conniving."

"Don't even go there," Claire warned, waving her hand. "Bye."

She overheard Simone ask Melissa, "What was that about?"

"Never mind," Melissa said. "You want to get dressed? Or you could come up here and let me taste you."

Claire closed the door, not waiting to see how long it might take the two women to dress. She had her own things to tend to.

She hustled to her office and found Max sitting on her couch. "Sorry I'm late," she said, before kissing him briefly. "Let me get my bag, and we can leave."

"You smell like sex. I didn't know you were working to-day."

She stopped and looked at Max—she saw no indication of censure at all. If anything, his mouth crinkled, holding back a smile.

She shrugged. "Melissa agreed to do a sketch of Simone. She wanted me to pose with her for a second sketch, and not surprisingly, one thing led to another." She winked at Max. "Guess I was the bridge that finally got them to connect."

Max stepped over to her, lifted her chin, and slanted his lips across hers. "Hi. I hope you didn't think I was prying. Sex is what we do. Sometimes we'll be together and sometimes we won't." He squeezed her butt. "I just hope you saved something for me."

"Oh, I did," she said, gently nipping the tip of his nose. She pouted. "They were so into each other, neither one of them even touched my pussy."

"You poor girl."

Claire laughed. "They asked if I wanted help afterward, and I said nope, I had a guy who I thought could finish me off just fine. So, can we go now?"

"We'd better, or we might not make it out of here the entire weekend. You grab your bag, and I'll bring your bike."

Claire straightened some items on her desk. She'd never been a fan of mess.

"Does Harry know about Melissa and Simone?"

Claire looked up sharply at Max.

"I think so. I hope so." She tried to think about what Melissa had said. "I'm sure he does. Melissa wouldn't hook up with Simone without telling him first." She flashed an eyebrow at Max. "I'm not positive, but I think Melissa is trying to get Harry to do a tape with her and Simone."

"That could be good." Max whistled softly. "Real good. If that happens, let me know. I'd pay admission to see that."

"She also agreed to work with you."

Max straightened. "Who agreed to work with me?"

"Simone."

"Damn, that old guy-young woman idea of Melissa's."

"That's right. And when you do that tape," Claire tossed him a smile, "I want to be there to cheer you on."

"So, did Melissa have to twist her arm to work with me?"

Claire chuckled and grabbed her bag and headed for the exit.

"Not after I convinced her age doesn't matter nearly as much as she thought it did."

CHAPTER EIGHT

The look of amazement on Claire's face along with her squeals at the sight of the four-poster bed pleased Max immensely, leaving no doubt about his choice.

Claire stepped to the bed, testing its bounce with her hand. She turned to him with a perplexed look. "This is a new bed, isn't it?"

"How can you tell?"

"It has that fresh smell of newness, and it's still very firm, as if it just arrived from the store."

"Do you like it?"

"I love it! I've never gotten around to buying a four-poster, but it's often part of my fantasy." She drew her lower lip into her mouth and shook her head.

Hesitantly, he took a step closer. She held her hands out to him, and he moved forward to hug her. He thought he felt her sobbing but chose not to comment.

Claire stepped out of their embrace, swiping at her eyes. "You did this because of me, didn't you?"

He shrugged his shoulders. "When I saw it in the store, I immediately thought of you."

She glanced back at the bed with admiration. "You are a man of many surprises." Her mouth broke into a shy smile. "I assume you haven't made love to a woman on this bed."

"Of course not."

Claire twirled around happily. "I look forward to helping you break it in." She sobered. "It fits me very nicely, but what happens if it doesn't fit your next woman?"

"I'll buy a new bed," he said, not missing a beat.

"You could go broke."

"That depends on the number of women I bring here, doesn't it?"

"Max," she said, running a finger down his cheek, "am I the first woman you've brought here since Agnes died?"

He nodded. It was his turn to choke up.

"I'm not sure what to say about that. I am honored." Claire stood on her tiptoes and kissed him briefly. "In case you're wondering, I've never been in your house before. I seldom leave Manhattan, and Agnes never invited me to visit."

His breath sharpened. Claire had just answered a question he'd probably never have found the guts to ask.

"I assume these mirrors are new."

Again he nodded.

"You are such a clever voyeur," she said. "I do love watching you make love with me. I expect it was past time for you to get rid of the bed you shared with Agnes. I couldn't be more pleased with your replacement."

She stepped back into his arms, and he inhaled the scent of her hair. His hands roamed over her back, then cradled her butt as hers did his. He kissed her hair. She tipped back her head, and he kissed her closed eyelids, her nose, then urgently covered her mouth.

Unexplained emotions welled up deep within his body. His lungs sought more air. Was he drowning in her scent? Was it the result of mentioning Agnes? He slid off her mouth, breathing deeply. She rested her head on his shoulder.

They both stood clinging to each other. He struggled with his own tears. It was time to get a new bed—it was time to move on. Not to deny his long-standing attachment to Agnes, but to move on. She'd want that.

He squeezed Claire tight. Hadn't Agnes been pointing him to this mysterious, sexy woman he now held in his arms? He blinked his eyes at the empty four-poster bed. There was plenty of time for that. He'd better figure out a way to get them out of his bedroom now, before he really made a fool of himself.

"Maybe you should show me your backyard," Claire whispered.

A jolt of electricity flashed across his brain. Had her thoughts been mimicking his? Had they both been on the brink of risking their fragile relationship by using *verboten* words or even considering unreasonable expectations?

He patted her bottom before taking her by the hand and leading her out into the hallway. "I hope you like the yard. While I hire people to get much of the heavier work done, I do get fairly involved with the flowers and shrubbery."

"It's like a park back here," Claire said as he escorted her across his patio onto the manicured lawn. "So colorful. So quiet."

"Thanks." He chuckled. "This is much more private than many parks. I often have an early-morning coffee on the patio and listen to the birds welcoming the day."

"Is that a tool shed?" Claire asked, pointing toward a small yellow building.

"No, the tool shed is the metal building in the far corner. The building you're pointing at is quite old. It was originally built as a stable."

"That is old!"

"Agnes and I were always going to fix it up as a little retreat place, but never got around to it." He frowned. "That was my project last summer. Come on, I'll show you."

"You must be handy with tools," Claire said, as they walked toward the old structure.

"I get by," he said, opening the screen door for her.

"How lovely," she mumbled softly. "This could be a lover's nest. Soft pillows. A desk. A couple of easy chairs.

What did you leave out?"

"A woman," he said, stepping up from behind to encircle her in his arms.

"You do have a romantic streak," she said, turning her cheek for him to kiss. "Between this and the carpet of a lawn, we might never use that bed." She turned in his arms and pointed again at the lawn. "Have you ever made love here, outside the house?" Her eyes gleamed.

He shook his head. "Agnes thought the neighbors might hear."

"And if they did?"

"She would've been mortified."

Claire shrugged. "I guess I left a few things out of her education." She kissed the tip of his nose. "I wouldn't be mortified."

He tapped his tongue against her nose. "I didn't think you would be."

"Maybe later," she whispered, holding his gaze. "I want our first lovemaking while I'm here to be on that four-poster bed." She flashed an eyebrow. " Then I think we should make love out here and in every room of your house."

He laughed easily. "Is this some sort of Feng Shui by Claire?"

"Maybe. That might help you reclaim your space for yourself."

"We can't do that in one weekend."

She pecked at his lips. "Maybe you'll have to invite me back."

Max kissed her forehead, then laid her head on his shoulder. "I intend to. You can count on that."

He closed his eyes and held her. *Slow down, old man. Slow down. Don't scare her off.* Maybe he wouldn't feel wound tight like a ball of string after they made love. "Maybe we should go out to eat before it gets too late."

"Do we have to? You must have something in the house to munch on. Even peanut butter will be fine." She stared back at the house. "I don't want to leave this place tonight. Let's eat light and save room for what we both are wanting." She squeezed his chin, then gave him a lecherous grin. "I don't fuck so well on a full stomach."

He nodded—that sure helped to lighten the mood. "I suspect I can find a little more in the cupboard than peanut butter, but I won't lay out a feast."

Claire rested her head on the headboard of the four-poster bed, trying to catch her breath after a lovely climax. Beneath her, apparently not sated, Max gingerly sucked her pussy lips into his mouth while his fingers massaged her buttocks as if he was intent on coaxing forth another orgasm. Her knees trembled around his ears as she squirmed across his face.

Heaving a sigh, she shifted back on her knees to settle on Max's chest. Her juices still covered his lips. She scraped a finger across his lower lip, then brought it to her mouth.

"Has anyone ever told you that you have a magical tongue?"

His lips curved up. "I believe a stunning older blonde woman has mentioned that on occasion."

Claire smirked. "Am I already forgetting what I've said to you?"

"I doubt you can repeat that comment about my tongue too often." He licked his lips. "And as usual, you offer up a very respectable aperitif."

"Thanks, but I believe you had a lot to do with offering it up. By the way, your mirrors are very well positioned."

Max chuckled. "I'm glad. I couldn't see anything but pussy and belly, which was fine with me."

"And I love this bed," Claire added. "I feel like a princess entertaining her paramour." She reached behind her to fondle his cock. "My, he's still soft."

Max nodded. "While I enjoy bantering with you, talk does seem to put him to sleep."

"And he has been up several times since we arrived, and I've neglected him." She winked. "Trust me. He will be no longer neglected tonight."

Claire slid down Max's body, settling on the mattress between his legs until she rested her head on his belly and could flick her tongue out at his cock. She curved her tongue under its head, then smiled as it immediately began to grow with anticipation. "Are you watching us in the mirrors? Look at how he's hardening. My, he is eager. A long wait does wonders for him. Watch him disappear," she said, taking him in her mouth.

She winked at Max in the mirror. She ran her fingernails over his testicles and chuckled to herself when Max's eyes closed. She ministered to his cock as thoroughly and tenderly as she knew how, but she didn't want to finish him that way. There was a more fitting way to initiate his four-poster bed.

Claire dropped him from her mouth.

Max's eyes immediately blinked open.

"I think this bed calls for an old-fashioned initiation, Max. Why don't you come on top? Pretend that you are my knight and I am your princess. You must love me for fear that you will be called away at any moment. Let's not think of tomorrow, Max. Love me tonight. As only you can."

She rolled onto her back. Max moved into position above her. The look of pure joy on his face nearly shattered her resolve. Surely he knew she was pretending. This was still just practice. She bit her lip. Wasn't it? It was the damn bed. It was the damn bed that had loosened her tongue and her senses. She placed her feet on the mattress and raised her knees, spreading them wide.

Max's breathing became labored as he knelt before her. She tilted her pelvis as his wide cock pried at her entrance. She inhaled when Max pushed forward, seating himself deep inside her. She lifted her legs to hug him tight. "Love me, my sweet Sir Knight. Love me good."

He nodded, then flexed back only long enough to regroup and forge ahead to fill her. She tapped her heels on his butt, encouraging him. His eyes glazed. Clearly, he had been on the edge most of the evening.

She slid her hand down the length of her body to their juncture. Her fingers brushed against his cock and her clit.

"Um, nice." He glanced quickly at her fingers clawing at her clit. He grimaced, closed his eyes, and if anything, quickened his pace.

"Go, go, go!" she wailed, hoping he wouldn't take too long, because she didn't think he'd breathe again until he climaxed or died trying.

"Good God!" he exclaimed, his eyes popping open and just as quickly closing. He huddled over her chest, sharpening his angle, driving his hips faster. His hot breath warmed her neck.

With her own orgasm assured, she wrapped her arms and legs around him. "You're making me come, Sir Knight. Come with me." She raked his shoulders with her fingernails. "To the hilt. That's it. I can't wait. Damn."

Ragged laughter rumbled from Max's mouth. He slowed.

"Don't stop," she said quickly. "You're so close."

He gave her a wolfish smile. "Come for me again, fair lady. I have enough here to fill you twice."

"Oh Max," she purred, kissing his forehead.

"Max?" he said, scowling at her while picking up his cadence.

"I forgot." She giggled. "Yes, Sir Knight. Make me come again. You don't need my assistance." She closed her eyes, concentrating on his cock filling and refilling her. Somewhere deep inside her, he'd found a button that yielded to his every thrust. "You're doing it." Each time he drove into her, an electrical charge jolted from his cock throughout her interior. She gasped and bucked against him, seeking her release, demanding his. "I'm coming again. Don't hold back this time. Give me all you have to give."

"Who's holding back?" he howled only inches from her cheek. "Holy shit, I'm coming."

Claire bucked her hips, matching his thrusts. His head jerked from side to side in concert with his spurting deep inside her. She didn't try to hold back her tears. She just held him. And when he settled against her breast, she never asked about the meaning of his tears.

"Damn bed," she moaned softly, beginning to drift off to sleep. It had not only loosened her tongue, it had nearly loosened her heartstrings. Hopefully, that was warning enough to convince her to take better self-protective measures.

Tomorrow would be soon enough. These practice sessions were getting out of hand. Starting on the Center tape might help both of them maintain their bearings.

The following morning, Max sat next to Claire, propped up against the headboard of the four-poster bed. While a sheet covered their lower torsos, Claire's breasts were not hidden from sight, thank goodness.

Claire made a show of chewing on a piece of melon. "This is delectable," she said, admiring the fresh fruit plate he'd prepared. Steaming coffee sat on the nightstand next to her.

He nodded, not wanting to break the spell of such a gorgeous view.

"There's never been a man who served me breakfast in bed."

His heart thudded. He wanted to know. Would she tell him? "Have you ever had a serious relationship with a man?"

Claire frowned and concentrated on peeling half an orange. "How long have you had the picture?"

Oh crap. Claire was a woman who believed the best defense was a good offense. "What picture?"

She gave him an incredulous look. "The one hanging in your downstairs office. One of the pictures Melissa drew of me posing nude in her studio easy chair."

"You didn't ask about it last night."

She set her fruit plate on the nightstand and arched an eyebrow at him. "I'm asking now. You're stalling. How long have you had it?"

He shrugged. "Probably since not long after Melissa drew it."

Claire scowled.

"It was Melissa's idea."

Claire cocked her head to the side, waiting for more explanation.

"She wanted me to agree to work with you on camera."

"And?"

"I refused."

"And she gave you the picture?"

"She said I could return it if I wanted to, but she wanted me to study it closely and see the real woman in the drawing."

"And you studied it?"

"You are a very multifaceted woman, Claire. Melissa did wonders at capturing more than you probably wanted."

"She usually does. So you hung it in your office."

"Eventually. At first, I hid it in my closet."

Claire couldn't hold back a giggle. "That's precious. So when did you bring me out of the closet?"

"Maybe a month or so after I brought it home. There was something about your image that haunted me, that gnawed

132

at me."

"You're not bad to gnaw on," she said, stroking his arm.

"You're not angry with me for hanging your picture in my office?"

"Why should I be? Melissa captures the essence of eroticism about as well as I've ever seen it done."

She gave him a quirky smile. "So have you jerked off studying that drawing of me?"

"Shit," he muttered. "Isn't there anything you won't ask?"

"I certainly hope not." She scowled down her nose at him. "Well?"

"Yes," he mumbled. "Often, if you must know."

He could feel his cheeks burning under her scrutiny. "Before we started practicing together?"

"Yes."

"Sort of a pre-practice, practice routine, I guess."

"So did you ever think about me that way before we started practicing?" He caught her smile before she quickly glanced away from him. He followed her gaze until he was watching her reflection in the mirror.

"I did take home the tape you, Melissa, and Harry did on three-way sex." She licked her lips. "Damn, that was a powerful video."

"And?"

"And I used one of my favorite vibrators imagining you were plundering my pussy and that you were deep in my ass." She turned back to poke her tongue out at him. "Does that please you?"

"I'm glad. I doubt many women do that while watching me perform."

"You might be surprised. Max," she whispered. "I know it's too soon after last night, but soon, very soon, I want you in my ass." She winked at him. "I've just about worn out that video."

"Too bad you can't slip a battery into me like you can with your vibrator."

She smirked. "It is, but I've not discovered a way of doing that. So maybe we ought to get dressed and take a bike ride. It seems that was the justification for my being here in the first place."

He nodded. "That, and the need for more practice."

"Uh, huh. Are you free Wednesday morning? Melissa and I thought that might be a good time to begin our taping."

"I'll be there. Do you know what we'll be working on?"

"Not positive. Depends on what Melissa wants."

"Let's not overdo it," Claire said over her shoulder to Max, who looked rather flushed. They'd brought their bikes to Old Croton Aqueduct State Historic Park, with trails overlooking the Hudson River.

She'd deliberately set a moderate pace and was determined not to bike too far away from where he'd parked the car. She'd had more than one experience of getting so involved with a ride she hadn't kept track of how far she'd ridden. The way back usually took at least as much effort as the first half of any ride.

Max nodded and grinned. "I'm doing fine, but we should be coming up on a picnic area fairly soon."

"Good, a little sustenance won't hurt. That must be it," she said, looking ahead.

They were in luck. There were three widely scattered tables in a nicely shaded clearing. None were occupied.

Claire selected the table furthest from the trail, hopped off her bike, and immediately reached for her water bottle. Both of them needed to pay attention to their water intake.

Fortunately, Max followed her lead without having to be reminded to take care of himself. She smiled to herself. She probably didn't have to be quite so cautious about him, given the stamina he'd already demonstrated in so many other ways. But given his rusty riding style, he probably hadn't been on a bike for years.

He'd made a lot of changes because of her. Why? Surely he didn't see them as some sort of item. Did he want to? Did *she* want to? That was the most important question. She blinked — no sense dwelling on a frivolous question.

She hadn't noticed Max removing cheese and crackers from his knapsack. She opened hers, adding fresh carrots, radishes, and two tomatoes to their modest meal. She'd brought a dark chocolate bar for dessert. Biking was one of those rare moments when she allowed herself chocolate. Its energy punch provided the justification, and she loved chocolate. Even she had difficulty with self-denial at times.

"This is a lovely ride," she said after the picnic was laid out and Max had had a chance to catch his breath. "You made an excellent selection."

"I doubt we could go too wrong on a day like this. Beautiful clear sky. Warm sunshine, but not too hot." He gave her a wide smile. "It feels good being on a bike again. It's odd how the body gets used to doing without and then picks it up with renewed gusto."

"Are you only talking about bike riding?"

Max's mouth crinkled. "Maybe."

"Are all English professors such romantics?" Claire reached across the table to wipe a dab of tomato from the corner of his mouth.

Max grabbed her fingers and brought them to his lips. He winked at her. "That's what a romantic would do."

"I'm glad you didn't cleanse your house of Agnes's pictures."

"What?" Max dropped her hand as if it had suddenly singed him. "That would be wrong."

"Of course it would. She was your wife for nearly thirty-five years. She loved you very much. You do know that?"

"Yes, I do. And she knew that I loved her, too. What are you trying to get at, Claire, other than quash a romantic moment?"

Claire studied the antics of a chipmunk sitting on the ground nearby begging for a morsel. She knew she shouldn't, but she reached into her snack bag and tossed a couple seeds at the little critter. She looked back at Max, who sat rigidly, masking his features, awaiting her response.

"Agnes and I weren't lovers. Not really." She smiled softly. "You two were lovers. Agnes and I were sex partners."

Max raised an eyebrow.

"I'm not saying we didn't enjoy each other. That would be a lie. We had some great times exploring each other. But you were her emotional, spiritual, and sexual partner. I was her sex partner."

"So in your way of thinking, can sex partners also become emotional and spiritual partners?"

Claire glanced away. She knew what he was asking, but she wasn't ready for that question. She didn't know if she had an answer. She redirected her attention toward the chipmunk, who seemed quite agitated and distressed with her for not tending to his needs. *He must be a male.*

"We lived together for a year. His name was Michael."

Max frowned. "Ah."

"It was right after college. He swept me off my feet. Michael was a romantic. I still don't know how it happened. One of us, both of us made a mistake. I got pregnant. We'd talked about marriage, but the pregnancy freaked Michael out. He convinced me that an abortion was the only option."

Claire rubbed her neck. Max sat like a rock. She had no idea what he was thinking.

"He was right. The timing was all wrong. We had no

money. We were flower children moving from one gathering to the next, experimenting with whatever we could get our hands on. It was no way to raise a baby — though people did. We decided we'd wait and have children later.

"As you can guess, there wasn't any *later*. Three months after the abortion, Michael split. I stepped out of a motel one morning and the van was gone, Michael was gone, what little money we did have was gone.

"I reached out to Phoebe, my former college roommate, who had started working here at the Center. The rest you probably know. She and I had an open relationship until she left me to go off and die."

"I've seen pictures and videos of her," Max said. "Melissa really does resemble her aunt. No wonder Harry was stricken with her. So were you and Phoebe lovers or sex partners?"

She squinted at him. "You can go for the jugular, too. We were lovers and always had been. It never mattered who else she was involved with, even Harry." She frowned. "It was so uncanny when Harry hired Melissa. Of course, he had no idea he was hiring the niece of his former lover.

"I guess I had gone into a self-pity shell after Phoebe left. Neither one of us had expected faithfulness from the other — that was our agreement. But I didn't expect we'd ever part.

"So I didn't seek a relationship again that might last more than a few hours." She paused. "I was still involved with your Agnes when Phoebe left, of course — but she was an exception. With her, I was always the teacher, and she was always the student. I think that was the way she, and possibly even I, justified our relationship. She wasn't cuckolding you. She was drawing on our relationship to strengthen what she treasured most, her love for you."

Max's expression sobered.

Claire shrugged. "As for me, there's not much I haven't tried sexually. I remain a firm believer in the right of adults to pursue their sexual interests in whatever way suits them that does not involve coercion. So ever since Phoebe left, I practiced what I preached without the remotest interest in intimacy."

Claire closed her eyes in a vain attempt to hold back tears. She didn't want to cry. Why did she cry so much around Max?

"Let me guess. Until Melissa arrived on the scene."

"Melissa pried me open." She chuckled. "Figuratively and literally. She sparked my renewed interest in working in front of a camera. You see," she said, curling her fingers in his, "for me, working on these tapes does require a certain level of relationship, perhaps even intimacy, in order for them to be genuine." She licked her dry lips. "Being sex partners involves some of all that."

"But not at the depth of lovers."

"Exactly."

"I understand. I'm sorry," Max said, brushing his fingers across the top of her hand. "I don't know what to say, other than that the woman who has emerged from all you've described is a very intriguing, sexy woman. And I'm extremely pleased to have her as a sex partner for as long as I can."

Claire nodded and peered at Max through blurry eyes. "You're making me blubber. Thank you for listening and understanding." She leaned across the space separating them to brush her lips against his. "Thank you for being you. For being my sex partner. Are you in a rush to get back?"

He shook his head.

"Do you suppose, after cleaning up here, we could go over to that overlook, sit on the grass for a while and watch the Hudson flow by? I'd very much like you to hold me if you would."

"I would very much like to hold you, Claire. Without a doubt."

Max sat on the knoll beside Claire with his arm tucked comfortably around her waist. Her head rested on his shoulder.

They'd said very little, each apparently content to watch the water ebb and flow from the north to the south.

He groaned inwardly. Sometimes, Claire sounded more like an academic than he did. How could she split hairs so thinly? Sex partners. Lovers.

He curled his fingers tighter around her waist. He doubted sex partners bared their souls to each other, then held each other to keep each other intact. He didn't feel like a damn sex partner. He felt like a lover. He didn't want to be a damn sex partner. He *was* a lover. He turned to briefly nuzzle Claire's sweet-smelling hair — his lover's hair. Even if his lover wasn't willing to hear his declaration — yet.

Chapter Nine

Feeling a little tense, Claire listened to Melissa's opening patter in front of the camera. She was a master at drawing the viewer into what would take place on the set, making all of the Center's products more personal. It had been her idea to open the videos with the performers sitting next to her on stools while she introduced the tape and interviewed the performers. She'd convinced Harry and herself that this more personal touch would enhance both market share and usefulness of the information to the viewer.

Claire glowed when she saw Simone and Inez join Harry to watch and support them. Simone might be in for a surprise.

Melissa glanced between her and Max sitting on either side of her. Smiling directly at the camera, Melissa pointed out, "As I've already said, this video will address some aspects of aging and lovemaking. You may be surprised to learn that some aspects of having sex are easier, while some can be more problematic. As you know from watching other Center tapes, there are many ways of lovemaking. The same is true for an older couple. Perhaps"—she again turned to grin at Claire and Max, including them in her introductory remarks—"being inventive and creative is even more of a premium as we age.

"Now then, you may have seen Claire and Max in other tapes, so they may already be known to you. So, Claire, without being specific, you are in your fifties?"

Claire nodded, tugging her robe around her legs. "Late fifties.

"And, Max. You're in your sixties?"

"Early sixties."

"We certainly want to be clear with our viewers that this tape is being made over a series of weeks. We don't expect Max to be superhuman." She gave him a gentle smile. "Older men may have more difficulty having orgasms and will likely ejaculate less frequently and with less volume than when they were twenty or thirty years younger."

"More difficult perhaps," Max conceded, "but well worth the effort."

"And there are some advantages. Right, Claire? Why don't you share with our viewers a couple of pluses of having sex with older guys?" Melissa smiled back at the camera. "We'll share more thoughts and tips with you as we go."

"Sure." Claire sat up straighter. "I find it a real turn-on to take a man in my mouth before he becomes fully hard."

Melissa laughed. "That's true. My guy wakes up with an erection. And if I can get to him while he's half-mast, he immediately grows stiff when I take him into my mouth. What's another advantage you're thinking about?"

Claire laughed. "This may sound selfish, but I can have as many orgasms as I want. I don't have to worry about squeezing my pleasure in before my partner ejaculates if I'm ready."

"Well, ladies," Melissa winked at the camera, "you may want to remember that. You do have something to look forward to with an older partner. Now, from your emails, you often wonder about whether our performers are involved with each other off camera or not. Max, you and Claire have a relationship off camera, right?"

Claire scowled at Melissa and Max. What the hell was Melissa doing? *We'll have to edit that question.* And how was Max going to answer? He didn't appear particularly flustered.

"That's correct," Max said smoothly. "At this age, more than a little practice is needed."

Good for you, Max!

Melissa winked at the camera. "I'm sure you want us to get started. Claire and Max, why don't you remove your robes and get set up on the bed."

Claire and Max nodded, then headed for set one. Melissa followed, continuing her patter. "We are going to demonstrate an important element of sex with older couples. Men and women need to become comfortable with the woman helping the man orgasm outside her body. Some men may be able to climax within the woman's vagina some of the time but not always. In those latter instances, the woman may want to find other ways to help her man come. Again, there is no right or wrong way. Your limits are only restrained by your creativity.

"Max and Claire lubed and did a little preliminary warm up before we went on camera. Adequate lube is even more important as we age. As you can see, Max is going to begin in the missionary position. Even if he feels himself about ready to come in Claire's vagina, we've asked him to pull out, so we can demonstrate one of the points of this scene."

Claire pursed her lips, trying to relax as Max slipped his cock into her pussy. He grunted once, then sank into her without difficulty.

"You okay?" Max whispered, seating himself securely.

Claire nodded, rubbing his bald head. "I'm fine," she whispered in his ear, looking away from the camera. "You handled Melissa's question very nicely."

"As you say, she can be too curious."

"You sure are feeling huge this morning." She grinned, kissing his nose. "Maybe we didn't have to abstain for the last couple of days. Now, let's get serious about this tape."

She lifted her legs straight up, knowing that was a turn-on for Max, as well as likely for many viewers. Max didn't hesitate. He began pumping in and out of her steadily. She smiled. Some young female viewers were going to be quite jealous as he simply glided along comfortably, obviously in no danger of coming prematurely. She glanced over at Simone, who looked quite entranced by what she and Max were managing.

Spreading her legs farther apart, she remained Max's wide-open receptacle. There would be other scenes where she would take the lead and they'd focus on the woman. This scene was to focus on the man. She ran her fingernails down either side of his spine.

His eyes rounded, and his hips flexed faster. She grinned as the force of his thrust propelled them up the bed an inch or so. His breathing turned ragged. Max had forgotten the camera. He was fucking her, and he didn't give a damn about the camera or Melissa's occasional patter.

Claire let her legs fall to the bed before wrapping them around his butt. When he drove into her, she assisted with her legs, pulling him harder each time.

She saw his eyes glaze over. "Let me know when you're ready."

"Now," he said, yanking out of her. He held his cock until she claimed it for herself with both hands. She smiled at him, then began slowly moving her hands over his length while holding him loosely, maintaining his edge. She cradled his balls. Max groaned and rocked back and forth on his knees, seeking release in her hands. Max shook his head, then stalled and gave her an odd half-smile. They both knew Melissa would want to keep their home audience informed.

"Claire has several options at this point," Melissa said. "And there is no particular rush. She could try all the options. Right now, she's prepared to bring Max off with her hands. Now you see her lower her mouth to cover the tip of Max's cock. She's left one hand on his cock and is using the other to fondle his ass.

"Ladies, the anus is incredibly sensitive for a guy. I hope you've watched our anal tapes and have become comfortable with anal play. For the older man, you can be very helpful by paying attention to his anus.

"Yes, Claire is dipping a finger into Max's anus. She's teasing him while keeping her oral attention on his cock. Watch Max squeeze his butt cheeks closed, then open. He wants more.

"Ah," Melissa moaned. "Her finger is all the way in. She's stimulating his prostate gland. Geez, guys, I'm creaming my panties." Melissa gasped. "We'll edit that comment out. Look. Max is getting re-involved. His hips are beginning to move." Melissa giggled. "Even an older man can wait only so long."

Claire smiled around Max's cock as he began to churn his hips. She could finish him this way, but she didn't want any viewer to think they had faked his orgasm. She raised her mouth off him, then quickened her hand on his cock and her finger in his ass. He gave her a wild look, breathing heavily.

She shifted slightly, so with any luck he'd spill on her breast. She kept her movements steady, monitoring his signals. He was coming. He just hadn't arrived yet.

"Come for us, Max," she whispered.

Max's thighs went rigid. His guttural response was a low growl.

"Yes," Claire said, feeling his surge nearing. "Cover my boob. Wonderful," she mewled as his come spewed forth. She milked him slowly. Satisfied that the viewer had witnessed a convincing ejaculation, Claire tucked Max back in her mouth and with great care took what remained.

"Excellent," Melissa cooed. "As you can see, Claire has been very inventive. She didn't stay with one thing. And from the look on her face, although this tape was more focused on the male partner than on the female, it doesn't look like Claire is going away unsatisfied."

Claire couldn't stifle a laugh. Without dropping Max from her mouth, she raised a hand and flashed an okay sign.

"Cut," Melissa said to the cameramen. "Fantastic, guys! Really, this is a great contribution to the tape."

Claire nodded and cradled Max's cock. "You okay?" she asked.

"Why wouldn't I be?" he said, cracking a wide smile. "As Melissa said, this should be a good start."

Claire handed him his robe, then they both got to their feet. It was only then that Claire realized not everyone had left the room. Simone stood a few feet away with a look of adoration that Claire thought the young woman reserved only for Melissa.

"You two were magnificent." Simone smiled shyly. "I wouldn't have believed this unless I'd seen it for myself. Maybe I won't be overly concerned about growing older."

"You have many years to go before you have to worry about growing older," Claire pointed out. "Simone, have you formally been introduced to Max?"

"Hi," Simone said, extending her hand to Max and smiling bashfully. "Can you really last as long as a woman wants?"

Max turned red. "Depends on the woman, I imagine. These old muscles do wear out in time."

Simone grinned at Claire. "I hope we can start that other tape Melissa was talking about real soon."

"You may have to stand in line. It does take Max a while to recover."

Simone stood on her tiptoes and pursed her lips.

Claire smiled and lowered her head, welcoming Simone's soft warm lips.

"Melissa was right," Simone murmured. "You two made me soaking wet. Feel me," she whispered, tucking Claire's fingers under her skirt.

"Goodness," Claire muttered as her fingers came into contact with Simone's moist, fleshy cleft. She grabbed Max's hand, interlacing their fingers. "Feel Simone and tell me your performance doesn't turn women on."

"Jesus," he mumbled. His eyes rounded at Claire, then at Simone, who lifted her skirt as if he had to see to believe.

Simone rocked against their fingers. "You two are fantastic," she breathed.

Max pulled away, leaving Simone gasping. "I'll never understand you women," he huffed, stalking toward the showers.

"What's his problem?" Simone asked, looking hurt as she glared at Max's back. "Doesn't he want to work with me?"

"It's not you." Claire chuckled. "I'm sure he'll work with you when the time comes. Max doesn't like getting involved with staff except on camera."

"But he's involved with you."

Claire turned quickly to wave at Max, but he'd already left.

She pursed her lips and looked back at Simone. "That's true, he is."

An hour later, Max entered Claire's office, slumped down on the couch, and glared at her.

She was leaning over a table, filling in the detail of a catalogue mock-up. She'd glanced up when he entered and smiled brilliantly. After one look at his face, her expression sobered, and she returned to her work.

"There," she said, "that'll work." She peered over at him. "How are you?"

"What was that about back there?" he asked, unable to keep exasperation from his tone.

Her brow furrowed. "What?"

"That little tease show with Simone?"

"Melissa wants the two of you to work together. Simone was hot for you. I didn't think it'd hurt for you two to play a little."

"With your help?"

"That's right."

"She spread her feet when you shoved my fingers into her pussy. She was inviting me to bring her off as she stood there."

Claire shrugged. "So—why didn't you?"

"We weren't working," he growled.

"So fine," she snapped. Claire shook her head. "You're going to fuck her silly sometime within the month. I don't see why a little play matters so much."

"I'm sure you don't," he said, rising to his feet. She flinched, and he felt immediate remorse. "I'm sorry, Claire. I'm still trying to fit in here, I guess. Simone is a beautiful young woman. Of course I'll work with her, if Melissa wants me to."

Claire didn't respond.

Max shrugged. "Maybe it would've been different if I wasn't so sated at that moment." He gave her a half-smile. "You did sap all the desire out of me. I hope Simone wasn't offended."

"Disappointed, maybe," Claire walked around the table, "but not offended. You probably only whetted her appetite more by not giving her what she wanted. I suspect Simone is used to getting what she wants. So when will I see you next?"

"Probably not until the weekend." His heart gave way. "You still want to come out to the house this weekend?"

"Why wouldn't I?" She clasped her hands at her waist. "You still have several rooms that need claiming."

"That's true." He laughed softly, then leaned over and kissed Claire's forehead. "Let me know when Simone is doing any on camera work. She's watched me. I think I'd like to watch her before hooking up with her on set. She could be a hellion."

Claire kissed his cheek. "She was wet, wasn't she?"

"Damn wet." He nodded at her. "You have my number if you need anything."

Max walked down the hallway and out the exit without stopping. He headed for his car, still trying to sort out his reactions to Claire and Simone.

How far would Claire have been willing to take things? Cripes, they'd just banged their brains out. Simone was seductively tantalizing, no mistake about that. When she'd lifted her skirt, he'd been surprised he'd gotten immediately hard again. Fortunately, neither she nor Claire had parted his robe. This place might be the death of him yet, if he hung around often enough.

Claire had expressed pride in her open relationship with Phoebe, apparently the only person she'd counted as a lover since the asshole Michael dumped her. Was Claire even capable of having a faithful relationship?

He climbed into his car. And why should that question bother him at all? He'd never expected an exclusive relationship with her, had he? Even Harry and Melissa continued working with other partners on camera on occasion. Max drew his hand over his bare head. What the three women had engaged in the previous Friday afternoon in Melissa's studio wasn't in front of a camera.

Yet he and Claire practiced as often as they could off camera.

So what was the difference? None.

He pulled out onto the street and headed for the bridge. He trusted that Melissa knew what she was doing. She'd become the glue that held the Center together. She wouldn't do anything to jeopardize it, and she'd clearly come to the decision to involve Simone in more of the Center's projects.

He'd seen no indication that Claire was hooking up with anyone outside the Center—nor with any other man, for that matter. That might be a matter of coincidence rather than choice. He sped up. He seldom reviewed any tapes he'd worked on, but he was looking forward to seeing this one. He'd watched Claire with plenty of other people on tape. Would she look any different marshalling her skills to bring *him* off?

Melissa examined the charcoal sketch of Simone lying in her arms. The younger woman lay spread eagled with her back crushed against Melissa's breasts. She'd canted her head until their lips nearly touched. The observer would have to determine if they had already kissed or were about to. The keen observer would recognize the well-loved look of both women. Melissa sighed. She probably wouldn't entitle the piece, but if she did, it would simply be *Bliss.*

She glanced up and waved at Harry as he entered her office studio.

He walked over to peer at the sketch, startling only slightly when he saw its subjects. "That's potent."

"Very," she replied. "Memorable."

He rubbed the base of her neck. "So have you set up a time for taping with Simone?"

"I thought we might try Friday afternoon. Have you decided whether or not to work with us? At this point, I don't know whether to prepare my comments for woman-on-woman or two women and a guy."

He shook his head, eyeing the drawing closely. "That's a hell of a lot to pass up, but Simone has to know if I work with her on camera, then I can't serve on any of her graduate school committees."

Melissa turned to her husband. "You'd still direct her research here?"

"Of course. And she'd still have access to all the data and resources we have for her dissertation. Damn," he said, scrutinizing the picture, "your body provides a pale backdrop that only serves to highlight Simone's contours."

"That's the intent." She smiled and turned back to the sketch. "Natural contrasts. I do believe this is the best work I've done from a photo."

"Maybe that's because you experienced the full impact of the photo."

"Probably. So when will you decide about Simone?"

"Are you pressing me?" He ran his chin through her hair.

"Not really, but it does sound like Simone should have a little more information so she can make an informed decision." Melissa clucked her mouth. "Not that I doubt her decision in the least."

Harry shook his head. "I'm old enough to be her father."

"So?" Melissa chirped. "You're almost old enough to be my father, and we're married. Simone will work with Max, and Max is old enough to be her grandfather." She scowled at Harry. "Didn't you once tell me that none of this is about age? It's about communicating with our viewers. It's about helping people."

"That drawing sure suggests Simone satisfied you quite nicely."

"Uh-huh. I enjoy sex. We all do, or I doubt any of us could do this sort of work." She pushed back from the desk and stood on her toes to kiss him. "Harry, you'll love working with Simone, trust me. I know you will."

He glanced back at the drawing. "I don't question your assessment, but we do need to let Simone decide first."

"You're not going to tell me your decision?"

"I may not know until Friday afternoon. A non-faculty member being asked to serve on a graduate student's committee is quite an honor. She won't start courses until next semester, but she already has an advisor. He's talked to me about serving on her dissertation when the time comes."

Melissa stuck her tongue out at her husband. "Dipping your tongue into Simone's pussy is quite an honor, too. I believe the three of us could come up with a variety of fantasy skits to showcase how two women can take care of each other and a guy as well." She frowned. "I can't make the decision for you, but please let me know as soon as you can."

"Speaking of dipping into pussy," Harry said, drawing her to him. "Are you wearing panties? I thought not. My, you are ready. Was it the drawing, or me?"

"Both," she squeaked.

"I don't think we should wait until we get home."

Melissa shook her head. "Too risky," she said, guiding him to the carpet.

"Isn't this where you hooked up with Simone and Claire last Friday?"

"Exactly," she murmured. "You can imagine, if you like, that they are still here with us," she whispered, cupping her mound with his fingers.

"Max?" Claire said into the phone.

"Who else did you expect? What's up?"

Typically abrupt. She smiled. She hadn't had many conversations with him over the phone, but he always sounded clipped and hurried. Some people nearly lived on the phone. Apparently, Max wasn't one of them.

"If you want to observe Simone at work, you might want to drop by the Center after lunch on Friday. We could go back to your place after."

"Sounds good. What's she taping?"

"At least woman-on-woman with Melissa. Maybe Harry will join for a three-way."

Max whistled softly. "She wants to work with everybody."

"Simone is eager. So will you be by?"

"I'll be there. Wouldn't want to miss it."

"Do you have thoughts about our weekend?"

Max was slow to respond. "A few. There are loads more bike trails, or we could drive up to the Mohawk Valley. I've been considering buying some property up that way."

"That sounds like fun."

"I think we should spend some time outside rather than being cooped up in the house all the time. We can do some walking along trails in the Mohawk region if you want."

Claire chuckled into the phone. "Walking isn't exactly the kind of outdoor activity I was thinking about."

"Oh."

"I'll work on some ideas before Friday. Max?"

"Yeah?"

"Would you like to share a little phone sex?"

"No."

His voice was suddenly raspy.

Claire chuckled. "I thought not. Another time, perhaps. See you Friday."

"Right. Bye."

Claire rolled over on her bed and howled with laughter. Max wasn't a high-tech kind of guy. He probably couldn't have switched the phone to speaker in order to free up his hands.

Sometimes he did show his age. Delightfully so.

CHAPTER TEN

Claire stood beside the cameraman on Set Two, glad she had a role to fulfill. She was to direct the camera if needed.

Melissa and Simone were sitting comfortably on a pair of stools.

"We're going to try a fantasy this afternoon," Melissa said excitedly, looking at the camera. "Some of our viewers learn more easily by being drawn into a fantasy rather than watching a tape focusing specifically on techniques. Simone, our newest staff member, will be joining me."

Melissa wet her lips, then tugged at the sash of her robe. "Before I set up the fantasy," Melissa said lightly, "let's get to know Simone a little. What attracted you to the Center, Simone?"

Sitting on a stool next to Melissa, Simone smiled into the camera and didn't hesitate. "You, of course."

Claire nodded, remembering Simone had said she'd been attracted to Melissa even before she met her, through her artwork. Given Simone's radiating face, her current interest seemed much more focused on the artist than on art.

"We'll cut out that question later." Melissa glanced at Claire as if pleading for help.

Claire merely shrugged her shoulders.

"So, Simone, why don't you briefly explain to our viewers why you chose this sort of work?"

Besides having some hot sex, Claire wanted to add.

"Because I believe working on videos like this one can be a way of helping a lot of people who want to learn more about sex and about how to express their unique sexuality." Simone turned surprisingly bashful. "And because I'm about to start a graduate degree in human sexuality, and I respect the Center's research capacity. I think we've reached an understanding whereby I will be able to express my sexuality while also contributing to the rich research database the Center has generated over the years. I am blessed to be able to pursue both interests in one workplace." Simone flashed a brilliant smile at the camera. "I am very pleased to be here with all of you."

Claire nodded thoughtfully. Most every viewer would believe Simone had singled them out individually with her infectious enthusiasm. And the viewer wouldn't be completely wrong. Simone reveled in being watched. Yet she didn't seem to get hung up on ego. She enjoyed sex — apparently, the giving as much as the receiving.

Reaching back to retie her ponytail, Claire made a mental note to decide how she might feature Simone in the next Center catalogue. Perhaps she should consider personal interviews for the catalogue like Melissa did with their multimedia.

She caught movement out of the corner of her eye. Harry and Simone must've come to an understanding about their future relationship. He entered the area wearing a robe. He appeared ready to go to work. She'd never doubted the Harry she'd known so well over the years would opt for working with his wife and Simone over serving on stuffy academic committees. Apparently, Simone agreed.

"And we are very pleased to have you working with us." Melissa briefly squeezed Simone's shoulder. "I'm sure our viewers will benefit from your work on camera as well as the research you will do off camera.

"So" — she arched her eyebrows at the camera — "here is the fantasy. Simone and I have only been lovers for a short time. We are making love in my living room. It is a Saturday afternoon. My husband is golfing. I am never certain when he'll return." Melissa pouted, already drawing the viewer into the fantasy. "And I don't know how he will react if he finds me in Simone's arms. He knows Simone; after all, she moved next door to us two years ago. He knows I'm intrigued with her, but not how much. We don't know if he will get home in time to find us together or not. Secretly, I hope he does.

"A footnote. We want you to see the fantasy unfold, but do keep in mind we are also demonstrating techniques. Woman-on-woman." She glanced over at Harry, who remained off camera. "And I believe two women and a guy." Melissa smiled at the camera. "We'll go get set up. Talk with you later. Enjoy."

Claire moved with the cameramen to follow the women toward Set Three. Several sex toys were randomly displayed on a low table. A couch and a couple easy chairs were the principle props filling out the set.

Claire and the small number of observers waited for the women to enter the set. They were disrobing offstage. Claire checked out the cameramen and signaled them to start, then heard Max gasping beside her. She looked up to see Melissa and Simone shimmy onto the set hand-in-hand. From their grins, it was rather obvious that this little skit had already begun offstage.

Claire tried to wet her dry mouth. Simone wore only white kneesocks. She'd never looked more naked. Melissa wore a gold chain loosely wrapped around her waist. Her breasts were partially clad with a flimsy pink bra that perfectly accentuated her swollen nipples.

The scene gave the impression that the audience was a little late gathering for the party. They were being dropped into the middle of a tryst. It was up to each viewer to decide whether the women had been loving each other for five minutes or for hours.

Melissa scattered several couch pillows about, then gestured for Simone to join her on the floor. Clearly, they had spoken about how they wanted to bring the viewer into the fantasy. If Harry did join the women, Claire didn't think he'd need a script.

The two women lay on their sides curled around each other, with Simone planting kisses on Melissa's mound. Glowing with her distinctive radiance, Melissa guided a vibrator along the length of Simone's dark pussy. Soft mewls escaped Simone's lips. As Simone continued to caress Melissa's buttocks tenderly, she leaned back, allowing Melissa to set the pace.

Simone's tight ebony bottom and pussy were the focal point of this pose, and Melissa didn't hesitate to show off their new staff person's treasures. She sank her teeth into Simone's hip while sliding the vibrator up one side of her pussy and down the other. The perceptive viewer would notice those pussy lips swelling and parting in anticipation. Simone's mewling turned into panting demands. Melissa smiled, then eased the vibrator into Simone's pink pussy.

Simone nearly shot out of her arms, but quickly steadied herself. Melissa raised Simone's top leg, giving herself better access to her clit and providing a clear view of how that little bit of hard flesh was growing immensely under Melissa's patient digital stimulation. With one of Simone's knee-sock-clad legs raised in the air and the other resting at an angle on the floor, Melissa had created an erotic visual picture like she did with her art, funneling the viewer's perspective to a pivotal, critical focal point — in this instance, the coming to life of Simone's sex.

Sighing, Simone began again to lap at Melissa's belly. Unfortunately, her curly head blocked Melissa's pubic regions from Claire's view. From the rhythm of Simone's elbow, she could tell Melissa's pussy was hardly going unnoticed.

Melissa jerked her head up, emitting a gasp. She widened her thighs, and Simone's head lowered, no doubt joining her finger. Claire checked the second cameraman. Good. The viewer, with some editing help, would have the opportunity to see both women exercising their oral talents. Melissa smacked her lips and blinked at the camera before refocusing on Simone's pussy. She turned up the vibrator, then sank it into Simone until it nearly disappeared from view.

Simone's white-clad legs shot straight out as she screamed. She was over the top. "Keep going!" she cried. "Good God."

Simone clutched Melissa's hips as if they were life preservers. She arched against the vibrator, while Melissa's fingers could be seen sliding a mercilessly deliberate pace along the length of Simone's exposed clit. Melissa seemed intent on slowly torturing her.

Simone quaked and twisted as Melissa remained relentlessly coaxing, calling forth the inevitable. "Come for me, girl. Come for all of us." Melissa leaned over, flicking her tongue across Simone's engorged clit.

"That's it!" Simone screamed, rolling away from Melissa.

Melissa chuckled, slowly withdrawing the vibrator. She waited a moment before turning about to gather her young protégé in her arms. Melissa's lips brushed across Simone's forehead, then slanted across her open mouth.

Simone eagerly returned the kiss, wrapping her arms around Melissa. She showered Melissa with kiss after kiss, then mouthed a single word. "Nice."

"That's it. I've seen enough," came a deep male voice from offstage. "Make room for me."

Startled, both women sat up, huddling together as Harry strutted on stage buck naked with his stiff condom-clad cock waving, looking as if any heat source would do.

Simone gleamed at Harry, her lips curving up into a smile. She'd clearly stopped acting, if indeed she ever had been.

"Look at him," she murmured, slightly awestruck.

"Hi, Harry," Melissa said softly. "I didn't know if you'd get here before we finished. You know Simone, our neighbor."

Harry grinned wolfishly at the two women and nodded. "Looks like you've done a nice job preparing her for me. I plan on getting to know her better. Much better."

"I want to get to know you better," said Simone, raising her arms to him.

"Come on down and join us, Harry," Melissa said, curling a finger at him. "I'll see what I can arrange to help the two of you get better acquainted."

The two women separated for Harry to lie between them. Once he was on his back, Simone rose to her hands and knees and moved quickly to cover his mouth with hers. They kissed greedily while Melissa flung off her flimsy bra. She grazed her nipples down Simone's back as she knelt behind her, then rubbed her breasts across Simone's elevated rump.

Claire wet her lips as Simone waggled her butt. She'd relished her own encounter with that tight derriere.

Melissa slapped Simone's bottom hard enough for the echo to reverberate around the stage. "You want me to share my husband with you?"

"Yes," Simone whimpered, pulling her mouth away from Harry and twisting her head around. "Spank my other cheek, too. I want to fuck your man. May I?"

Had Claire ever witnessed eyes that pled more than Simone's?

Instead of answering, Melissa reached between Simone's legs to encircle Harry's cock with one hand while the other pressed Simone's thighs back until she had the cock head gliding along Simone's damp cleft.

"Simone, I give you my husband," Melissa intoned. "Husband, I give you our neighbor, Simone. Better late than never. I believe you two can take over from here."

Melissa swatted Simone's bottom once more before moving to the side. For her part, Simone rose up on her knees until she squatted over Harry's cock. She raised her fists in the air, then settled down, swallowing Harry's shaft with her pussy until it disappeared from view.

"Oh yeah. So full." Simone grinned at Melissa. "You're a lucky woman. Thank you, neighbor."

Simone's look of triumph had to touch anyone watching.

Harry moaned as Simone waggled her butt, securing their joining. Claire knew Simone had to be a tight fit for him. Given the sparks flying between the three performers, Claire wondered how long this little scene could last. Having been there before, she knew none of the participants had any awareness of the cameras or even that they were being watched. They had been transported into the fantasy — and ultimately, that was what would make this tape so valuable for viewers.

Apparently satisfied with the connection she'd made between Simone and Harry, Melissa scooted around and knelt beside Simone, keeping the couple between her and the camera. She wrapped an arm around Simone, then kissed the corner of her mouth while fondling her boobs.

Harry groaned, seemingly mesmerized by his wife, who had clearly taken over the direction of their erotic play.

Melissa reached down to brush against Simone's enlarged clit. She teasingly used her tongue to wet the woman's ear. "Any time you're ready."

Simone smacked her lips. "I can't believe you're both loving me."

"We'd like to try," Melissa chuckled, "if you can unlock yourself enough to move."

"Oh my." The words were breathy. Simone rose up on her knees, then quickly crashed down around Harry, who grunted his pleasure. She rose again.

"That's more like it," Melissa said, smacking Simone's butt sharply. "Fuck my man. Show him what you're made of, girl."

Simone raised her arms straight up, then swayed back and forth. Each time she rose and fell, she moaned more loudly. She bit down on her lower lip and shifted into a corkscrew motion. Her arms flapped loosely. Simone was drawing her lovers and the viewers into her own private world.

Up to this point, Harry had been the passive recipient of the byplay between the two women, evidently unfazed by the visual display Melissa and Simone so cleverly orchestrated.

The way his face contorted, Claire was sure Simone had found a way to squeeze his cock while maintaining her energetic dance over him.

"Oh hell," Harry groaned loudly, joining the fray. His hips failed to keep up with Simone. He reached up to steady her, but she slapped his hands away, then leaned back, farther out of his reach. She shook her head, and Harry settled back, apparently resigned to his fate.

Simone giggled, then leaned forward on her hands and knees to kiss his wide-open mouth. "I can't take you any deeper. Now be a good neighbor. Fuck me good."

Harry didn't seem in the mood to debate.

Claire smiled. Simone had him on the verge of finishing much sooner than he'd planned. There was much more to demonstrate to the viewer.

"Now," Simone barked, driving her tongue into his mouth.

She raised her head, waggling her butt against his cock. "Do I have to do all the work? Show me what you've got, big man."

Harry grunted and his hips lurched upward, threatening to dislodge Simone. She grinned, then bore back against him, holding her ground. Harry's hips churned over and over until they began to spasm.

Simone fought to hold her position while crying out her joy. "I've got him!" she screamed to Melissa. "He's filling me."

Melissa sat back on her heels and became a cheerleader with everyone else in the room. The ending of this little skit had hardly been in doubt from the moment Simone began her gyrating aerial ride.

Simone crashed to Harry's chest. She alternated between soft moans and wails, greedily accepting the impact of every thrust. Harry wrapped his arms around her back, then began pumping faster as if he were attempting to drench her pussy from some untapped reservoir hidden in his loins.

Claire wiped perspiration from her brow. At last the tableau ebbed and quieted. For a long moment, the only sounds were haggard breathing. Not a sound came from anyone standing around the set.

At last, Harry twisted around to lock his focus on his wife. She must've been smiling, because Harry's mouth turned into a large grin.

"Guess we can still get it done," he murmured. "A little too quick, though."

Melissa leaned over and kissed him. "I never had a doubt."

Melissa turned to the cameramen.

"That's enough for today, guys. We'll probably do another sequence or two during the next week." She grinned back at Simone. "Perhaps we'll all be able to exercise a little more patience and last a little longer, now that we have this one under our belts." She turned to Simone. "When you're ready, we can go get cleaned up."

"Thank you," Simone said to Harry as she hoisted herself off him. "I'm sure this will be a very useful tape. I've always loved fantasies." She hugged herself. "I wish *my* neighbor was so well hung. Good God, this is a fantastic place to work!"

Claire smiled at Max.

He shook his head as they left the set. "She's something, huh?"

"Wild and unbridled."

He turned, and Claire caught a hint of a smile. "She'd better have a power drink when she works with me. She won't be bringing me off nearly as quickly as she did Harry."

Absorbed in his book, Max looked up when he heard Clair's voice.

"This is such a splendid bed," Claire said. "I'm so pleased you wanted me to help initiate it."

Max peeked over his reading glasses at her. She'd set the novel she'd been reading on her lap. Her breasts still had a pinkish afterglow from their recent lovemaking. He leaned back against the pillows and closed his book. "Is your novel boring?"

She chuckled, then squeezed his arm. "No, but it's not nearly as exciting as we are."

"Too bad I'm not younger. We could make love all night long."

Claire frowned at him. "I hope you're not troubled by not ejaculating. I'm not sure I could come again if I wanted to."

"I could probably prove you a liar about that, but"—he yawned—"I do want to save some energy for the rest of the weekend. Reading in bed like this . . ." He gave her wry grin. "Isn't too domestic for you, is it?"

"Not at all. I'm not thirty either, if you recall. I take it you and Agnes weren't all that frequent even when you were thirty."

Oddly, the change of subject didn't irritate him. Talking about Agnes came easier now, without sending him into a tailspin. "Agnes probably told you that sex for us was pretty much a Saturday morning thing. Then it didn't interfere with sleep, and we didn't have to rush off to work. However, sex seldom delayed my yard work for long."

"Too bad." Claire made a face. "I hope you're not planning on any early morning yard work tomorrow."

"Can't say I ever considered it. Of course, after Isabelle was old enough to walk, Saturday morning sex was most often replaced with cartoons." He shrugged his shoulders. "In those days, the cartoons were more creative than our sex."

"And more enjoyable?" Claire asked.

"Often. Too often."

"That makes me sad for both of you. So, does Isabelle know about your work with the Center?"

Max reached behind him to straighten the pillows. He scowled at the picture of his daughter on a nearby wall.

"Agnes was so excited about us contributing to the sexual well-being of humankind that she eagerly confided in Isabelle. She thought she could help Isabelle and her husband have better intimacy than we had had. Our daughter wasn't nearly as enthused as Agnes naively expected.

"Since Agnes's death, Isabelle has pretty much kept me at arm's length. I expect she thought the entire renewed interest in sex was my idea, not her mother's. She lives in Oregon, seems to have a good husband and a stable middle-class life. We're in touch at major holidays and birthdays. She hasn't been back here since Agnes died."

"That's a shame."

Claire studied the other picture on the wall.

Max could have predicted her next question.

"And your granddaughter? I've forgotten her name."

"Rosanne. I'm not certain what she knows. She doesn't ask questions, and I don't tell."

"Sort of like the military."

"Something like that. Rosanne is in college in the Boston area. She's about as far away from her mother as she can get.

I do get to see her more often."

"She must be a little younger than Simone."

"Probably. Rosanne is twenty." He smiled. "Some days, I think she's twenty going on forty, and other days, she behaves like an adolescent."

"Sounds like a woman."

"Right. I forgot."

"I believe Simone is twenty-three. Melissa is twenty-six or twenty-seven. There are days when I'd like to be that young again." Claire gave him a pout. "But not many. I was probably lucky to survive those raucous years."

"Hmm, I might like to be younger than I am, but I wouldn't want to be twenty again."

"Damn, Missy and Simone were good yesterday." Claire yawned. "They each bring an uncanny, genuine quality to this work that captivates anyone watching."

"I noticed. Do you think Simone caught Harry by surprise?"

Claire nodded. "I know she did. None of us had seen Simone work with a man before." She smiled at him, then pecked at his nose. "She's got some surprise moves. Even I wasn't aware of her subtle corkscrew twists."

"Yeah, if Harry's eyes were any clue, she had him incredibly turned on. He didn't have a prayer for stretching out that scene."

"You're going to have to be careful with her," Claire chided, "if you're going to uphold the reputation I've raved about to her."

"Maybe you women shouldn't talk so much." He tapped her nipple with a finger. "But you're right. I'm going to have to keep my wits about me with Simone. She may be nearly as challenging as you are."

"Now who's stretching it? And for your information, I'm putting my money on you. If she's able to bring you off as quickly as she did Harry, I may have to step in and take over."

Max laughed. "And I don't doubt you'd do that." He glanced at his granddaughter's picture. "You'd like Rosanne. In her own way, she's a free spirit, too. Loves to sail. Is totally wrapped up in the green environment movement. Can't abide large corporations abandoning worker pension plans. If there is a cause lurking about, Rosanne won't be far behind. She'll amount to something someday."

"Like her grandfather."

He shrugged. "I've had a good life. Few complaints. I'd still like to finish some more manuscripts."

Claire giggled. "I don't think I told you. I searched your name on the Internet. Looks like you've been quite prolific."

"Most people aren't particularly interested in English literature. I'd like to finish a piece I've been writing about hybridizing roses."

"Why don't you?"

He grimaced. "I have to make time for it."

"Maybe we should collaborate on a piece about sex for older couples."

He eyed her curiously but couldn't figure out if she was kidding or not. "As long as it's not one of those sterile sex manuals."

Claire gave him the evil eye, then slid her hand under the sheet to cradle his soft penis. "Can you imagine me doing anything regarding sex that is sterile or boring?"

"Not hardly," he admitted, before chuckling.

"If you're done reading, why don't you hit the light? I'd like to go to sleep holding you like this."

Max switched off the lamp, then turned on his side, appreciating the warmth of Claire's pussy nestling against his butt and her fingers protectively cupping his testicles and penis.

Did Claire have any idea how loving her touch could be?

Claire drained her coffee and got up from the kitchen island to refill their mugs. She grinned—Max's eyes followed her every movement.

Domestic? Given last night's bedroom coziness, that ugly word might be more apt than she'd like to believe. But *domestic* wouldn't spoil their weekend, if she could help it. On her way to the kitchen, she'd already secreted her anal lube in a desk drawer of his home office.

Max had risen first and pulled on a pair of Levi's and a polo shirt before coming down to make the coffee. She'd slipped on the shortest skirt she'd brought with her, then slid into one of Max's white shirts. She'd knotted it below her breasts, not bothering with any of its buttons. Nor had she seen any need for underwear.

Domestic. Damn, that word had gnawed at her much of the night.

"It's Saturday morning," she said evenly. "Do you plan on yard work this morning?"

"I told you I wasn't."

She nodded and wet her lips. "Grab your mug and follow me."

Claire left the kitchen heading for Max's office. She smiled when she heard Max's footsteps behind her.

Without uttering a word, she strode quickly to his desk and began moving stacks of paper to the floor. Claire had the desk nearly cleared before Max spoke.

"What are you doing, Claire? I didn't think you'd want to spend Saturday morning cleaning my office."

"I have no such plans," she said, crawling onto his desk. She stretched out on her side, resting her chin on her elbow. "Office desks have many uses." She flipped up her short skirt and reached around her butt to slip a finger in her exposed pussy.

"Have you ever fucked a woman on your desk? Maybe one of those cute coeds who flash their panties at you from the front row of the lecture hall?"

Max's fingers trembled fumbling at his belt buckle. He shook his head. "Never."

"Too bad, though I love being your first at most anything. Well, Professor, why don't you think of me as one of your older students looking for a little extra credit?"

She smiled as he kicked his jeans aside, then quickly tugged his polo shirt over his head. His stiff cock swung wildly.

"My, my, he is ready. Maybe I should've brought along some classmates." Claire shifted to her hands and knees, crouching low over the desk. "Do you see anything he might want?"

"More than one." Max squeezed her butt, then palmed her pussy.

"Would you like a little taste, Professor?" she asked, wagging her butt seductively.

Max grunted.

She couldn't see him, but she felt him spreading her outer pussy lips with his fingers and his tongue laving at the opening.

"Jesus," she mumbled.

He reached around to tweak one nipple, and she tugged on the other one. "Incredible. Can you tongue my ass?"

His fingers on her nipple shook, then he let go of her breast.

Max clasped one butt cheek with each hand and spread them. "A most fetching bottom," he said in a husky voice.

He kissed one cheek, then the other. His tongue toyed at the crease of her buttocks.

"I'm so open," she moaned. "Don't tease me, Professor. I've dreamed about you in my ass for so long." His wet tongue tapped at her portal. "Goodness." She pushed back against him.

He chuckled as his tongue entered her full bore. He gripped her ass cheeks tightly and thoroughly tongued her ass.

"Oh hell," she squealed.

She hadn't counted on coming, but she wasn't about to hold back. He wrapped his arms around her thighs, holding her in place. She came over his wrists.

She heaved a sigh as he stood, then twisted her head and grinned. "Spectacular. Why don't you get him wet in my pussy?"

She winked. "And then finish him in my ass." She swore his cock stretched out an extra inch or so.

"You're a little too high up," he groused, trying to enter her. "I won't be able to stay on my tiptoes like this for long."

Claire crouched lower, trying to give him a better angle.

"Wait one moment. I'll get my huge dictionary."

She snickered as he dragged the oversized book to the end of the desk, then hefted it to the floor and stood on it.

"You have such a scholarly approach. A rather unique use for such a book of knowledge," she quipped. "But at the moment, I can't think of a better use."

"There," he said. "Targets are in range. Are you ready?"

"Professor, I've imagined this little scene since the first day of class. You had such a mesmerizing voice. I had you stripped naked before I even saw the syllabus."

Max's fingers dug into her back as his cock slid along her pussy folds until she felt him sinking easily inside her.

"Perfect. Remember, don't overdo it. I want you in my ass. I want all the extra credit I can get."

"Don't worry." He flexed in and out of her and scraped his fingers down her spine. "You're working on an A already."

She shivered as Max dropped kisses across her back, tugging on her ponytail as if it were connected to a bell. "Are you trying to ring my chimes, Professor?"

"I'm not *trying* to. I *will*. I promise."

She gasped when he reached under her to fondle her clit. "Goodness, you're going to make me come again."

"And that's bad?"

Trusting that he had himself in check, Claire twisted her head from side to side, pushing back against him. He never altered the pace of his hips banging into her, but the speed of his fingers strumming her clit increased.

"Tug on my ponytail again."

He twisted the fingers of one hand in her hair while the fingers of his other hand whipped across her engorged clit. His hips maintained a steady staccato pace.

"Stop. Wait."

He stilled immediately. She arched her neck back, shuddering in his grasp, hoping he had some appreciation for the warmth enveloping her body.

She blinked her eyes shut, then open. She inhaled sharply. "That was good. Now my ass!"

"So soon?"

"I don't want to lose you."

"I'm not going anywhere. Don't be so greedy. Take a couple more breaths."

Claire breathed through her nose and nodded her head. "Now, Professor Wilson," she purred, getting back into her role. "Don't make me wait any longer."

Max squidged out of her pussy, and she smiled at him over her shoulder. He skimmed his hand up and down his cock several times, then nodded, indicating his readiness.

Claire rested her head on the desk and waited.

"Your asshole is stunning," Max murmured. "You couldn't be more open."

"For you, Professor. I'm glad I'm not disappointing you. I just knew a man of your learning would know how to satisfy a woman. You'll find the lube in your top desk drawer. Fill my ass, Professor. It's all yours for the taking."

The lube was still cool, but quickly warmed as he spread it around and into her opening. She did her best not to wince when the head of his cock squeezed in.

"Nice," she murmured, realizing that Max was being extra cautious.

He pressed forward a little more.

"Give me a moment," she breathed. "I'll open more."

Perspiration beaded her brow. She'd forgotten how wide Max could get. "Try again." She smiled as her anal opening expanded, accepting more of the fleshy invader.

Max paused.

"More," she moaned. "I want all of you." She flexed her buttocks, trying to create more room for him. "I won't accept less. Ah, yes!" She felt her interior expand, accepting Max until his hips nestled against her rear. "Welcome."

"Are you sure you're okay?" Max moaned into her ear, leaning over her back.

"I'm fine now. We'll need to do this more often. Pull out a little and ease back in." Goosebumps climbed her arms. "Perfect. Professor?"

"Yes?"

"Are you enjoying the view?"

He chuckled. "Very much. I'm not even certain Melissa's flair for artistry could do this justice."

She waggled her butt. "If you've imprinted the sight of your cock buried in my ass, maybe it's time to pump your seed into me. Don't hold back. Believe me, any squeals you'll hear from me will be squeals of joy."

She heard him suck in air, then felt him withdraw a little and ease back in, testing their connection. His next stroke was more complete.

"That's right," she said. "Pound my ass, Max."

She blinked, quickly realizing she'd stepped out of the fantasy she'd arranged for them. To hell with the fantasy. This was better than any fantasy could ever be.

"This is new territory for us, Max. Explore. Plunder. Take me higher and higher."

Her voice rose shrilly as he did indeed take her higher with every stroke.

Realizing he must be close to ejaculating, she clinched her anal sleeve and concentrated on that little ball that bounced deep in her body looking for a way out. It grew.

"Good God," she yelped. "You must be right behind my belly button. Oh, Max," she cried out. "Love me. Don't let me climax without you."

He grunted. "I'm trying. Jesus."

"You're almost there, Max. Join me. We're on the edge of the cliff. Leap with me."

She howled, and to her delight, his howl nearly overpowered hers. His cock jerked in her ass.

"I'm coming!" he shouted. "I can't believe it," he moaned, clutching her body tight, ramming in and out of her. "I'm coming in your ass. You are so tight. So incredibly hot."

He slowed. She felt the heat of his breath on her shoulders. He pulled partially out, only to slam back into her once more. She heard a mixture of laughter and cussing, as if Max couldn't quite comprehend what he was doing.

His hips continued to slap her butt long after he was empty. "Humongous."

She giggled. His laughter mingled with her giggles. They must be riding an adrenaline high. "Beautiful. You were beautiful, Max. Do I get my extra credit?"

Warm air from his harsh breathing soothed her back.

"You can have as much credit as you want," he moaned. "I'll never be able to give you everything you deserve. Will we ever be the same?"

Claire rested her head on her hands, refusing to think too deeply about that question. He must know lovers were never the same from moment to moment. If they were, they'd cease being lovers.

She raised her eyes and blinked at the picture he had of her hanging on the wall. Which view of her was most accurate — that domestic image of happily reading in bed next to Max, or the drawing of a slightly imperialistic, frankly hungry sex goddess spreading her thighs to entice a lover?

Trembling, she closed her eyes. *Is it possible to be both?*

CHAPTER ELEVEN

M ax set down his trimming sheers, stealing a moment to peer over a shrub toward Claire. She was clad in a pale blue bikini, reading on a chaise lounge. He found it very hard not to believe she belonged on his patio. This wasn't the first twinge he'd experienced about something more permanent, but it was the most powerful.

They'd both been quite exhausted from their rather robust office tryst and had agreed to forego the trip to the Mohawk Valley—another day, perhaps. Not only could Claire be creative and spontaneous, she wasn't opposed to altering plans. Once Agnes had made up her mind, there'd seldom been room for change.

He returned his attention to the shrub but couldn't shake the possibility that he and Claire deserved more time together than weekends. What would it be like living with her on a full-time basis? He chuckled softly. He'd never know what he'd find when he entered a room. He might walk into the kitchen and find her cooking a meal or splayed out across the island serving up a little pussy delight.

Damn, her ass was hot—and tight.

Max stood and surveyed his work. He nodded his satisfaction, then headed toward the patio, where he poured himself a glass of lemonade. Claire didn't look his way until after she'd apparently finished a page. He leaned over and kissed her forehead. "You rival the scent of my flowers."

"You're being romantic again," she said, beaming at him. "Be careful."

He nodded, quite aware that her caution didn't have the same kind of bite it once had. Was she softening? Has she fantasized about more than weekends and office trysts? Should he ask? Probably not. "Good book?"

"Delicious. Though I expect you could write better love scenes."

"Doubt that."

"Maybe you should try your hand at it. I'd love to see how you'd write this morning's little escapade." She eyed him benevolently. "Even after showering and relaxing, my butt is still humming."

"I assume from your expression that's not a bad thing."

"You must be kidding. I'm sure any of your coeds would be pleased with your efforts to be fair and equitable with grading and dispersing extra credit," she quipped. "Maybe we should go to your campus office someday." She inhaled deeply. "The only thing that would be better is if you were still in my ass."

He laughed easily. "Not this soon. I can guarantee that."

"You looked like you knew what you were doing out there with that clipper in your hand."

"Not much nurtures my soul more than working with shrubs and flowers."

"I could see that."

He tried to appear as natural as possible. "This has been an exceptional day for nurturing the soul. Making love with you does more for my soul than anything I can think of."

"Ah, Max," she said, puckering her lips.

He dropped to his knees, accepting her soft kiss.

She slipped her mouth off his lips, then settled his head on her breasts. She repeatedly planted kisses on his bald pate. "What am I going to do with you?" she murmured.

Had she intended him to hear those words? Her question was a strained plea. She probably didn't want an answer—at least not from him.

They cuddled until his muscles began to complain of stiffness. The gentle rise and fall of her breasts reminded him of the ebb and flow of the ocean at Monterey. They'd come a long way since then. How much further would they go?

Her fingers grazed his head. He had little doubt that Claire's resistances were eroding. Max smiled, then drew his index finger across her belly until he rimmed her navel. Her heated skin warmed his fingers.

"Don't start something we can't finish," she warned, covering his fingers with hers. "We have the fundraiser for the Center on Friday night. You remember, the one featuring some of Melissa's art?"

"I remember."

"Melissa wants us to do a little more taping for the aging and sex video Wednesday afternoon."

He grew aware of Claire's lungs expanding as she breathed deeply before continuing.

"Why don't you plan on coming by Wednesday after work and staying over through the weekend? That should be less hectic than dealing with the traffic."

Was that her heart beating faster, or his? "I'd like that," he managed to say. "But I will have to bring along more than one change of clothes."

Claire's belly shook as she giggled. "I think we are beyond that. Maybe you haven't noticed, but I've taken over more of your second bedroom closet than I should have."

He grinned and nipped at the curve of her breast. "I've noticed. I'm not complaining."

"Are you comfortable enough like that on your knees?"

"Never more comfortable," he said, trying to calm his straining thighs.

"Good. I feel like I'm floating." She drew his fingers under her bikini bottom until they cupped her mound. "Don't get too excited," she said. "But I don't want to deny you entirely from contact with a bush. You did come out here to work with your bushes. Though I must admit, this is a rather tiny bush."

He grinned into her breast, appreciating the heat spilling over his fingers. Like a perfect gentleman, he resisted moving his fingers. "You do keep it trimmed nicely. And I don't have another bush that even comes close to matching this one."

"I should hope not," she teased. "I certainly hope not. It's beginning to feel like nap time again. I do seem to nap more out here than in the city. Maybe it's the fresh air."

"That and all the exercise," Max murmured, closing his eyes.

"That, too." She yawned. "Luxuriant exercise."

Max smiled as her body relaxed beneath his. He'd die before he moved a muscle to disturb her. He stifled a yawn and settled his cheek against her bosom. He couldn't imagine a better surface for napping.

"Now, ladies," Melissa said into her mike, "if you haven't done anything like this before, it may take a time or two for you to feel comfortable with being so completely exposed to your man. You might prefer using pillows. Claire finds that a seat rest, similar to those used for sitting around campfires or at other outdoor events, works quite fine for these purposes. She and I believe this little chair provides more reliable support than pillows. You'll want to discover what works best for you.

"You've been watching Claire teasing Max with a full frontal display while her labia engorge with anticipation. Even the camera is picking up on how wet she's become, and she hasn't invited Max to do a thing other than watch.

"She knows she's leaning back far enough to display her anus as well as her pussy. Even that forbidding portal is visibly opening. Don't you love how Claire lazily drags a thumb up each side of her pussy, then down again? Doesn't that give you the shivers?"

Melissa chuckled. "If anyone ever doubted the appropriateness of the word *flower* to describe a woman's vulva, that person should witness Claire's pink vulva opening for Max. By the way, guys, it can require a lot of willpower on your part to keep your hands to yourself until the woman invites your participation in this exercise. Notice how Max skims his fingers over his half-hard penis now and then to stay in the game.

"This is an excellent way for older women to tend to their bodies without having to depend on the man to maintain an erection for a long time, while at the same time not excluding him. As usual, make sure you have plenty of lube handy. Again, lube can be important at any age, but becomes more and more important as we age."

Melissa nodded at Claire. It was time to move on.

"Don't you love the way Claire sticks her tongue out at her man when she dips a finger into her pussy? Oops. Make that two fingers.

"Just in case Max is blind, Claire is tantalizing him and herself by scraping an index finger across that incredibly sensitive ridge between pussy and anus. She hasn't even touched her anus, but you can see that passageway is becoming quite aroused. Again, ladies, such responsiveness might not happen for you on your first time or your tenth, but eventually, your body will begin to anticipate and express its desires much more without censure. Remember, for some women who have very tight vaginas, the anus may offer a less constricting avenue for intercourse.

"Now what is Claire doing? She has asked Max to prepare an anal toy for her. He is lubing a delightful little toy which, if you haven't used, you may want to try. Don't be put off by its long, narrow rod shape. It vibrates and is good for beginners. It won't take long before you'll be ready for thicker toys.

"Claire is nodding at Max. He will no longer be merely a voyeur. He is placing a dab of lube on her dark portal. Now he's bringing the toy to bear on Claire's entrance.

"Even though Claire is very experienced with anal play, she and Max are taking their time. Notice her tilting her hips, giving him a slightly better angle. He takes his lead from her. She nods, and he propels the toy in farther—there! It's in place.

"Max is turning on the vibrating function. Look at the broad smile spreading across Claire's lips as she flexes her hips against the purple invader. And you're wondering if she is enjoying this?

"Ah, Claire is reaching for another vibrator. She is wetting it with her mouth. Now what do you suppose she's planning to do with that one?

Melissa blew a kiss at Claire, who lowered the vibrator to her vulva.

"Now, ladies, you may have wondered what it would be like to have two cocks serving you at once, but if you either haven't had the opportunity to try it with two men or didn't want to, this is a way for you to approximate how it feels.

"Claire first covers Max's hand so she can control the anal toy as she places the tip of the pink vibrator between her very wide open vulva, then pushes the toy steadily inward.

"This takes some doing, because everything down there is fuller and tighter. Claire's furrowed brow is perspiring. Look at that grin. Oh my. Both vibrators are in play. Claire nods at Max as he resumes gently drawing the anal vibrator back and forth.

"She matches his strokes with her own. What a gorgeous view. You have a ringside seat. Claire's eyes are rounding, and her breathing is less steady. I'm going to be quiet and let you watch. This needs no explanation."

Melissa dropped the mike to her side, focusing on Claire as she crumbled in front of the camera.

Claire whimpered, rolling her eyes. "Stop," she moaned. "No, don't stop. Oh damn," she muttered, jamming the pink vibrator in as far as she could. "I'm coming!" she wailed. "Don't move."

Melissa listened to the soft hum of the cameras as she waited for Claire to return. She debated about turning the cameras off, but her intuition told her to wait.

Claire raised her eyelids slightly and her lips parted into a satisfied smile. "Pull out slowly."

Max withdrew the anal toy as Melissa began to speak into the mike.

"In case you haven't seen any of our anal tapes, I want to reiterate here that it is extremely important to remove anal toys slowly. Claire's anal area is very sensitive by this point and also may be quite dry.

"Now Claire is removing the pink vibrator. Her juices are rather evident, in case you thought she was faking any of this." Melissa's sudden intake of breath was audible. "Oh my! This wasn't part of the script. Apparently, Max has decided his woman's juices shouldn't be wasted and that her incredible frontal display has earned more rewards. Look at Claire. Now there is a satisfied woman. Now what?

"She's pushing his head lower. Goodness, she's rubbing her wet pussy all over Max's bald head. She's bucking against his head. Damn, she's coming again," Melissa gasped.

"I never thought of that. Claire is giggling, and it sounds like Max is too." Melissa turned to face the camera.

"When Claire begins to giggle like this, she usually has a difficult time stopping. You've probably seen enough—certainly more than I expected." She grinned. "Once more, perhaps one of the most important lessons to take away from any of our tapes is to be open to your own creativity. Be willing to surprise and be surprised. Bye for now," she said, giving her signature wave to the camera.

"Wow!" Melissa cried, turning to see Max and Claire hugging each other, trying to contain their laughter. "I won't bother writing a script next time. That was absolutely stunning."

Seated at the board room table, Claire nodded, graciously accepting the accolades of the Center's management. Harry, Melissa, and Bev Anderson, chair of the Center's Board of Directors, were pleased with the mock-up of the latest Center catalogue. Max, who was sitting in on the meeting, patted her thigh. He seemed genuinely pleased for her, and she was glad he could celebrate her professional successes as well as her sexual prowess.

"Thanks everyone," she said. "I've had a lot of help, particularly from Melissa and Inez. Of course, the two of them take the lead on our web catalogue. Still, it's important to market the old-fashioned way."

"That was an insightful interview with Simone," Bev said. "Looks like she's been a good addition to the Center staff."

Claire peeked at Melissa and Harry. They both smiled. "She's going to be exceptional," Harry commented. "She's quite talented."

Bev's eyes sparkled. "Yes, Melissa showed me the edited version of the three of you. Quite splendid." Bev chuckled. "I believe, in the vernacular" — she glanced at Harry — "she smoked you."

Harry steepled his fingers. "I won't deny that. She can be a whirling dervish. But we do need to be careful with Simone. None of us can afford to have her thinking she can simply have her way at the Center."

Claire was glad to see there was no disagreement about that.

"I hope you're better prepared for her antics then I was," Harry said, turning to Max. "She's eager. She wants to do everything at once, and she prefers to do it her way." Harry tilted his head to the side. "She actually has an excellent research mind. Part of what we're seeing from her with her desire to work with everyone is her way of doing research. The best way to learn about the Center is to get in there and work with everyone, and hopefully in the process become indispensable."

"No one is indispensable," Melissa said. "None of us are, really."

"We know that. Simone will be a better staff member once she learns that's true for her too. And the first step," Harry looked at Max, "is for you to keep the upper hand when you work with her next week."

"Thanks for the added pressure, but I am aware of the potential problem. Simone is that proverbial diamond in the rough. Losing her would be a real loss. Having her rampage through the Center could, in the long run, be even more disastrous."

"Exactly. Now then, we're not having very good luck adding to our male staff." Harry scowled. "My priority is to identify an African American or Asian guy." He shook his head. "At this point, I've been interviewing a host of guys regardless of race, and I'm coming up empty."

"Are we that picky?" Bev asked.

"We want a guy with a good head on his shoulders as well as a guy who can give head." Harry bowed to the ladies.

"Harry's right," Claire said, looking at Bev. "Before Melissa joined us, we were beginning to drift away from the kind of quality that makes our products stand above those of competitors. Even Harry wouldn't work on set with our regular guys. I think at some level, that was another reason I gave up working on camera until Melissa convinced me otherwise. From the beginning, we wanted to be about more than sex."

"That's right," Melissa chimed in. "All of our staff must be committed to certain values."

"I know." Bev smiled sheepishly. "I helped you write the new mission statement. I'm not complaining about your search results, but clearly you need to cast a wider net."

"Or a narrower one," Harry said. "Max, you talked to me once about an African American colleague at your college who expressed some interest in our research program. Do you think he'd be interested in helping us out?"

"Boyd Roberts? We've joked about my work at the Center. I think he's more curious than he'd like to let on. From what he's implied, I expect he's purchased some of our materials." Max shrugged. "I invited him to tomorrow night's gala featuring Melissa's art, because he's been curious about our work."

"What does he teach?" Bev asked.

"He's a fairly new sociologist. Probably in his early thirties, but I'm not sure he's all that serious about the Center. He may be much more interested in our research program than in our educational videos."

"We'll take it slow. Why don't you and Claire escort him around the gala?" Harry laughed, glancing at his wife. "If he trips over his tongue when he looks at Melissa's artwork, he probably won't work out."

"If he fails to react at all," Claire added, "he won't work either."

Harry nodded. "Depending on how that goes, let's talk with him. If he's interested and passes our health testing, then we might have him do a demo with the two of you."

"Both of us?" Max asked.

"Why not?" Melissa broke in. "We've wanted to do an older woman younger guy, and we've wanted to do two guys and a woman." She grinned. "This could be an actual twofer."

"We'll take it one step at a time," Claire said. "He may not be at all inclined to work with us on camera."

"Once you see him," Max teased, "you may hope he is inclined. Boyd is as bald as a billiard ball."

"Damn." Claire swallowed hard. "I'm not sure I'd know what to do with *two* bald heads."

Melissa's eyebrows rose. "I'm sure you'll come up with something, if called upon."

Max shot a glance at Claire, still unable to take his eyes off her for long. She'd chosen a striking wardrobe, fitting for the codirector of a Center on sex practices. The snug yellow dress dropped to mid-thigh. Its scooped-out back stopped just short of the rise of her rear. And no one was left to wonder whether she wore a bra. He wasn't sure how she kept her breasts from spilling out. He did know she wore panties. At least she had been when they'd left her condo.

She'd drawn appreciative stares from men and women alike, but she'd made a point of hanging on his arm. A couple times, she placed his palm on her butt. On second thought, he wasn't at all convinced she had on panties. "Have I told you in the last five minutes how damn striking you are in that dress?"

Claire patted his arm. "Maybe three minutes ago, but I won't tire of that. Am I making you horny, or is it Melissa's art?"

Max nodded at the artwork and grinned at a sketch of Claire with a dress down to her waist, caressing a breast and tugging on a nipple. "The art is seductive, but it doesn't hold a candle to you in the flesh."

She batted her eyelashes coquettishly. "I am glad you prefer me to my picture." She rubbed her hip against his. "If we weren't in the middle of a damn crowd, I'd help you with your horniness. Later." She stuck her tongue in his ear and slid his fingers down her backside.

When had she dumped the panties?

"Just for you," she murmured, "you are by far the most handsome guy here."

He had the vague thought that at his age, his ego couldn't balloon like that of a randy teenager, but it sure as hell was.

"Is that tall black bald-headed dude in the entryway Boyd?" Claire whispered in his ear.

Max grinned and waved at him. "Yeah, that's him."

"Did he play basketball?"

"College ball. His knees didn't hold up for more than that."

Claire whistled softly. "Knees are not exactly the part of his anatomy I was trying to fathom."

"No doubt." Max chuckled, then possessively placed his hand on the rise of her rump. "Come on, let's give Boyd the tour." After introducing Boyd to Claire and exchanging pleasantries, Max led Boyd toward the first of Melissa's paintings while Claire went to get a round of champagne.

Both he and Boyd turned to watch Claire's butt swing back and forth as she made her way to the bar.

Boyd whistled low. "Damn, is that the woman you were talking about? She's your squeeze?"

Max felt his cheeks warm. "Claire and I work together, and we spend a fair amount of time outside the Center together too."

"I've seen some of her work. She had shorter hair then." Boyd swallowed. "And you're willing to share her?"

"We work together." He looked sharply at Boyd. "What we do at the Center is one thing. What we do outside the Center is another."

"Got it," Boyd said, nodding. "Sharing doesn't go beyond the Center."

"That's correct, at least for me. So does your question mean you've decided to give us a try?"

Boyd shook his head. "No. But I am a man. Who wouldn't be tempted? But I don't really need another job to get enough sex. Though I would like to talk with your research director about future directions he sees for the Center's research program."

"Harry will be happy to talk with you about that. You know, Boyd, you don't have to work on camera to work with the research program."

"Did I hear something about not working on camera?" Claire handed a champagne glass to each of them.

"Boyd hasn't decided yet." Max smiled. "But you do tempt him."

"Well, isn't that nice to know? You probably say that about all women."

Boyd smiled, easily getting into the banter. "And you would tempt more than one dead man."

Claire tipped back her head and laughed. "I've never had a man I thought was dead. Anyway, you'll probably find some of our younger staff more intriguing."

"I find older, experienced women quite attractive, actually."

"So what do you think of Melissa's art?"

"Sensuous. Provocative. Seductive. Artsy. She's a very talented woman. Her work on canvas matches her work on videos."

Claire looked sharply at Boyd. "You've done your homework."

"That's right. I wouldn't be here if I didn't share some of the principles you all share."

"So you've seen Melissa work on tape. Does that mean

you've also seen me working on tape?"

Boyd bared his straight white teeth, then bowed deeply. "You are an expert with your body. You are as talented as the artist we honor this evening."

"I see."

She was firing up—could Max head her off at the pass? "Maybe I should find Harry and Melissa so we can introduce them to Boyd."

Claire riveted him in place with a glare before redirecting her attention to Boyd.

Max knew what irritated her. She thought Boyd was a little too smug. Maybe it was his professorial style. Max grimaced, remembering how he'd turned her off until she got to know him.

"Do you have any idea how much work is involved in performing before a camera?" Claire asked, flashing an eyebrow. "This is about more than generating orgasms."

Boyd took a step back. "I realize you're not doing porn here."

Claire heaved a sigh. "And what makes you say that?"

"Your work is obviously educational in nature. Not that people can't learn something of value from a high-quality porn film." Boyd frowned.

Max expected his friend was trying to extricate himself from a hole that he couldn't quite see.

"Especially, the recent work of the Center is very consistent," Boyd added quickly. "It's clear the performers actually like each other. Melissa's voice-overs really add a richness to the videos. And you guys seem to laugh quite easily."

Claire nodded at him. Color rose along her throat. "I'm sorry. I may have misjudged you. You are quite observant. That should make you a decent contributor. If you want to see what it's like on set, you may want to drop by Tuesday morning around ten o'clock. Max will be working with one of our younger talents. You might be in a better position to decide if you want to try out with us after seeing how we actually work on set."

She coolly turned to Max. "I'll go round up Harry and Melissa."

"Is she always that welcoming?" Boyd asked when Claire was out of earshot.

"She can be frosty and quite businesslike. I'm not sure what that was about. Claire prides herself on being a professional. She's worked as hard as anyone for the survival of the Center over the years. If you want to work with us, treat Claire like a professional, and she'll enjoy working with you and you'll enjoy working with her. But make no doubt about it, if you appear to devalue her or anyone else at the Center, she'll hand you your balls. And they won't be on a silver platter."

Standing in Claire's bedroom later, Max finally asked, "Are you going to tell me why you shifted from hot to cold when you were talking with Boyd?" He thought he saw the air whoosh from Claire's lungs.

"I've felt badly ever since. I was a bitch." Her eyes teared up. "When it was clear he'd already seen my work and started calling me an expert and comparing me to Melissa, I about flipped out." She heaved a huge sigh. "I know I'm good at what I do. And I've worked hard at developing my craft. But it's meaningless to compare me to a younger woman. Each woman is different. Period." She shook her head forcefully. "If you must know, Boyd's style of banter transported me back to an earlier time — to Michael's banter. I may not have made it clear before that Michael was African American."

"Damn." Max looked around for an escape. "It might've helped if I had known."

"I may have felt shame because of my relationship with Michael, but not because of his race. He left me. Black. White.

Asian—it didn't matter. I felt shame. I felt like I wasn't good enough when he left me."

"But you are so more than good enough, Claire," Max said, reaching for her. To his surprise, she didn't resist his comforting overture—instead, she sobbed against his shoulder. He massaged her back, encouraging her to let it out.

She leaned back, giving him a half-grin. "Sometimes I'm such a mess. How can you stand me?"

"Just fine," he said, trying to hold himself together. "We can get Simone to work with Boyd if he wants to cut a demo."

"Hell no," Claire snapped. "She'll have to stand in line. I've had other African American men since Michael. It's just that none of them reminded me of him in such a stark way."

Max nodded. "Maybe that was important. At least if for no other reason, because you were able to talk about Michael with me."

"That might be true," she said. She pouted. "You do seem to find a silver lining in most anything. Do you think Boyd will still want to work with me?"

"If he decides to link up with the Center, he will. He is a man, and you are one hot lady."

"Good. So do you think you can help me out of this dress so you can demonstrate just how hot you think I am?"

"Gladly, but first," he whispered, sliding his hand up her thigh. "What the hell did you do with your panties? They wouldn't even squeeze into that tiny purse you carried."

Claire grabbed his wrist, holding his hand in place. "They're in the wastebasket by the bar. I wonder if someone went home with a souvenir."

Between chuckles, Max whispered, "Come on, woman, let's get you ready for some loving."

"Oh," she cooed, shrugging out of the top of the dress. "You sound like a man who wants to have his way with me."

He cradled a breast with both hands, lifting it to his lips.

He pulled on the lengthening nipple with his teeth.

"Not want, lady — *will* have his way with you. A little haste might be in order."

"Yes, Master," she murmured, shoving the rest of the dress down over her hips, wiggling out of it, then dropping to her knees. She pulled down the zipper of his tux pants and reached in for his cock.

Max fumbled with the studs on his shirt.

"Don't take it off," she said. "You look incredibly potent in a cummerbund. I've been wanting to do this all night."

The heat of her mouth warmed his enlarging penis. She bobbed rapidly, lengthening him with each stroke. He tried not to dwell on why it was so sexy for her to be naked and for him to still be in his tux. There hadn't even been time to remove his shoes.

Too soon, she dropped him from her mouth and stood. With one hand, she fumbled with enough studs to open his shirt and ran her lips across his chest, all the while ministering to his cock with the other hand. She lifted her head, winked at him, then led him toward the bed, holding his more-than-ready cock.

She turned and knelt before the bed.

Puzzled, Max watched her fumble under the bed before pulling out some sort of paddle. She thrust it at him. "I want you to paddle my ass." She laid her head on the bed, arching her bottom upward.

Max blinked a couple times at the paddle. It might've passed for a soft ping pong paddle.

"Do you suppose Boyd undressed me in his mind tonight?" She lay before him with a cheek on the covers, her eyes closed and her mouth curved into a curious grin.

He stared at her. "Of course he did. I doubt there was a man there who didn't, unless he was gay."

"How about the women?" she purred.

"Them, too."

"I removed my panties in the middle of the crowd. I deserve to be paddled, don't you think?"

He smiled, at last understanding her game. "You might at that. And I'm just the man to do it." He squeezed a butt cheek as if testing it.

"Oh my."

He drew back the paddle, then tapped it against Claire's butt.

"I hope you're more man than that," she chided.

His nostrils flared as he raised the paddle and smacked it more firmly against her flesh.

"Now we're cooking," Claire said with a sigh.

Max tried to remember what she'd said about spanking: firm, rhythmic, methodical. He bit his tongue as he worked on one buttock until it reddened from his attention.

"That stings nicely," Claire moaned. "Don't leave out the other cheek."

He nodded, paying equal attention to both. Once it matched the color of the first, he began alternating strokes. First one cheek quivered, then the other.

Claire's groans intensified. She lifted her head from the bed, arching her neck. She waggled her butt, but he never missed a stroke. She reminded him of his childhood days in Nebraska, when a mare in heat would tease their stallion unmercifully. The crisp smack of the paddle slapping flesh was deafening. His cock ached with desire.

"You've got me on the edge, Max," Claire squealed, heaving and sighing before him.

Sparks flew across his brain. He had to feel her flesh. He tossed the paddle aside and slapped her butt with his hand. The heat coming from her ass made him pause, but only for a moment. Max fought for control. Her wet cleft blurred before his eyes.

Her asshole opened. Too many choices. If she was on the edge, where the hell was he?

No time to remove his pants. Quickly, he stepped up to her twitching rear end and shoved his burgeoning cock into her slick pussy.

"At last," Claire groaned. "Take me. Be my wild stud."

Gripping her ass with both hands, Max rocked back and forth on the balls of his feet, tantalizing her with several short strokes, then rearing back and slamming forward, propelling both of them to oblivion.

Her howls were like spurs biting into his flesh. He hadn't come this quickly for a long time. Claire's fingers curled into the bedcovers. Her wails turned to whimpers. "Take me. Take me. Take me."

His legs shook. His thighs tightened. "Claire!" He corkscrewed into her once, twice, three times, emptying himself with each thrust.

Max collapsed, covering her quaking back. They lay glued together by perspiration for what seemed like an eternity.

She remained surprisingly silent.

He swallowed, searching for his voice. "You okay? I didn't hurt you, did I?"

She squirmed her butt against his crotch. "You were wonderful." She chuckled softly. "You wielded that paddle as if you knew what you were doing."

"I played a lot of ping pong in college."

"To my utter delight. You know that was the quickest you've ever come in me."

Max laughed. "I nearly came before I could get in you. Amazing. This tux will have to go to the cleaners."

"Hope we didn't ruin it, but I do love a man in a tux."

Max leaned over her back, lifted her hair and planted a kiss on her neck. "And I love a woman who loves a man in a tux."

CHAPTER TWELVE

Claire nestled herself in a chair she'd drawn up close to the bed. She tightened the sash on her robe and sipped her morning coffee. Her focus never strayed from the sleeping form of Max, stretched out like he didn't have a care in the world. Perhaps she'd overtaxed him last night.

She shivered under the robe, but her shivers had nothing to do with the temperature.

Max stirred. He cracked an eye open. He seemed a little surprised to see her sitting there, watching him, then a small smile worked across his lips. "Are you a vision?" he asked. "Or are you real?"

"Max, do you love me?"

"Son of a bitch."

Max scrambled into a sitting position.

"Son of a bitch is not exactly what a woman wants to hear when she gets up the courage to ask a guy if he loves her."

"Of course I love you," Max grumbled, raking his fingers through his hair. "It's just — I wasn't anticipating the question. Hell, I was trying to figure out a way of telling you without causing you to run."

"As you can see, I'm not running."

"Do you have any more of that coffee?"

Claire nodded and rose to fill a cup for him.

"Cripes, you even brought the coffeepot up here. How long have you been waiting for me to wake?"

"About an hour."

She handed him the coffee.

He took three large swallows, as if he needed the caffeine to kick in as soon as possible.

She sat back down. She'd discovered what she needed to know.

"So, do you love me?" His eyes had grown huge.

Her heart hummed. This was not a time for coy. "I've only used these words with two other people. I love you. I didn't want to fall in love with anyone again."

"Michael and Phoebe ?"

"Yes."

Max's fingers trembled slightly. "I'm happy you were willing to change your mind. What made that happen?"

"You." She shrugged. "I can't explain it. I certainly want space between us, but when you're not there for a night, I'm missing something. Something very important."

"I help you stay warm."

She nodded. "Physically. Emotionally. And spiritually."

"Ah, the holy triumvirate."

"That's right. I didn't think it was possible, but you made the impossible possible."

"Not true," he corrected. *"We* made the impossible possible."

"I like that. We do make a fantastic team."

"So." Max pursed his lips. "Are we talking marriage here?"

"Heavens no!" Claire patted her racing heart. "That never occurred to me. I'm too old for marriage," she stammered, not liking the laughter evident in Max's eyes.

She had to talk fast, or she'd disintegrate. "I was thinking about sharing living space. Who knows how many years we have left? We shouldn't waste a one." She shrugged her shoulders. "Beyond that, I don't have a specific plan. Exclusive relationship?"

"Of course. I haven't been with a woman since I met you other than at work. What about work?"

"I've given that some thought." Claire wrinkled her nose trying to find the right way to present her idea. "At present, I'm only committed to screw one other man. And that's Boyd, if he decides to do the demo. After last night, that seems doubtful."

"I'll put my money on Boyd on that one." Max cocked an eyebrow. "What does he have to lose? It's only a demo. We won't use it unless he signs the release forms. And he gets to fuck the most beautiful woman at the gala."

"And you're not jealous?"

"Absolutely not. It's part of the package. It's what we do."

"I've decided that after Boyd, if there is a Boyd, I won't agree to work with another man."

Max threw her a questioning look.

She smiled. "I don't need more than one man, not really. Not when you can meet my fantasies of a gentle man, a strong man, and" —she flashed a small smile—"a slightly rough man."

Max nodded at the space where he'd stood when he's paddled her and taken her roughly from behind. "You did get me to cross a line last night. I can still feel my hand stinging."

"You didn't cross that line too far," she responded. "But far enough. So I'd been thinking about possibly cutting back at the Center even before Melissa joined. Actually, Melissa reinvigorated my waning interest."

"So no men. What about women?"

Claire gave him what she knew was her best provocative pout. "Let's not get carried away here with exclusivity. We have to build our relationship on realistic expectations, or it will fail for sure."

"And what are your expectations for me?"

Claire chuckled softly. "Well, I doubt you're going to suddenly develop a passion for guys. I expect you to continue working at the Center. I get a kick out of watching you with

other women. But," she said sternly, "no other women outside the Center, unless I am with you — that would be entirely
different — or I'll serve up your balls on a tarnished silver platter."

"Those balls you love to cradle so much?"

She nodded.

"Funny, that reminds me of a conversation with Boyd. But
I can live with those expectations. I'm not sure how much
longer I'll want to work on camera, but I'm sure Melissa has
more plans for me. And Melissa and Harry do seem to have a
happy marriage and still work on set from time to time."

"So maybe the young can be role models for their elders.
But we're not talking about marriage."

"Of course not." Max smirked. "Wouldn't think of it."

"You're good at a lot of things, but you don't lie well." She
gave him a half-smile. "You are more old-fashioned than I am.
Welcome to the modern world, Max. Let's agree to play house
together." She rose to her feet and kissed him on his bald
head.

His arms wrapped around her waist, and he rubbed his
head back and forth across her robe, finally cradling his head
against her bare breasts. He kissed one breast, then the other.
He lifted his lips to meet hers. "I haven't played house since I
was a kid and played with the girl next door."

Claire chuckled. "So did you get around to playing doctor?" Max shook his head. "We were a little slow, I guess."

"I'll be your nurse anytime, Max. You might be surprised
how nicely I fill out a nurse's uniform."

"I can only imagine."

Max cradled his head in his hands as he lay on the carpet of
set two, giving himself over to the visual and tactile show
Simone was displaying for him and the cameras. Tension

etched across her features as she shifted from side to side, re-positioning herself on his cock.

Once the cameras were going, she'd been very quick moving through the preliminaries until she had his cock where she wanted it. Would she ever appreciate finesse? He ran his hands along her thighs as they flexed, propelling her higher.

Simone had energy to spare. She gave him a frustrated look as she gyrated with her arms above her head, twisting up and down his cock.

She'd nearly surprised him once. He'd met her thrust for thrust, then had pulled back to let her do the work and steel his own response. Her smallish boobs bobbed freely, as did her frizzed hairdo. She inhaled air through her nose as her lips thinned. When had this become a battle of wills?

Long before they'd taken off their robes, he'd known she didn't want to work with him. Claire had told him about the bargain Simone made in Melissa's office—Max for Melissa, and Claire was thrown in as part of the package. He knew Simone respected him more since she'd seen him work, but she probably thought she could dispense with him quickly, as she had with Harry.

No way. No fucking way. "You're going to wear yourself out if you don't breathe now and then." Max gave her a languid grin.

Slowly, Simone stilled. Her lips formed a pout. She leaned forward, and his cock popped out of her. She drew up close to his ear so only he could hear her whisper.

"I know what you're doing. You want to fuck me." She flicked her tongue at his ear as he cradled her butt in his hands. "I nearly had you."

"Never," he whispered back. "That was your imagination. I noticed you didn't come."

"I didn't want to."

"And now you do."

"Just fuck me and we'll see."

"Any time, you two," Melissa interrupted. "The cameras are running."

Max smiled at Simone, then rolled her onto her back. He looked down at her startled face. "Okay, little girl, let me show you how an old man makes love."

He slid down her body, pausing to nip at each dark nipple. Simone stifled her response when he bit the first nipple, but not the second.

"Yes," she moaned. "Do that again."

He smiled. This was more like the vocal, expressive woman he'd seen perform before. Without much effort, he closed his mouth around one of her small breasts. At the same moment, he curled two fingers up inside her, searching for her hot spot.

"Christ," she yelped, bucking against his fingers. "That's not fair." She grabbed his shoulders, holding on tight, quaking beneath him.

Max dropped her breast from his mouth. Without looking at her, he licked his way down her trim, dark belly until his lips brushed against the hard nubbin standing sentry at the apex of her triangle.

"Crap," she mewed. "I'm coming again."

"I noticed." He lifted his head to wink at her.

Her large round eyes made him chuckle. Her head bobbed back and forward, matching her hips as they worked against his fingers. "Good God," she moaned, going slack.

Max withdrew his fingers and lowered his mouth to capture her juices. He sucked her pussy lips into his mouth, gently nibbling on them, then chuckled when Simone again took off like a rocket. She bucked so hard he feared for his teeth. He set her butt back on the carpet and rose to his knees. He leaned forward, grazing his lips across hers until she was licking her own juices.

"Claire's right. You have a magical tongue," she whispered

with a trace of awe.

"You're not the first to make that claim," he said, nibbling on her bottom lip. "And you are incredibly expressive. Who wouldn't want to love you just to hear you squeal?"

"So, are you going to fuck me now?"

Max drew in a deep breath and nodded. "I'm sure as hell going to try."

He moved back down her torso. She tilted her pelvis as he slowly entered her. Perspiration beaded his forehead. She was damn tight.

Once he was in to the hilt, Simone smiled at him. "Go for it, old man." She wrapped her legs around his waist as he began a steady cadence. She bounced her butt off the carpet, meeting him stroke for stroke. They both kept their eyes open, daring, challenging.

Max cupped her bottom and lifted her ass. "You must not even weigh a hundred pounds. I haven't been able to lift a woman like this in years."

"Damn, damn, damn," she chanted shrilly as she snapped her head around, her fingers clawing at her clit.

Max maintained his pace, smiling as she shattered underneath him. She was something to watch from a distance, but up close, every corpuscle, every muscle participated when she climaxed. She was mesmerizing.

"You want to try another position? Maybe getting on your hands and knees?"

She shook her head lazily. "No way. I'll cry uncle if you want. My thighs are burning. I don't have much left. My pussy is worn out, but it's sure singing words of praise."

Max didn't move to stop her from pulling away from him. She swung around and rolled the condom off his cock. Her small, dark palm provided a stark contrast with his pale cock.

Simone winked, then blew him a kiss. "This old boy still deserves some attention. I owe him—big time."

Max remained kneeling and settled back against his heels, granting her more space.

"Don't hold back," she said, giving him an evil eye. "Please. I lost count of how many times I came."

He nodded. "I won't hold back on purpose, but there are no guarantees."

Simone gave him a devastating smile. "As long as you don't purposefully hold back or die, I'll issue the guarantee. This guy will come for me." She promptly popped him into her incredibly warm, moist mouth, locking her fingers behind her back. Without using her hands, she bobbed up and down, apparently testing his length.

He was about to question her bravado when her mouth slackened and she inched him down her throat. When her lips kissed his loins, he didn't doubt her guarantee for a moment longer.

She slowly raised and lowered her head, teasing him. He knew — and she knew — she could have him whenever she chose.

"Damn, you are exceptional." He twined his fingers in her curls.

Simone kept her hands clasped behind her back, but never stopped bobbing along the length of his shaft. Almost imperceptibly, she quickened her movements until he was entirely at her mercy. He groaned. This was the beginning of the end. She sensed it, too. There wasn't going to be any retrograde orgasm this time.

Simone's dark curls became a blur as she drew forth his essence. His hips strained for release. He held them in check, letting Simone work her special brand of wonder.

"Christ!" he yelled. "Here he comes."

If she heard his warning, she didn't heed it. If anything, she took him deeper as he spasmed down her throat. Her throat muscles milked him thoroughly until she was apparently satisfied that she'd claimed everything.

At last she dropped him from her mouth, settled back on her heels, smiled broadly, and licked her lips. She raised a palm up for a high five.

He managed to smack her palm before crumbling to the carpet. "Damn." His lips curved into a smile. "That was beyond my imagination."

She stuck her tongue out at him, then settled down beside him, draping a leg over him as if they were longtime lovers. "I told you I'd guarantee you'd come. I never lost a blow job contest in college."

"I don't recall such contests when I was in college."

Simone smirked conspiratorially. "I didn't think they even had colleges in your day. Oh!" she exclaimed, turning to face Melissa as if she'd completely forgotten the cameras. "I was supposed to let the audience see some of his sperm so they'd know we weren't faking."

Melissa smiled happily at Simone. "We do that often with these tapes focused on aging, but I don't think any viewer is going to assume for a second that either of you were faking. Tremendous. Both of you. We might have to try that again." Melissa winked at Max. "Simone, would you be willing to hook up with Max again?"

"You better believe it," Simone chirped. "I wonder how long we could last if we really tried."

Max flopped back, blowing air through pursed lips. Maybe he should retire from his Center activities while he still could. He turned toward Claire, who still stood on the sidelines. She was giving him two thumbs up—way up. Hell, he must have several more good years in him, at least.

"So what did you think?"

Claire turned to Boyd. He'd entered the set just in time to

hear Melissa introducing Simone and Max on camera and walked directly to Claire. During the shoot, she'd paid close enough attention to know that Boyd got turned on more than once. But then anyone in the room would have to be stone-dead not to respond to the performance they'd just witnessed.

"Fascinating," he began, his eyes sparkling at her. "At first I thought I was witnessing some kind of battle between the sexes, and then it turned into something quite lovely, almost like a ballet." He glanced around the room. "Nice set up. Everyone on the sidelines seemed quite professional." He chuckled. "I didn't see any orgies breaking out."

Claire laughed. "And you won't, at least not in here. So have you decided to do the demo with me and Max?"

"Do you want me to?"

Claire put on her poker face. "That's not for me to decide. I'm codirector of the Center. I do what I think is best for the Center. If you want to cut a demo, I'm willing to work with you, as is Max. If not, that's fine, too."

"And Max is okay with this?"

"Did I look jealous watching Max and Simone?"

Boyd shook his head.

"It'd be quite another matter if they tried anything outside the Center."

"I've talked some with Harry," Boyd said. "He's got some exciting research ideas. I think I could help him gain access into some communities that might otherwise question the value of this work." He smiled easily.

Claire relaxed as the conversation shifted to more neutral ground. She expected they had come to a certain understanding. She was on-limits on the set only.

Boyd looked back at stage two, where Simone and Max had just finished. "If I work for the Center, will I be able to work with Simone?"

Claire broke into a smile. "She's hot. Sure, if she's willing."

"Damn hot." He nodded thoughtfully. "I might have to work on that."

Claire saw no reason to tell him he probably wouldn't have to work hard at hooking up with Simone. She squeezed his hand. "There is the matter of the demo before we make a final decision."

"I'm meeting with the Center doctor after lunch."

"Good." Claire brushed back a wisp of hair. "I'll check with Melissa for scheduling. Assuming the health stuff is okay, we should be ready for you Friday of this week, or Wednesday or Friday next week. There's no particular hurry."

"I teach most of the day on Fridays. Wednesday is an open day. Most anytime will work on Wednesday."

Claire stood on her tiptoes and pecked his cheek. "We'll let you know for sure." She winked at him. "Don't lose any sleep over this. We won't be trying anything too fancy for the demo."

Boyd shrugged his shoulders. "Strange, isn't it? It's not like I haven't had sex with my share of women, but this is different. Thanks for trying to put me at ease. See you. Probably, Wednesday."

She stared thoughtfully at Boyd's back as he left the studio. He didn't seem nearly as cocky or into himself as he had Friday night. Maybe he would work out. He'd certainly been taken with Simone.

Claire shook her head. When had she ever been the gateway to another woman? Maybe Melissa's matchmaker penchant was rubbing off on her. Of course, Melissa would probably claim that the matchmaking had actually begun with her.

Melissa ran her finger across the Center's master calendar that she maintained on her desk, pleased at this development. She glanced up at Claire. "Wednesday morning looks fine for the demo."

Claire nodded.

"I'll make the arrangements. It will be a closed set. Harry and I will operate the cameras. You'll direct. If Boyd releases the tape and we decide to use it, I'll do voice-over later. So do you think he'll work out?"

"Hard to say." Claire's shoulders rose and fell. "I saw more potential this morning than the other night."

Melissa hooked her tongue in her cheek. "Given the dress you wore to the gala, I'm not convinced you could hold him responsible for not trying to impress you with his smooth composure."

"We'll see. Max and I will be ready."

"Speaking of Max, he certainly held up his end out there with Simone."

"He did, didn't he?"

Was that possessive pride coloring Claire's response? Melissa smiled. "You two look like you're progressing nicely."

"Pry. Pry. Pry," Claire teased. She nodded, unable to hide a broad smile. "We're talking about playing house together."

"All right!" Melissa bolted around the desk to hug Claire. "I couldn't be happier for you." Melissa caught her breath. "Any implications for the Center?"

"Probably. We're talking about that. Neither one of us wants to completely sever our ties with the Center." Claire looked around the office somewhat wistfully.

Though she didn't often think about it, Melissa suddenly connected that this had been Aunt Phoebe's office.

"This place has been a part of most of my life. I don't want to give it up entirely, and Max doesn't expect that."

"Good, we'll definitely continue to need your presence here. And Max, too. Goodness, did you see how Simone blew him?"

Claire chuckled. "I'm not blind yet."

"I've never seen a girl blow a guy holding her hands behind her back like that. She must possess incredible suction capacity in her throat."

"She was awesome. They both were."

"I may have to ask Simone more about how she manages that." Melissa went back to her desk and scratched out a note. "We haven't done any videos recently on oral sex. Simone and Max could certainly demonstrate some advanced skills. Maybe you'd like to join them," she said, winking at Claire.

"Maybe." Claire didn't make eye contact as she turned and left the office. If anything, she looked a little confused.

Melissa grinned. If she didn't know better, Claire might just be a tiny bit jealous of Simone. If her suspicion was true, she was confident that twinge would pass, for Claire was nothing if not a professional. But it was amusing to finally see a chink in Claire's emotional armor.

"Do you always bring sunflower seeds with you when you come to the park?"

Claire ignored him while she paid close attention to the needs of a finch.

Once the bird hopped off, Claire turned and smiled at him. "Of course I do. I've developed a relationship with some of these feathered friends over the years." She snickered. "Well, if not the same birds, maybe their relatives." She leaned back against the park bench.

Max placed his arm around her shoulders.

Claire kissed his cheek. "Hopefully, you're not jealous of the attention I give my bird friends."

Max gazed across the wide expanse of Central Park. It was good to see people of all ages out for early evening strolls. During daylight hours, at least, the park was a gathering place for New York City's rich diversity, and he never tired of watching it stream by.

"That's another thing we share," Claire said, following his gaze. "We both enjoy people watching."

"You don't think that's a result of getting older?"

"Watching people? I've people watched since I was a little girl." She cuddled closer, repositioning his hand so it cradled the top of a breast. "Better," she whispered.

"And who is the romantic?" Max teased, grazing his thumb over the rise of flesh.

"Umm. Oh, look at the little girl with the blond pigtails chasing the puppy. Oops. The puppy is chasing the girl. And here comes the daddy to the rescue."

"That brings back memories," Max said, stifling a sigh. "Only Rosanne was a redhead, like her mother and grandmother. She was so innocent then."

"But they grow up."

"I guess we all do."

"There sure are a lot of power walkers out this evening."

Max chuckled. "Do you suppose they're power walkers, or are they just people in a rush to get somewhere?"

"Good point. I imagine I used to rush like that."

"But not anymore?"

Claire shook her head, cradling his hand. "Not anymore. Time is rushing faster than I can manage. Don't stare, but take a peek at the young couple at about two o'clock braced against the tree making out. They do seem to enjoy kissing."

Max looked, then nibbled Claire's ear. "Who's staring? You do have radar for lovers."

"Cripes, she's riding his knee. Oh my, a girl after my own heart. Max, she's hanging onto his shoulder for dear life, but she's not surrendering her perch on his thigh for anything.

"He's looking around. Oops, I think he caught me watching. Ah." Claire sighed. "She stopped, now they're kissing wildly again." Claire squeezed his fingers on her breast. "That girl had a damn good ride. Oh, to be young lovers again."

"Being old lovers isn't bad." Max dipped his fingers under the fabric covering her breast.

"If that couple were to look across the way at us, they'd never guess I'm sitting here with my man caressing my nipple. And" — she turned and kissed his cheek — "that I'm wet as hell."

"You could probably hump my knee and they wouldn't even notice because they don't expect it. That's one advantage with age. People don't expect us to be horny or do outrageous things."

"So true. And there's something quite gratifying about defying their limited expectations. Perhaps we should go over and share our wisdom with the youngsters."

Max shook his head. "I doubt they'd listen. So, are you nervous about tomorrow?"

"Nervous?" Claire gave him a puzzled look. "Heavens no. Excited some, but not nervous. Being with two guys can be an incredibly powerful experience for a woman. Probably not much different than for a guy with two women. I must say I enjoy both, but the former is probably a bigger high for the ego. There's no need to share with another woman."

"Maybe we'll have to revise our expectations."

"What?"

He kissed her nose, then tweaked her nipple. "If you find two guys so enjoyable, maybe we should at least make room for that occasionally in the future."

"Ah," she said slowly as the meaning of his words sank in. She smiled sheepishly. "Maybe I was a bit rash overgeneralizing about exclusivity. You wouldn't mind sharing me once and a while?"

"If that makes you happy and" — he raised an eyebrow — "if I'm included. I wonder if Boyd has ever been involved in a three-way."

"I doubt it," Claire said. "I had the impression listening to him the other day that this demo might be stretching him a bit."

"Ready to head back?" Max withdrew his fingers from the top of her dress.

"We should," she acknowledged. "No loving tonight, Max. I want to keep my edge for tomorrow."

"Understood," he said, grinning. He wondered if Boyd had any idea what he was in for.

CHAPTER THIRTEEN

Settling herself comfortably on the carpeted floor of set two, Claire looked up at the crew. "Everybody ready?" she asked, taking control of the set. "Cameras?"

"Camera One, ready," Melissa replied.

Harry nodded. "As is Camera Two."

"Good." Claire glanced between Max and Boyd. Each man knelt beside her, still wearing green robes. "As I said earlier, I'll direct the demo. We're not going to try anything too fancy or too athletic — no double penetrations, nothing embarrassing, nothing beyond your experience." She smiled easily at Boyd. "Well, not too far out of your experience."

Boyd nodded, keeping a tight smile in place.

Claire knew tension when she saw it. They'd better start before Boyd burst. "Let's see what you've got to work with," she said to Boyd, untying his robe. His lips thinned as she reached in to withdraw his very stiff cock. She smiled. "At least I won't have to spend time getting him up." She hefted his sizeable cock with the palm of her hand, showing him off to the camera. She nodded. "He should do."

Boyd gasped.

Claire chuckled and winked at him. "I've had smaller and I've had larger. What matters is how well you use him. Time to fit him with his own personal raincoat." She laughed softly, coiled her fingers around his shaft, and slipped on a condom. "He's bound to get soaked where he's going. And Boyd . . . you can talk. If we wind up using this tape, we can edit sound quite easily."

"Thanks," he croaked. "Guess I'm a little tight. Tell me what you want me to do."

She dipped her head and lightly kissed the soft crown of his cock, which snapped to attention in response. She shrugged off her robe. "You're doing fine. I've had guys try out who fainted by this point, or who ejaculated and couldn't continue."

Boyd's chuckle was deep, and his mouth crinkled into a smile. "Then I'm ahead of the game."

"Why don't you guys get rid of those robes? We'll begin with something easy. Kind of a getting-to-know-you exercise." She grinned broadly at both men. "I think I'd like a mouth on each breast. Remember, the object of a two-guys-and-a-girl tape is giving the girl pleasure. I expect you two to enjoy yourselves, but my pleasure comes first."

Claire stretched out on her back. The carpet provided a comfortable surface. Max and Boyd lay at right angles to her, Max on her right and Boyd on her left. She must look like a cross with one white crossbeam and one black crossbeam.

Boyd watched Max lave at a breast, then he followed suit.

"Scrumptious," Claire said.

Boyd continued to mirror Max's actions. She'd give Boyd credit for patience. She shuddered as both men chewed on a breast, then clamped a nipple gently between their teeth.

Claire rubbed her fingers over both bald heads—one black and one white. "Two mouths. Two bald heads," she murmured. "What more could a girl want?"

Both men stopped nibbling.

"I know, I know—two cocks. We'll get there. If you both could just take in a little more boob. That's right. Pull gently. Yes," she chirped. "I believe I'm going to have a little O. And we've only just begun." She held her breath, measuring the breadth of the orgasm sweeping over her. She squeezed each man's shoulder. Once her head cleared, she turned to Boyd.

"You doing okay?"

Boyd's smile came readily. "Much better. I think I'm getting with the program. What next?"

"So we know you're a breast man," she said, peering at him. "Why don't you travel north so I can find out what kind of kisser you are while Max travels south to kiss a different set of lips?"

Claire waited for Max to get in position, then wrapped her arms around Boyd's neck and drew him into a kiss. She shivered delightfully as she felt Max's tongue slide the length of her crevice.

She licked the corner of Boyd's mouth. She liked the way his eyes smiled. Max dipped his tongue into her, and she pushed hers into Boyd's mouth. He clamped down on it and groaned. She withdrew her tongue, and he chased it. His tongue filled her mouth and she sucked on it before it could retreat.

Boyd didn't seem to have any plans for a quick retreat. He plundered her mouth just as Max plundered her pussy. She squeezed her eyes shut to focus entirely on appreciating both tongues.

Relentless in his quest, Max lifted her legs over his shoulders, then thrust his tongue deeper.

She gasped when two fingers entered. Max was cheating. She'd never said anything about fingers.

Boyd took advantage of her momentary lapse by covering her lips with his mouth, inching his tongue in farther. She twisted her head from side to side without breaking away from Boyd. Her hips bucked. There was no escape from the tongue—not that she wanted to escape. Her head threatened to explode. She pounded her fist against Boyd's broad back as he held her while her juices cascaded over Max.

Fortunately for her, Boyd eased away, allowing her to take a deep breath. By the time she could open her eyes, Max knelt alongside her, grinning broadly. Boyd knelt on the other side. From the look of things, she had much more to do.

Claire clutched each man's cock and beamed.

"Looks like these guys are feeling a little left out. Boyd, I want to try this fellow out in my pussy." She glanced at Max. "If you'll stay right here, I can tend to my favorite cock orally."

Moments later, Claire sucked in air and flattened her belly. "Very nice," she murmured as Boyd's cock began filling her.

She tilted her pelvis, taking more of him until his loins settled against her crotch. She wrapped her legs around his butt and squeezed.

"So wet," Boyd murmured.

"Don't finish in my pussy," she warned him. "I have other plans for his finale. Some self-control is a must with this work."

Boyd grunted and flexed his hips, not waiting for more instructions.

Claire smiled up at him. "Enjoy the ride. I plan to." She turned to Max's cock and pouted. "You must feel neglected." She flicked her tongue at it and laughed as it dodged away.

Max helped her by guiding his cock to her lips, and she took him in. She palmed his balls and was soon alternating her strokes with Boyd's. When he pulled partway out, Claire slid down Max's cock. She pulled back on Max as she accepted Boyd's full length in her vagina.

Two cocks. Two *slick* cocks. She inhaled sharply through her nose. She couldn't lose track of what she was doing. This was her show. She trusted Max wouldn't come in her mouth, but she was less certain that Boyd could hold himself in check.

Out of the corner of one eye, she saw Boyd's cheek muscles twitch. Other than that, he wasn't showing much of a strain. His action was smooth. Twice, his strokes lifted her ass off the carpet. She didn't doubt he could be quite athletic if she gave him permission to finish where he was.

But she hadn't done that. She grinned mischievously. No better time to test his control. Claire let Max pop out of her mouth, then curled one set of fingers around the base of his cock. She locked her gaze on Boyd's eyes and moved her free hand to her clit.

Boyd's eyes rounded and his hips pumped faster.

She shook her head. "Just me," she whispered. "You can't come with me."

Boyd groaned, then nodded, slowing to a steady pace. His focus remained glued on her fingers as she kept stroking her clit. Max drove in and out of her fist while keeping his gaze trained on the juncture where she stroked and Boyd flexed in and out.

Claire grinned at Boyd, then at Max as she raised her legs straight up and spread them wide, playing to both her men.

"Damn," Boyd whispered, stopping mid-stroke.

Claire nodded to acknowledge his attempt at self-control, but she was soaring, gone, over the top.

Boyd stayed in place, letting her plumb the universe. She clutched Max's cock tight as if it were a tether. She permitted herself a little time to soar among the clouds. The camera could wait. This was too precious to waste—at any age.

Slowly, she settled back into her surroundings. She stretched, and Boyd took that as his cue to uncouple. His cock drooped a little.

"Poor boy," she said, climbing onto her hands and knees and turning to face Boyd. "It's time. This guy is quite talented. He deserves a little more for his efforts." She winked at Boyd, then slipped off the condom. She clutched his cock in both hands, pulled back its dark skin and rubbed its sensitive head across her cheeks and lips. "Don't you agree?"

Boyd smacked his lips and ran his fingers through her hair. "I'd be pleased." His voice was husky.

"Hoped you might." Claire turned to grin at Max and wiggled her butt. "If you'll bring up the rear, so to speak, I'll proceed with Boyd. We'll see what he's been saving up for me."

Max needed no further instruction. Soon, his cock entered her pussy with little fanfare. He leaned over to kiss her back.

"Nice," she purred, fondling Boyd's shaft and cradling his balls. She ran her tongue along its length. "Don't get too carried away, Max. It's getting more difficult for me to concentrate on both of you. Just stay with me. Hug me."

Cupping a breast in each hand, Max seemed content to cover her with his body.

"Now you," she said to Boyd, squeezing his cock. "My, he does look ready."

Boyd chuckled. "I think he's been ready for some time."

"I may not be as limber as Simone was the other day with Max, but I bet I'll get the job done."

Boyd's teeth gleamed. "I'm betting on you, lady, without question. I've seen some of your classic tapes. I'm honored."

Claire nodded, unsure what to say. She opened her mouth to cover the tip of his cock, then rested her head against his hard abs. Should she feel honored that he obviously appreciated her work, or should she feel old? *Classic?*

She inhaled. Maybe he'd said classy. She didn't have enough energy left to bother with finesse. She wrapped one hand around his dark cock and continued feeding more of him into her mouth. She cradled his balls, then began gliding up and down his length. He slid easily down her throat.

She smiled as his fingers raked through her hair. He was very close. She couldn't tell if the men were watching each other or not, but Max started fucking her pussy with renewed vigor. Wow! She had to drop her hand from Boyd in order to remain in place. On hands and knees, she braced for Max's onslaught and bobbed her head up and down Boyd's shaft. Claire didn't think Max was going to come, but there was no doubt about Boyd. He cupped her head between his large hands as she felt him expand, preparing to erupt.

"Good God!" Boyd shouted. His thighs flexed, matching her efforts.

Claire felt him building, then he cascaded into her. She swallowed rapidly to keep up with him. She smiled to herself, pleased that she'd been able to take all of him. He quickly began to soften in her mouth.

Her eyes snapped open. She'd forgotten about Max. She shuddered.

He hadn't forgotten about her. He stroked her clit steadily until she showered his cock. She shivered. She'd have to pay him back later. She was done.

Claire dropped Boyd from her mouth, then winked at him. "At least you passed the taste test. Was that classic or classy you said earlier?"

Boyd shook his head at her, ignoring his limp cock. "You are one classy lady. And you," he said to Max, who had pulled out of her to kneel beside them, "are one hell of a lucky guy."

"I know," Max said, leaning over to kiss her cheek. "What do you think, did Boyd pass the tryout?"

Claire beamed a smile at both men. "You know he did. Unless something I didn't see shows up on the screening, I don't see any reason why we wouldn't want Boyd to join our team." She looked toward Melissa and Harry for approval.

"Quite impressive," Melissa said.

"You'll be a welcome addition," Harry added. "I hope you want to join us."

Boyd followed his partners' lead by putting on his robe. He knotted the sash, then smiled a little self-consciously at everyone. "I should probably think on it longer. And I'm not quite sure how I will explain this to the dean if I ever have to, but there's no way in the world that I wouldn't want to join your team after this."

He gave Claire a half-smile. "And this wasn't fancy?"

Claire shook her head. "Not at all."

"But pleasurable?"

"Oh yeah," she said, hugging herself. "If you'll sign the release, I believe we've just created a scene that clearly demonstrates how two guys can leave a woman very pleasure-filled and satisfied. Unless the video lies."

She yawned and stood. "Now, if you don't mind. I think I'm going to go shower, then head to my office, where I plan to curl up for a well-earned nap."

Claire flounced a curtsy, and both men bowed. She waved, then left to a round of applause. For the moment, she felt like the slightly imperialistic sex goddess that Melissa had sketched.

By the time she reached her office, she yearned for Max's four-poster bed, one of his special back rubs, and a very long nap. She didn't care if that did sound overly domestic.

After showering, Max entered Melissa's office to check in with her while Claire napped. Claire had looked quite exhausted, but then she'd worked harder during the taping than either he or Boyd.

Melissa looked up from her desk and gave him a broad welcoming smile. She got up and hugged him. "I understand you and Claire are moving in together," she said, ushering him to a seat on the couch.

"I didn't think she wanted to tell anyone yet."

"Girl talk," Melissa replied. "Girl talk isn't exactly like broadcasting the news."

"It isn't?"

"So, when are you going to do this and how?"

"We haven't set a timetable yet." Max grinned. "Maybe

we're doing it by osmosis. There are fewer nights apart, and I can't keep track of where my clothes are."

"I remember that phase quite vividly. So when are you going to ask her to marry you?"

"Melissa!" Max shook his head. "Do all women simply barge ahead? Or is it just you and Claire?"

"You probably know that better than I do."

"Right," he said, remembering that it would've been better if Agnes had asked questions more often. "Maybe it's just women who work at the Center."

"You may be onto something there, but you didn't answer my question."

Max shrugged. "Claire's made it quite clear she's not interested in marriage."

"And you're satisfied with that?"

"I can live with it."

Melissa tilted her head.

"So I'm old-fashioned enough to want marriage. But I'll take Claire any way I can get her."

Melissa reached over and squeezed his fingers. "And she's lucky to have found you, too. But I do hope we aren't going to lose the two of you."

"We'll always be your friends. Yours and Harry's," he said, lifting Melissa's chin. "You did a lot for an old guy's ego, and I don't forget easily. At least not yet."

"Bah. You helped a young woman find her place here in the Center. And I won't forget that, either. And you're not that damn old. So you'll continue working for the Center?"

"Some. At least for the foreseeable future. Some days I feel older than other days. I think Claire would like to cut back some. I don't work all that often anyway. She was good out there this morning, wasn't she? She knows how to put a guy through the paces without letting him get very uptight."

"Claire is always good when she wants to be. I'm pleased I

had a small part in the two of you actually getting together."

Max nodded. "You were persistent. When you sent us off to Monterey to the conference, I wasn't betting on either one of us staying for the whole thing."

"But you did."

"Yeah, we sure did. Thanks. I'll let you get back to work. We're planning on leaving a little early to avoid traffic. I think Claire is going to work from her laptop at the house for the rest of the week."

"That works for us." Melissa returned to her desk. "Enjoy. See you next week."

Saturday morning, Max shook his head as he studied Claire, on her hands and knees, scrubbing the closet floor. He didn't think anyone bothered with scrubbing closet floors. Apparently, once Claire decided to go on a cleaning spree, nothing was safe from her eagle eye.

He'd been polishing furniture for what seemed like hours. She'd scoured the bathroom until it glistened and smelled fresh. They'd stripped the bed down and turned the mattress over. She'd shown him how to clean mirrors without getting them dirtier than they were when he'd begun.

She'd taken great care cleaning their rapidly growing collection of sex toys—some of which truly amazed him. He'd never realized the extent to which Claire was Ms. Clean.

He knew he should feel better about this flurry of activity—maybe it was part of Claire's way of nesting. She was subtly claiming part of his space—and he couldn't be more pleased.

Max glanced at her rear rotating in concert with her scrubbing motion and smiled. She did look more than a little fetching in black shorts and a pink tee shirt. Usually, he preferred working outdoors in his yard, but then he wouldn't be able to appreciate how Claire could become so absorbed in her work.

Maybe he should enlist her help with the flowers, but he

rather liked having her on the chaise lounge watching. She would probably over-trim the roses anyway. Sometimes she didn't know when to stop. Like right now.

Max stepped over and tapped her rear.

Claire jolted straight up. "Damn, don't scare me like that." She looked up at him, and a smile spread across her lips. "How long have you been standing there watching me slave away on this floor?"

"Long enough."

"Looks like long enough to get some ideas." She sketched the outline of his arousal with an index finger and shook her head. "Not yet. I'm not nearly done with my cleaning."

"You've been scrubbing, polishing, and vacuuming for two days now. When are you going to say enough is enough? And I don't really think closet floors need to shine."

Claire looked at him one more time, then burst into tears. "I'm trying," she sobbed. "I'm trying to make this work."

Max cradled her close to his chest. "Make what work?"

"Being your . . . partner," she blubbered.

"My partner!" Max stared at her. Slowly, he began to understand. He kissed her forehead, then gingerly removed the scarf from her head. "I don't care if you are my partner or my wife. I'm not in love with you because you can keep my closet floor clean."

"You're not?" she whimpered.

"You know I'm not. Sometimes, I believe you lose track of who we are and what we are."

"I do?"

He nodded. "We're lovers. We share adventures. We share dreams and joys and pains. And yes, we clean house from time to time, but not for days on end. I love you for who you are. Don't try to fit into a stereotype that I don't even care about."

"Oh damn, sometimes I am a mess."

"I won't deny that." Max grinned. "But then I get to be the shining knight and ride in to rescue the fair maiden."

"Now who's wading in stereotypes?"

"At least mine's more pleasant."

She nodded.

"Come on," he said, helping her to her feet. "Why don't you take a long shower? I'll set out a bite to eat. Maybe we'll take a nap on the patio afterward. And then come back up here and love the rest of Saturday afternoon away."

"You really want to?"

"I really want to."

Claire nodded, and a wisp of a smile parted her lips. "I'm not sure this is going to work, but I do enjoy your way of going about it better than scrubbing the closet floor." She shook her head. "When we invite Melissa and Harry over for dinner some weekend, I'll make sure to show them your closet floors."

Max smirked. "I'm sure they'll be envious."

"Max, you awake?"

Max peeked at Claire out of the corner of his eye and smiled. He reached across the space separating their lounge chairs and squeezed her fingers. "I am now."

"Do you think often about death and dying?"

He closed his eyes and took his time before replying. Claire seemed intent on dealing with heavy stuff today. Was all of this because of their decision to move in together? Was she reconsidering their commitment?

"I try not to dwell on it," he said, pushing himself into an upright position. "The death part doesn't bother me much. Something either continues after death or not. If not, then I won't be aware of it." He frowned. "I'm not looking forward to the dying part. Why do you ask?"

Claire smiled self-consciously. "I can't say I think much

about after death, but I worry about getting really old." She emitted a half-chuckle. "We kid about being old, but we're really not."

"Some days I feel older than other days."

"I don't want to get so old that I'm asexual."

Max caught a fleeting glimpse of sudden fright on her face and froze.

"I don't want to be sexless. I can't imagine going on without some sexual response. I work at staying trim, but even imagining my body deteriorating doesn't paralyze me." Her eyes turned misty. "I don't have to orgasm to tremendous applause, but I can't fathom feeling nothing."

Max intertwined their fingers. Her fingers were oddly cold. "I have difficulty imagining a time when we can't cuddle," he said quietly. "Maybe I'll cover your pussy with my palm, or cradle a breast, or kiss your lips or your eyelids. We'll always have each other and our memories."

"I wish I could believe that." She averted her eyes. "We can't even count on our memories. So many people are outliving their minds."

"Maybe realizing our fragility will help us cherish each day and each moment we have together."

"You," she said, swiping at tears, "are nothing if not a romantic."

"I'll accept that critical acclaim. And speaking of romance, isn't it about time for us to go upstairs and frolic on our favorite four-poster bed?"

Claire nodded. "Past time."

"I'm going to take a quick shower. Why don't you pour us some wine, and I'll join you."

Feeling refreshed and eager, Max didn't bother with a robe before entering the bedroom. Upon entering, he came to an abrupt halt. His stomach lurched and his cock went rigid. A grin worked its way across his lips as he let his eyes rove over his long-legged Claire lying on the bed wearing only a tentative smile and strap-on dildo. She remained silent.

The next step was clearly his. He closed the distance between them, then sat on the bed beside her. "I was wondering when we were going to get around to this."

"You're not upset?"

"Do I look upset?" He shook his head at her. "I saw you taking extra time with it this morning when you were cleaning the toys. If you hadn't found a natural way to introduce it, I would've mentioned the dildo sooner rather than later." He was pleased to see Claire visibly relax. He tugged on both of her taut nipples. "Wasn't it Melissa who commented to the viewers during one of our anal tapes that a man who expected to screw his woman in the ass should be prepared for her to do the same to him?" He kissed her puffy lips. "I've claimed your ass many times, Claire. It's about time you claimed mine."

She nodded, running a hand over the false cock. "This will require a lot of trust."

"I love you, Claire. I trust you with my life. Don't ever doubt that. I certainly trust you with my ass." He reached for the lube sitting on the nightstand. "This is quite the contraption." He chuckled, slathering lube around the false cock. "You do know how to use it?"

Claire tilted her head and raised her eyebrows.

"Strike that question. What position do you want me in?"

Claire held the base of the dildo in one hand and rearranged pillows with the other. "Let's try you on your back with your rear propped up on a pillow or two. That way, I can see your face if anything becomes too painful. And"—she eyed his erection—"either one of us can help your cock when the time is right. I want to watch you come with me in your ass."

"The way he's reacting so far, that might not be a problem."

Max moved into position and studied the dildo swinging back and forth between Claire's legs as if it had lost its moorings. Claire steadied it, then inhaled deeply. Her eyes lowered, no doubt sighting in her target.

Max's mouth went dry, and he tried without much success to keep his buttocks from clenching.

"Maybe you should pull your knees up to your chest and spread your buttocks some until I'm in."

Max nodded and did as she suggested. Had he ever risked being this vulnerable with anyone before? He shook his head to clear it of second thoughts.

"Very inviting," Claire purred. "First, I'll apply a little lube on you."

Her finger stretched his anus, then slid quite easily inward. The lube was cooling. Maybe he should have her apply some to his forehead.

She ducked down and wet his cock with her lips. The dildo flopped against his balls.

"Perhaps you should get on with it," he whispered hoarsely.

Claire nodded, hovering over him. The next thing he felt was a hard object stretching his anus wider than any finger or vibrator ever had. He gritted his teeth and shut his eyes.

"The tip is in," Claire said softly. "We'll wait for you to open more."

Max wasn't convinced he could open wide enough, but he wasn't going to tell her that. Instead, he nodded. He managed a small smile when he realized he was indeed opening.

"More?" she asked.

"Yes," he whispered, opening his eyes to give her a tiny smile.

"Very slow and easy," she said as if she were soothing a child. "We're past the outer ring. The rest should go smoothly enough." She beamed him a smile. "Not too painful?"

He shook his head, but she sat back and rested again. "We're not in a hurry," she said, squeezing his cock. "And this fellow can be patient a little longer. We're halfway. I'll apply a little more lube."

Max groaned as she pulled a little way out to slather on more lube.

"There. Here we go again." She held her breath, then flexed forward.

Damn. He wanted to shout for joy. He knew his face broke into a wide smile when she settled against his loins. Had his ass ever felt so full? Or so loved?

"You did it," she squealed. "I'm all the way in. Let's do a little testing." She pulled partially out and slid back in gently.

It was getting difficult to distinguish pain from joy. His entire pubic region was alive in ways it had never been before. Claire did some more testing, and he wet his lips. They were beyond testing. His prostate gland must be taking direct hits.

She slowed long enough to lean over and chew on his lip. "I love you," she whispered. "Forever."

"And I love you. Now fuck my ass, lady."

"My guy."

Claire settled back to drive the false cock home.

Max grunted. He reached for his cock, hesitated, then looked at Claire.

"Go ahead. I want to watch you come."

He didn't think she'd have long to wait. She continued to fill and refill his ass while he pumped his cock. Their gazes locked on each other's until he was on the brink.

Without holding back her efforts with the dildo, she cheered him on. "Come for me, Max. Come for us. It's me fucking you. Come for us, Max."

A howl started deep in his body, then surfaced as he began to spurt. His hand wouldn't stop.

"Incredible."

He closed his eyes and lay back to appreciate the afterglow.

Claire slowed her motion. "So much, Max. You were wonderful. You . . ."

"Good God, Grandpa, what are you doing!"

"What the fuck!" Claire screamed at the top of her lungs.

Claire's yelling and yanking the cock roughly out of his ass brought Max back to his senses. He heard two women shouting at him. His eyes sprang open. Where the hell had Rosanne come from?

"Rosanne!" he yelped, belatedly pulling the sheet over him.

Out of the corner of his eye he saw Claire kneeling on the floor beside the bed trying to hide.

"Rosanne!" he said again. "What are you doing here!"

Even to his ears, that sounded like too rational a question, given the shrieks and pandemonium unfolding in his bedroom.

His wide-eyed granddaughter stood in the bedroom doorway dressed in a miniskirt and tee, holding a carry-on bag in one hand, with her other hand cupped over her mouth. Her eyes seemed about the size of silver dollars.

Her brow furrowed more as she saw Claire peeking over the edge of the bed. "You're *Grandma's* lover. How . . ."

"Don't you ever lock the fucking door?" Claire shrieked.

Max could almost see a spring snap in her.

"I've never been so humiliated, so mortified!"

"I'm . . ." Rosanne began. "I didn't mean . . ."

"Rosanne," Max said evenly, "go downstairs to the office."

"Both of you go downstairs!" Claire hollered. "I don't want to ever see or talk to you again!" She stalked toward the bathroom door, paying no heed to the false dildo swinging like a divining rod from between her legs. The bathroom door slammed shut, rattling its hinges.

Max grimaced, then looked toward his granddaughter who, for her part, looked ready to crumble. He shook his head at the bathroom door. Clearly he had one too many women to deal with, if not two too many.

"Go on down to the office, Rosanne," he said, surprisingly calm. "I'll get dressed and join you there."

"I'm sorry, Gramps," Rosanne squealed through tears.

"Go. Everything will be fine."

Once Rosanne left, Max stood and quickly dressed. He rapped on the bathroom door. "You okay in there?"

"Get out!" was the response. "Don't you understand the word never?"

Max felt rather than heard an object crashing against the door about eye level. Sighing, he headed downstairs. Maybe the second woman in the house would be a little more malleable. He pinched the bridge of his nose. What timing! Cripes, his ass still hummed and burned, and now he had to go be a reasonable-sounding grandfather.

Claire scrubbed her face and glared at her reflection in the mirror. How had things gone so quickly from near perfect to beyond ugly?

Where did his granddaughter come from? For a moment, she'd looked like a young Agnes coming back to accuse her husband and former lover.

Why the hell didn't Max lock his door?

And there she was fucking the girl's grandfather in the ass with a strap-on. She was beyond mortified. No word adequate to describe her rage materialized in the fog of her mind.

She hurriedly stepped into the bedroom and grabbed her purse. The first thing to do was get a cab. Claire punched the numbers into her cell phone and ordered one for immediate pickup.

Next, she made a quick search of the room, throwing as many of her things as she could into her overnight bag. Whatever she couldn't fit would have to stay — she wasn't about to come back for any of it. They were only things. She could always buy more things.

On her way out the door, she glanced over her shoulder at the four-poster bed. Tears streamed down her cheeks as she sneaked quietly down the stairs — thankfully, Max's office was down the hall from the entryway. She desperately hoped they couldn't hear anything.

She tried to breathe evenly when she stepped out on the sidewalk and was elated to see the cabbie waiting for her. Only after she climbed into the cab and sped away did she realize that she'd left the strap-on in the bedroom. Tears welled again. At least Max had a souvenir.

CHAPTER FOURTEEN

Max heard the entry door slam shut, and a minute later, the sound of a car pulling out of the driveway. He grimaced. He'd have to deal with Claire later. Right now he had a fairly remorseful, frightened granddaughter crying on his office couch.

He raised his hand to stop her from telling him one more time how sorry she was for interrupting. She'd used her key to get in and was taking her stuff to her bedroom when she'd walked by his room. And of course, that door was open. And of course, one thing led to another.

He was running out of patience. He didn't need to hear again what he already knew.

"Okay," he said, sitting across from Rosanne. He crossed his legs at the ankles. "I understand how that little fiasco happened. I accept your apology. I am not going to discuss my love life with you. And I do not apologize for anything you might've seen or heard that you weren't supposed to see or hear. So why don't you tell me what brought you here in the first place? You don't often just pop in."

"I was infuriated with my mother," Rosanne said tartly. "And I wanted to tell you in person."

"Tell me what?"

"I'm in love."

Max's heart fluttered. "You're in love. Well, I'm happy for you. Tell me about the lucky guy."

She shook her head vigorously.

How many more studs could she get in her left ear? He

counted five before a tiny light bulb of recognition switched on somewhere in his brain.

"She's not a guy. Her name is Lucinda. And we love each other very much. And," she wailed, "I knew you'd understand."

Max rose to his feet to gather his granddaughter in his arms.

He took several large breaths, then let Rosanne sob against his shoulder. Where was Claire when he needed her? She'd know better what to say and do than he would.

"Of course I understand, and I'm happy for you—and for Lucinda." He leaned back to wipe tears from her eyes. "I take it your mother isn't so understanding?"

Max smiled to himself as Rosanne shook her head. Her reddish hair was the same shade as her grandmother's.

"My parents disowned me. They won't be chipping in any more for my college. I'm not welcome in Oregon."

"Shit." Max settled Rosanne back down on the couch, then took a seat beside her. "Don't worry about college. I'll cover that." He gave her a big hug. "And I am pleased you trusted me enough to come and tell me in person."

Rosanne sniffled. "My timing could've been a little better."

"It would've helped if you had called to let me know when to expect you. No more apologies," he reminded her, when she opened her mouth to speak. "So tell me, how did you know Claire was Agnes's lover?"

"Once, when I was visiting—I was probably fourteen or so—Grandma Agnes took me to the city, and we stopped at the Center. I stayed in the waiting area while Grandma went down the hall." She shrugged her shoulders. "Of course I got tired of waiting. As I cruised the place, I came across a room with a small window. When I peeked in, there was Grandma kissing a beautiful, tall, blonde woman. It was the same woman with you upstairs."

"I see."

"I wasn't born yesterday. I only hung around long enough to see Grandma slip a hand under the blonde woman's skirt. Barely minutes later, looking a little flushed, Grandmother picked me up from the waiting area. It wasn't until we came back here that she told me she'd seen me spying on her in a mirror on the opposite wall."

"So she told you about Claire."

"About Claire and how loving Claire was helping you and her. She showed me pictures of Claire — fully clothed, I should add — and talked about the important work of the Center. She was very proud of the work you and she were doing as volunteers for the Center.

"Surprisingly, Grandma wasn't ashamed at all by my discovery of her and Claire. It was as if she had a secret she'd wanted to share with me for some time and this was the opportunity to finally tell me about what was important to her."

Max furrowed his brow. Agnes could be quite determined. "Do you think she staged that scene for you so you'd have to talk about it?"

Rosanne grinned. "I've wondered about that, but I don't think Claire had any idea I saw them kissing. Grandma had always been my confidant, but after that morning, she opened up to me about girl things. Something Mom never did. Grandma got me my first birth control stuff, bought me a couple of books on sex, a vibrator, and generally wanted me to own and honor my body."

"Your mother didn't know about any of this?"

"Oh, she knew about Grandma and Claire, but she didn't and doesn't know that I know. Mother was infuriated and was so horrified that Claire came to Grandma's funeral. I don't know if Claire knows that Mother knows."

Max winced. "She does now."

"So, do you love her?"

Max sighed. His granddaughter certainly was a bold one. "Yeah, I love her."

"Does she love you?"

"She says she does. Or at least did."

"So are you going to marry her?"

Max arched his eyebrows at his rather naïve granddaughter. "Did that woman upstairs look like someone who was going to marry me?"

"No." Rosanne giggled. "But she did look pretty funny trying to strut across the bedroom with dignity with that strap-on flopping so wildly."

Max shook his head but couldn't contain a small laugh. "That's right, but you'd better not tell her that."

"Maybe I should," Rosanne said, rising to her feet. "That's it. I do need to apologize to her. I can make things right again. It was just a big mistake. My fault, totally."

Women! Max couldn't even find the strength to stand. "I wish you wouldn't," he said, fully aware he might as well be pissing against a sixty-mile an hour wind.

The look of determination on Rosanne's face was identical to a familiar look he'd seen on Agnes—for that matter, on Melissa, Simone, and Claire.

He shook his head. His granddaughter's zeal only meant there would be more pieces for him to pick up later.

Rosanne tugged on her short mini.

"Do you think you could've found a shorter skirt to wear?"

"Gramps, sometimes you sound like an old fuddy-duddy."

"I've seen women with longer panties than that skirt."

She shook her head at him. "They were called bloomers, Grandpa."

"I'm not that damn old."

"Oh, just kidding," Rosanne countered, smiling devilishly. "I'll go put my stuff in my room."

Max watched fondly as his revived granddaughter

sashayed out the door. Somehow, he expected it was going to take much more than a conversation to revive Claire.

The rain splattering against the bedroom window provided the kind of protective cocoon Claire longed for. She curled under the blankets, unsure if she'd ever again welcome sunshine.

She glanced at the clock next to the bed. Three o'clock in the afternoon. She sighed. It was still Sunday. Time dragged glacially. Maybe she should get up and go in to the Center. Work had always been her lifeline when her personal life fell apart. Why should this time be any different?

But she couldn't find the energy to budge. She'd only managed coffee, toast, and bananas since returning to her condo. Sleep had eluded her much of the night. She'd developed a different appreciation for one of her old favorite tunes: "Twist and Shout."

Mercifully, exhaustion led to sleep. But sleep didn't last nearly long enough. She'd never considered how fortunate hibernating animals were.

She sat up long enough to punch a fist in a pillow, rearrange it, and flop back down on the mattress. Then she groaned, sat up, and swung her legs over the bed. No one was going to bring her coffee.

She did her best to ignore her reflection in the mirrors. She wasn't ready for that.

Claire made her way slowly to the kitchen. Even the kitchen seemed sterile. Going through the motions brewing more coffee, she couldn't completely avoid the self-chastisement her brain continued to whip up against her.

She nodded, then sighed for the umpteenth time. She'd really made a mess of things. Ms. Cool-and-Sophisticated had totally lost it because of a young redheaded waif of a girl.

She'd attacked viciously out of shock. How many times had she told people to be open to surprise? She shook her head at the coffee streaming too slowly into the pot. Did surprise include shock?

Where had that girl come from? And she still couldn't understand why Max didn't keep his doors locked. Anyone could've come in and threatened their lives. Newspapers were full of such stories. He'd left them vulnerable.

Her shoulders slumped. Vulnerability was an emotion she hadn't often let herself feel. Lately, she'd had far too much of that nagging feeling. Why else had she bothered to scrub the closet floors? Cripes, Max was right on that one. She'd been trying to live up to an image that neither one of them probably gave a damn about. If they did decide the closets floors needed cleaning, they could hire it done.

She poured more coffee, then shut her eyelids as she brought the cup to her mouth. Never had she talked to anyone about death and dying. She'd shared anxieties with Max that she wasn't sure she'd ever named before.

She'd been on an incredible emotional high once Max had made it clear he was not only willing, but wanted her to claim his ass. She'd expected to have to tease and cajole, but he'd simply offered himself to her, no reservations.

Tears stung her eyes. The look of adoration and praise on his face when she'd finally entered him completely was unforgettable. His howls of pleasure as he splattered across his chest still rang in her ears.

She shook her head. Why couldn't she erase those memories?

Her eyes sprang open. She'd lost Max, but she didn't want to lose her memories of him.

How many times in the last twenty-four hours had she replayed that grotesque scene? They'd been at the pinnacle — then one scream had shattered everything.

She couldn't blame Rosanne for screaming, but she did blame Max for being so lax as to let her enter the house without knocking. And she did blame the girl for not immediately backing out of the bedroom. She'd seemed rooted in place, unable to move at all.

What must've gone through her mind when she saw the strap-on and realized what she'd walked in on? Maybe the girl was made of the same kind of grit that so characterized Max and Agnes. Some young women would've fainted or launched into a tirade.

Claire scowled. She hadn't actually taken the time to listen to what Rosanne might have been saying. She'd only seen one escape, and that was locking herself in the bathroom as quickly as possible.

Only after she'd caught her breath in the bathroom had she considered how ridiculous she must've looked waddling toward the bathroom still wearing that damn strap-on.

She wasn't exactly sure what she'd screamed in her rage. She sighed. It wasn't pleasant, that was for sure. Max looked dumbfounded, angry, and more concerned about his granddaughter than about her.

Had they had a good laugh about the crazy blond who'd stormed out of the house? What else could she have done?

It was still difficult to fathom a different immediate solution. Maybe she should've simply strutted over to the girl and said, "Hi, I'm your grandfather's lover. It's good to meet you. Now get the hell out of our bedroom."

Max wouldn't have tolerated that. When the chips were down, she was only the most recent lover, and Rosanne was the granddaughter. The girl looked vulnerable herself. Why the hell had she shown up without even calling?

Claire refilled her coffee cup and headed back to her bedroom — her sanctuary.

She sat upright against the pillow and picked up her most

recent novel. The words blurred on the page. No way could she concentrate enough to care about some fictional character's troubles. She already had enough of her own.

She picked up the cell phone from the nightstand. There were no messages—though eight calls had come in from Max's home phone. She'd turned off the ringer. It wasn't just that she didn't want to talk to him—she had no idea what to say to him.

It wasn't until the middle of the night that she'd awakened with a start, recalling Rosanne's words—*Grandma's lover.* Those words still stabbed at her. How did Rosanne find out about her and Agnes? Had Rosanne's mother told her, to spite her own mother and father?

She couldn't remember Agnes ever introducing the two of them, so how would the girl even recognize her? She had gone to Agnes's funeral but had remained on the edges of a rather large crowd. And she'd made a point of avoiding the family receiving line. She'd gone out of respect for Agnes, not to cause a scene.

It was uncanny how closely Rosanne resembled her grandmother—more so in person than in pictures.

Claire slid down under the covers. Could Agnes possibly have talked to Rosanne about her? Would she have shown a picture of her female lover to her granddaughter?

Possibly. Claire allowed herself a small smile. Agnes had become so zealous about the Center's work and so grateful for finding renewed romance with her husband. It wasn't beyond question that she might share her newfound sense of purpose with her granddaughter. That didn't mean she'd tell her about her lover, though.

But somehow, Rosanne had recognized her.

Claire tried as hard as she might to bring back the image of Rosanne standing in the bedroom doorway. The girl had registered shock, but Claire couldn't recall horror or censure.

With her brain fried, Claire squeezed her eyes shut, rolled over and squeezed a pillow between her legs. She couldn't do this incessant rehashing anymore. She drifted in and out of sleep. With any luck, the next time she woke, it would be time to go to work.

Melissa sat next to Claire at the small round table in her office. She squeezed her friend's fingers and nodded again. She'd been listening for nearly a half an hour. It was important for Claire to tell her story as she remembered it.

Melissa sighed. There were significant discrepancies between Claire's story and the one Max had told her last night on the phone. But one element each story shared was blame and self-blame.

It surprised her a little that neither Claire nor Max blamed the granddaughter much. Melissa shrugged. Maybe that was a grandparent-type response. For her part, she would've sliced Rosanne up into ribbons. How dare she prance around her grandfather's place like she owned it without even letting anyone know she was coming! Then, when she did see Max and Claire in the heat of lovemaking, Rosanne hadn't had the good grace to simply back out of the room.

But the granddaughter wasn't her problem. Max and Claire would have to deal with her.

Max and Claire's future—that was her problem. They weren't even talking to each other. Would either of them hear the depth of agony and love in the other's voice if they couldn't stop self-pity long enough to listen?

Claire had definitely lost her moorings. She'd wanted to come to work to get away from herself. Melissa smiled a little. She wasn't a stranger to that strategy. Her painting had held her up through very trying times.

"Are you listening?" Claire asked, hooding her bloodshot

eyes.

"I'm trying," Melissa said. "But you are repeating your-self."

"Sorry."

"Don't be. It's okay. But I do think you're whipping your-self far too much about it all." Melissa acknowledged Claire's look of doubt. "I'm not saying your feelings are unfounded, but at some point, you have to think about moving on. Or maybe how to reclaim what you and Max share."

"Which is nothing," Claire spat out.

"I don't believe that for an instant, but what I believe is un-important. But, Claire, there were three people involved in this situation. I doubt you need to take on more than a third of the blame."

Claire shrugged her shoulders.

"And there are two of you principally responsible for turn-ing things around. Neither one of you can do that alone." Melissa scowled at her friend. "You do want to turn it around, don't you?"

Again Claire's shoulders rose and fell. "I didn't think I did." Claire gave her a mournful look—so unlike Claire. "But I do love Max. The bastard. He should've locked the doors."

Melissa groaned and jumped in quickly before Claire had a chance to spin on that sore point again. "Do you even know that Max didn't have the doors locked?"

"What do you mean?"

"There is such a thing as a spare key."

"I don't know. Max can't love me after what I said."

"Defiance is probably better than self-pity. I'm sorry, Claire, but I do have an appointment coming in from out of town. I know you want to get back to work. Could you do me a favor?"

"Sure. I need to stay busy and focused."

"Good. Would you review this tape for me?" Melissa

picked up a tape from the table. "It's the scene with me and Simone and Harry. I'd like your input about editing before we go further."

Claire nodded. "I can do that. How soon do you need it?"

"As soon as possible. I'd appreciate it if you could work on it right away."

"I don't have anything better to do. I'll go down to the screening room and review it right away. If the tape does justice to the work you three did, it should be quite good."

Melissa gave her friend a half-smile. "The tape doesn't lie."

Half an hour later, Claire sat in the screening room feeling useful again. She, like Melissa, had a good eye for stripping away redundancy to keep a tape moving. Sometimes things took longer to develop on set than one could allow for on tape. One of her criticisms of much erotica was that scenes often lasted far too long. Then there was that little trick of re-looping scene segments that the Center never resorted to.

Claire watched Simone in white knee socks riding Harry's cock. She sighed. Harry's face contorted, as if he thought he could actually resist Simone's frenzy. Foolish man.

She chuckled at the sight of Harry giving up, then driving into the young woman so hard that Simone was left to ride him like a bull rider. The moment Simone turned wide-eyed to Melissa and shouted, "I've got him! He's filling me," was as spectacular on tape as it had been firsthand. More than one couple ought to be inspired to replicate that scene. There might even be a run on white knee socks.

Claire took a few moments to wrap up her edit commentary before rising to turn off the tape. Her brow furrowed as the screen fluttered and a new image came into view.

She plopped back down in her chair, trying to breathe. She was on the screen sitting in her camping seat, splayed wide open in front of Max.

She couldn't move. The video continued to run. Her eyes teared up as she saw herself opening for Max. She could feel the vibrator he held in her ass and the one she held in her pussy as if Max was in the room with her. He'd been so gentle, watching her, letting her tell him verbally and nonverbally what she wanted.

She crushed her breasts when she saw the image of her riding Max's bald head, then smiled at the sight of a tiny stream of her juices spreading across his pate. She hadn't realized that would be caught on tape, but she saw no need to edit it out.

She sighed heavily as the scene ended. Melissa could be very deceptive. *This* was the reason she wanted her to review the tape and to do so as soon as possible. Her comments on the three-way would be helpful, but this was why Melissa sent her to the screening room.

She was right. The tape didn't lie. What she and Max shared was beautiful. It was a kind of intimacy and love neither she nor he had probably ever expected to find.

The screen continued to flicker after the scene ended. It looked so stark without color, without images.

Stark. She didn't want the rest of her life to be stark because she'd panicked in one moment. But would Max still want her?

A knock on the screening room door pulled her back to the present. "Come in," she said.

"I need to talk with you."

Claire winced at the sight of the young redhead. Did Rosanne ever wear anything but the shortest miniskirts available? Did she even own a bra? Her nipples were nearly as evident as the row of studs in her left ear. *Ouch.*

While she'd rather talk to Max, maybe the granddaughter could at least provide her with a clue about what was going on with him. She nodded, then gestured toward a chair and turned off the machine with the remote. "How did you find me down here?"

"Simone, the little cute African American girl, showed me the way."

"Ah, Simone. The ever-present, ever-observant Simone." Claire scowled. "You may be lucky you made it this far," she added under her breath. "What's on your mind, Rosanne? I don't think we were properly introduced." Rosanne seemed surprised when Claire reached over and shook her hand. "I am Claire Johnson, and you are Max's granddaughter."

Rosanne nodded. "Grandmother said you could be incredibly cool and poised."

"Not quite like the other day. You did catch me at, shall we say, a vulnerable moment. What do you want to talk about, Rosanne?"

"Me, you, Gramps."

"You've got the floor."

Claire listened for what felt like long minutes as Roseanne told her story in a very straightforward manner. She sounded apologetic but didn't lean toward the histrionic. Rather, she came across as very genuine — much like her grandfather and grandmother.

So she did have a key to the house. Melissa was right. Again. Claire watched Rosanne pull several pictures from her purse. Claire's heart fluttered at the sight of Agnes's beaming smile. When Agnes was happy, she glowed. There were photos of the two of them. On several occasions they'd asked a tourist to take their picture when they were in a park or at a museum.

"I wish Agnes had introduced us." Claire looked wistfully at the photos. "Maybe we would've avoided this recent disaster entirely. So, seeing your grandmother and me that morning didn't freak you out?"

"Funny." Rosanne chuckled. "That's almost exactly what

Grandma Agnes asked when we got back to the house that day. Not really. I'd already kissed a few girls during sleepovers. And . . ." Rosanne blushed a little. "We did do a little more exploring than that. I understood what she was after under your skirt."

"I see," Claire said, before clearing her throat.

"But I must admit I was a little surprised that older women were attracted to each other."

"Well, I guess that's something."

"Would you like to see a picture of Lucinda?" Rosanne said with a look of expectancy.

"Of course I would," Claire said, encouraging any shift of conversation.

Roseanne handed it to her.

"She's lovely," Claire murmured, picking up the photo to take a closer look. "Absolutely stunning."

"I often feel drab next to her," Rosanne admitted.

"Nonsense!" Claire handed the photo back. "You are a very attractive young woman. I doubt anyone would ever describe you as drab."

"Lucinda has such a rich skin tone. Her mother is Puerto Rican, and her father is African American."

Claire nodded. "I suppose your mother wasn't too pleased with that fact, either."

Rosanne shrugged. "I never got around to describing Lucinda's ethnicity. My mother's tirade made that impossible. And then the phone went dead."

"I'm sorry," Claire said, reaching over to cover the young woman's hand. "Life is tough enough when we don't have the support of those we love."

"Thanks."

Claire withdrew her hand.

"Gramps said you'd understand. And I knew he would."

Claire caught herself looking toward the screen where

she'd so recently witnessed Max loving her. "I'm sure he does." Her eyes misted. This was not the time for *cool and sophisticated* to slip away.

"He loves you very much."

Claire snapped her head around to stare at Rosanne.

"He does. I wish I could help you understand."

Claire laughed. "You can't put Humpty Dumpty back together again."

"Bullshit!"

Claire flinched.

"You helped my grandparents get their marriage back together when it was at its rockiest. You were able to help my grandmother find herself, can't you help yourself?"

Claire struggled for her voice but couldn't seem to locate it.

"You've probably helped thousands of people through your work at the Center."

Claire frowned. "How much do you know about the Center's work?"

"Enough." Rosanne smiled easily. "I am twenty, and the Center sells to anyone over eighteen."

"Damn."

Rosanne laughed. "You are a gorgeous woman, Claire. When I get to be your age, I hope I'm half as attractive as you. And that I'm half as comfortable in my skin as you are." A tiny grin worked across Rose's lips. "Watching you and Grandmother was like watching a symphony being created."

Claire gasped. "You saw . . ."

Rosanne shrugged. "Like I said, I'm over eighteen, and the Center didn't reject my credit card." She winked. "Don't tell Gramps, but I think he's very nicely hung for a man his age. If I want a man when I'm that old, I hope I find one like Gramps."

"But . . ."

"But," Rose held up a palm to prevent Claire from inter-rupting, "you should know that while I think I could grow to like you a lot and I respect your work, you do nothing for me sexually. You don't trip my trigger."

"What? Trip your trigger? Oh."

Claire shrank into her chair, chagrined that they were even having this conversation. She inhaled sharply. Maybe it was needed to clear the air. She stifled the laughter coming to her lips and shook her head.

"You don't trip my trigger either. When I look at you, I see a lovely young woman who happens to be Max's grand-daughter."

"Good." Rosanne clapped her hands gleefully. "Now that we've cleared that potentially difficult matter, maybe we can be friends. Just friends. I have missed my talks with Grandma Agnes a lot."

Claire arched her eyebrows. Had she been so direct and straightforward when she was twenty? Maybe not, but then Phoebe was still opening her up to a vast new world at that age. Apparently, a world that Rosanne already knew quite well. She squinted.

"You're not trying to be a matchmaker, are you? I've got matchmakers up to my ears."

"Then maybe one more won't hurt. Ever since Grandma told me about you, I've always considered you part of the family. Not someone I could approach, but still a member of my family."

"That's a beautiful thing to say," Claire said through tears. "If nothing else good comes out of the last forty-eight hours or so, maybe finding a new friend makes it worthwhile."

"As long as you don't lose Gramps in the process. I have to run, Claire, but I do have one more question."

"What's that?"

"Where would I find a strap-on dildo like the one you had

242

on the other day?"

"What?" Claire nearly popped out of her seat. She looked sharply at Rosanne who stood there waiting for a response to what she'd clearly considered a perfectly reasonable question. "How long were you standing in the doorway?"

Rosanne lips parted into a tiny smile. "Long enough. I couldn't decide who was enjoying themselves more. That looked incredibly powerful. I think Lucinda and I would like to try that."

Claire felt herself giving up. She couldn't go back and change what Rosanne might've seen or heard. She nodded.

"Check at the desk on the way out and pick up a catalogue. You should be able to find one that suits you and your lover." She grinned. "Make sure you use plenty of lube."

"Thanks," Rosanne said, softly. She leaned over and kissed Claire's cheek. "That's the kind of advice Grandma Agnes used to give me." Rosanne leaned back and chuckled. "I'm sure you don't see yourself as a grandmother type, but I wouldn't mind having a grandma I could talk to again. Bye."

Claire remained speechless long after the screening room door closed behind the young redhead. So Max's granddaughter was on her side, but that didn't mean a thing about Max.

How did Rosanne know Max still loved her? Had he confided in his granddaughter? Was it woman's intuition? Or was it merely the child within the granddaughter longing for a grandmother?

And how did that make her feel? Surprisingly, glowing in a way she'd never quite experienced before. She realized her work probably had helped a lot of young women, but she'd seldom heard about it in such a firsthand, matter-of-fact way.

That praise had come from the lips of Agnes's and Max's granddaughter? Amazing. Did Claire have the patience required to even be a stand-in grandmother?

Claire bit her tongue. She couldn't be much worse at being a grandmother than Rosanne's mother was at being a mother.

Claire flipped the tape machine back on and replayed the scene between her and Max. She appreciated on the second screening how comfortable she and Max appeared, almost domestic. And yet, how sexy they were together.

By the time she finished reviewing the scene again, she'd come to one resolution. She wasn't about to lose Max without putting up a fight.

But this was a fight with which she had very little experience. She felt like an utter novice. Would she know what to do?

CHAPTER FIFTEEN

Max scratched his unshaven face and studied the picture of Claire hanging on his office wall. Funny, Rosanne hadn't even mentioned the picture.

Maybe he should storm Claire in her sanctuary. She was probably holed up in her bedroom. Or he could simply show up at the Center tomorrow like his granddaughter apparently had today. He shook his head. He didn't want to risk embarrassing Claire any further by airing their pain in front of coworkers.

Had Rosanne really told Claire she thought she'd make good grandmother material? After that, he'd be lucky if Claire was still in the city—or in the country, for that matter. The thought of becoming an instant grandmother probably scared her more than the memory of being discovered Saturday afternoon.

Max reached for the phone, but his fingers formed into a fist instead. Why would she bother to take his call this time? He'd tried her at least a dozen times with no answer.

But she'd talked with Rosanne.

Would she talk with him? What did he have to lose? He wanted her. Damn if he was going to be put off this easy. Life was too damn short for giving up.

Even Rosanne had tweaked him by wondering if he was too old to fight for his lover. Why the hell didn't he have a grandson? He seemed badly outnumbered these days by women who had his best interests at heart.

His eyes traveled back to the nude of Claire staring back at him. Her wide-open thighs showed off her swollen labia, parted, as if waiting for his tongue. The shadow of her darker portal also beckoned. Her breasts lay back on themselves, with nipples standing alert and tall.

Yet all of those erogenous zones directed the eye on a line to her face. No smile. Sharp eyes. Confident. Nose slightly raised. She projected an aura of self-assurance and being in charge, seducing him with a sexy air of superiority.

Max unzipped his pants. His stiff arousal sprang out, seeking relief. He skimmed his fingers over its length. When did she not have that effect on him?

Max grabbed the phone and punched in her numbers. Only then did he glance at the clock. It was nearly midnight. Rosanne had long since gone to bed.

"Hello." Claire's voice sounded strained. He didn't think she'd been sleeping.

"You wanted phone sex."

"Max?"

"You laughed at me when I said I wasn't into that."

"But . . ."

"I'm sitting in my office, Claire. I'm jerking off while studying the painting of you and listening to your voice. Join me, Claire."

"This is absurd."

"No more absurd than much of what we've done. You weren't able to sleep, were you?"

"No."

"Let me help you fall asleep, Claire. It's the least I can do."

"Are you drunk?"

"Only on you."

"Cripes." He heard her gasp, then hesitate. "We have so much to talk about."

"We can always talk, but first you need to get some sleep. Rosanne told me you looked like you hadn't slept in days."

"She told you she talked to me?"

"Not now, Claire. My cock is screaming for release. I want you to catch up with me. I'll wait, but not for long."

Silence droned on.

"Tell me what you want me to do."

"That's my girl. Are you in bed?"

"Yes."

"Why don't you pull on your nipples? Imagine my fingers twisting them and pulling them to their fullness."

"I am."

"Good. My cock is shaking with need. I won't last long. Use your fingers to tease your pussy."

"I'm already wet. I've got two fingers in. Oh my. I wish you were here."

Max chuckled. "This will have to do."

"You're really jerking off watching my picture?"

"Have I ever lied to you?"

"No."

"Claire." His voice rose. "Strum your clit for me."

"I am. God, I'm almost there."

"Don't wait for me. He's building. Claire, meet me for breakfast in the morning."

Her laughter filled his ears.

"Are you telling me you think the way to my heart is through my pussy?"

"Sounds good to me." Max grunted. "Here he comes. Hot damn."

"I'm gone," she said, sighing into the phone. After several moments, her voice filled his ear. "This was good, Max. I would never have thought of this. Breakfast at eight, my place."

"That'll work. I'm going to have to hang up. My neck has a crick in it, and I have to get my handkerchief to clean up."

"You didn't use the speaker phone."

"Can never get it to work. Sweet dreams."

"I'm going to sleep well. Bye."

Max laid the phone in its cradle, rotated his neck, and cleaned himself up. He smiled at Claire's picture and the mess he'd made. He had no idea how many times he'd jerked off in his lifetime, but probably none of them, other than perhaps the first time he'd ejaculated, was more momentous than this one.

Max filled all her orifices at once. Her mouth. Her pussy. Her ass. He'd wormed his way into her heart — her soul. Her entire being soared. Claire hugged a pillow tight to her chest. Her ears rang with Max's piercing cries of ecstasy.

Ringing. Reaching blindly for the phone, Claire forced her sleep-filled eyes open. Four a.m. Cripes, what else did Max want from her?

"Hello," she whispered, her throat still raw from crying.

"Claire?"

"Rosanne?" Claire shot straight up. "What's wrong?"

"It's Gramps." Rosanne's strained voice couldn't seem to speak fast enough. "We're at the emergency room. The doctors are trying to figure out if he had a heart attack. He's asking for you."

"I'll be there as soon as I can." Claire was immediately on her feet haphazardly grabbing clothes from drawers. "How . . . how is he?"

"Feisty. Demanding. Pissed that I called the ambulance. The staff here is telling us that this is exactly where he needs to be."

"Give me the address." She scribbled the information on a pad. "I've got to call down to the doorman to get me a cab. Oh. Have you called your mother?"

Claire heard Rosanne sniffle.

"I tried. She hung up as soon as she recognized my voice."

"Bitch! Sorry."

"Don't be. I'm scared, Claire. I need you."

"I know, honey. I am too. I'll be there as soon as I can get there."

Barely an hour later, Claire half-walked, half-ran toward the swinging emergency room doors. Rosanne must've had one eye on the doors, because just as soon as Claire stepped into the cavernous emergency room, Rosanne was in her arms. She held the girl tight. She was here now. Suddenly, there was no need to rush. Claire let Rosanne sob on her shoulder until she found words.

"Thanks for coming," Rosanne said. "I've never been so scared," she rattled on. "The doctors don't think he had an actual heart attack, but they're concerned that this was a warning. We've got to get Gramps to listen to them."

"Take me to him," Claire said, holding Rosanne's hand. "You did a good job getting him here."

"He can be stubborn."

Claire chuckled softly. "Tell me about it."

Rosanne ducked around a screen, and Claire followed. Her eyes misted when she saw Max propped up on a hospital bed with three or four monitors beeping and humming, gleaning vital information.

Max shook his head when he saw her.

"Sorry," he quipped. "Looks like I may be a little late for breakfast."

Claire didn't hesitate. She stepped over, brushed her lips across his, and squeezed his hand.

Still clutching Claire with one hand, Rosanne reached out and cradled her grandfather's other hand.

"How are you?" Claire asked. "You have pretty good color

for having gone through this."

Claire didn't miss the trace of fear that flashed across Max's eyes before he responded.

"Looks like I'll live. Might not have to be here if my grand-daughter hadn't been prowling around the house in the middle of the night to find me doubled over in the hallway. I was returning from the bathroom. Next thing I knew, an ambulance was on the way."

"What do the doctors know?"

Max huffed. "Probably more than they're telling me."

"We'll sort this out, Max. We'll get you in to the city if we need a different hospital."

A young doctor pulled back the curtain and squeezed into the small space. He looked at Claire and frowned slightly, then nodded.

Did she have scarlet woman emblazoned on her forehead'?

"Are you his wife?"

Claire didn't miss a beat, nor did she look at Max. She shook her head. "Fiancée."

Max and Rosanne each squeezed a hand.

"Close enough," the doctor said with a hint of a smile. "You can stay." He turned to Max. "Your preliminary results are providing us with a good news-bad news story."

"Sounds like life," Max retorted.

The doctor ignored Max's comment. "You did not have a heart attack."

Max gave Rosanne an *I told you so* look.

"But you could have one at any moment. You're lucky your granddaughter had enough sense to get you in here." The doctor glanced at each of them before continuing. "We don't believe you are in any immediate danger now. You've responded quite well to our efforts to stabilize you."

"But . . ." Max said.

"But we do want to keep you in here for at least a few more

hours, possibly overnight. We're getting a bed ready for you now."

Max scowled. "Damn. That's it?"

The doctor shook his head. "The angiogram shows significant blockage. We'll need to do a bypass procedure."

Claire squeezed Max's hand as Max turned quite pale.

"This procedure is quite routine these days." He must've noticed the skepticism in the room. "I realize it isn't routine for you. Your situation does not constitute an emergency. We can schedule the procedure for probably two or three weeks from now."

"But I thought he was close to a heart attack?" Claire blurted out.

"He was. He isn't now. We'll provide you with appropriate medicine. A dietician will talk to you about his diet, and he should exercise regularly, but"—the doctor's gaze dropped below Claire's chin—"nothing too strenuous."

Claire caught herself glancing down. Good grief. In her haste, she'd forgotten to put on a bra. Her nipples were on full display. No wonder the doctor kept giving her odd stares.

She thrust out her chin. "Rest assured, Doctor, that Max is in good hands. I'm sure we can set up an exercise routine that won't overtax him too much," she said sweetly. "But it will be hard to keep him down."

The young doctor blushed, then nodded at Max. "One of us will check in with you upstairs after you've settled in."

"I don't want to be here any longer than absolutely necessary."

The doctor gave Max a wry smile and glanced at Claire. "I think I understand."

Claire checked her watch and glanced back at Max, whose eyes remained closed. It was nearly noon. They should know fairly soon if he had to stay the night. She hoped not. Max was already grouchy enough. She hadn't expected him to be such a poor patient.

Thank goodness he'd taken a nap shortly after moving into a regular hospital room. There was only one monitor still attached to him. She and Rosanne had taken his nap as an opportunity to make some decisions. There was no need for both of them to stay with Max. Rosanne had been up most of the night and needed some rest. Unfortunately, the girl had to return to Boston in two days to start the new quarter.

Claire grinned a little. That would provide Claire with enough time to move what she needed most to Max's house. Max didn't know it yet, but she and Rosanne agreed it would be best for Claire to stay with Max until he recovered from the bypass procedure.

"Sorry if I've been a bear," Max said hoarsely, breaking Claire's concentration.

She walked over to the bed, kissed his forehead, and took his hand. "Maybe we should hibernate."

A smile crossed his lips. "Where's Rosanne?"

"I sent her home. She's beat."

"Yeah. This was a lot for her to take in."

"She was quite shaken, but she'll rebound quickly."

"The advantage of youth."

"Something like that. So, how are you feeling?"

"Ready to go home."

Claire cocked her head to the side. "You're going to have a houseguest for a while. Until you're fully recovered from the procedure."

"Procedure—hell. Why don't they just say open heart surgery?' So who's going to be my guest?"

Claire caught the twinkle in his eye but didn't rise to his bait. "I have a nurse friend who should be able to meet your needs."

"Ah. Does she look at all like that gorgeous blond nude

hanging in my office?"

Claire brushed her lips against his. "She could be mistaken for her double."

"Thought you might use this little episode to move in."

"Max?" Now she was confused. He didn't look like he was joking.

"We had an agreement, an understanding, before you ran off last weekend. You broke it."

She nodded. "But I thought after last night?"

"Ssh." He placed a finger across her lips. "I'm willing to live up to every stipulation of our prior agreement, with one added stipulation."

"What's that?" she croaked.

"I want you to be my wife." He brushed his hand across her cheek as her heart raced. "Let me clarify. I need you to be my wife, Claire. It's working for Melissa and Harry. It can work for us. But . . ."

She placed a finger across his lips. "No buts. I reached the same conclusion in the back seat of the cab as I tried to get the driver to drive faster and faster." She cocked her head to one side. "I don't like to lie. And I did tell that young curious doctor that I was your fiancée."

Max smiled broadly.

Claire covered his smile with hers.

"That doc was tripping over his tongue. Can't blame him. You look so tantalizing when your nipples swell like they are right now." Max encircled a nipple, then pulled on it playfully.

She slapped his fingers away. "Max, no strenuous exercise."

Max's laughter warmed her heart. She hadn't heard him laugh since the previous Saturday.

He nodded. "I love you, woman. And I don't think tweaking your nipple can be considered strenuous exercise."

She chuckled. "I love you, too, Max. And I know how one thing leads to another." She winked at him. "I am looking forward to being your nurse for years to come."

"Nurse Claire." He scrunched his mouth. "I'm not sure that fits my image of you."

"I don't believe I've described my nurse's uniform," she said, parting her lips with the tip of her tongue. "Given how traditional I am, I begin with the classic nurse's hat. Let's see, I add to that white stockings held up with a white garter belt."

Max's face crinkled. "My kind of nurse."

"Sometimes, I'm able to locate my short white dress that buttons down the front. But I never have been able to find a bra or panties that seem to coordinate with the outfit."

"You can stop looking for them."

She shook her head. "There won't be time to look for them if I'm tending to your needs. I am a firm believer in alternative healing strategies. How about you?"

"Me? I'm just firm."

Claire laughed, then kissed Max on the cheek. "Sorry. I hope that doesn't count as strenuous exercise."

"So, do you have thoughts on a wedding date?"

"Yep. Worked it through on the ride over here."

"You must've been quite convinced I'd make it."

She blinked tears away. "I was willing you to make it. How about Thanksgiving weekend? We'll have a small but tasteful wedding. Rosanne will be on break."

"Honeymoon?"

"I thought that was the groom's responsibility." She grinned. "But I do think an island somewhere would be nice. We only truly became aware of one another on the beach in Monterey."

"I'll work on it when I get out of this place."

"We have time, Max. Let's take our time."

Two days later, Claire beamed at Rosanne hugging her grandfather goodbye in their entryway. Her carry-on bag lay on the floor. Apparently, one advantage of miniskirts was they didn't require much space.

The three of them had enjoyed a fine time since they'd brought Max back from the hospital. Grandfather and granddaughter had entertained her with stories of Rosanne growing up. No one seemed at all uncomfortable talking about Agnes and how she doted on her granddaughter. Isabelle, Rosanne's mother, was seldom mentioned.

They were awaiting the cab. Rosanne had insisted on taking a cab rather than having them drive her to the airport.

She backed out of her grandfather's arms, fighting back tears.

"I love you, Gramps. You mind Nurse Claire real good." Rosanne turned to Claire, holding out her arms.

"Don't you dare call me Grams," Claire said, drawing the girl into her arms.

Rosanne laughed and pecked at her cheek before stepping back. "I'm so looking forward to the wedding. It's exciting to have you officially in the family. Can I bring Lucinda to the wedding?"

"Of course you can," Max said.

Claire brought herself up short. "Why would you even have to ask?"

"Will my mom be there?"

"Oh." Max curled his fingers around Rosanne's hand. "She'll be invited, but there's no way in the world she'll come to the wedding."

"And if she does," Claire said, "we'll deal with her. Lucinda and any of your friends will always be welcome in our house."

"Good." Rosanne peeked out the door. Still no taxi. She glanced back at them, suddenly looking quite shy. "One more thing—I'd like you to help me get a job next summer, between my junior and senior year."

"Of course," Claire said immediately. "It will be great to have you in the city. You can stay with us, if you'd like."

"I want to work at the Center."

"What?" she and Max responded in unison.

"I'll have another year of college left, but I want to begin seriously looking at what I want to do after college."

"Not the Center," Max huffed. "Impossible."

"But you and Grandma Agnes and Claire have done so much to help others. I might want to pursue a research career like Simone is doing. She sounds thrilled with her choices."

"Jesus." Max ran his hand over his bald head, then stared helplessly at Claire. "Say something, please."

"I think your grandfather is right, Rosanne. You should think of some place other than the Center to work."

Hurt and anger vied for space on the young redhead's features, then she suddenly became very calm. Claire tried not to smile at Rosanne, but this was a tactic with which she was quite familiar, and she expected her grandfather was in over his head. Way over.

"I won't fight with you about it now." Rosanne gave both of them a pert smile. "There is plenty of time for that. But"—she scowled at her grandfather—"if you're telling me I can't work at the Center, then you are telling me that you are ashamed of what you and Grandma did—and you are ashamed of Claire's career?"

Claire clutched Max's hand. His granddaughter might not be looking for a fight, but she wasn't hesitating about going for the jugular.

"How about you Claire—are you ashamed of who you are?"

"Of course not, but . . ."

"But nothing. Think about it." Rosanne gave them a smile

that could melt butter. She brushed back a lock of hair that covered her studded earlobe.

Claire couldn't help but wonder if Rose had other piercings.

"I'm not ashamed of either of you. I often tell my friends about you and Grandmother."

"You do?" Max sounded totally incredulous.

"Why not? I'm proud of who you are and what you're doing for people. And" – she arched her eyebrows – "if I decide I want to follow a similar career path, I expect you to be equally proud of me."

The taxi horn prevented any further discussion. Rosanne gathered up her carry-on bag and blew them a kiss. "Talk to you soon," she said over her shoulder before taxi the door shut behind her.

Claire looked carefully at Max. She'd never seen him so dumbfounded. "Come on, Max. Let's take our coffee out to the patio. You look like sitting down is a good idea."

Max never said a word until they sat next to each other looking out across the yard. He interlaced his fingers with hers, then sighed several times before speaking. He turned and grimaced at her. "You know I'm not ashamed of you?"

Claire smiled and nodded. "I know that."

"And I'm not ashamed of the work Agnes and I did for the Center."

"I know that, too."

"But my granddaughter." He scrunched his mouth.

"It is a little mind-boggling, isn't it?"

"A little? I should've just said hell no, no way."

Claire shook her head in disagreement. "That would've been like waving a red flag in front of a bull. As you've said, Rosanne gets into causes. This week it's freeing the world of its sexual hang-ups. By next summer she'll probably be onto something else."

"And if not?"

"We may have to bargain with her. Maybe she'll be able to work with our research team, but absolutely no work on camera."

Max groaned.

"She'll be twenty-one, Max. It's not exactly like she can't go find similar work elsewhere." She smiled. "Some of those places have much lower standards than we do."

"Damn. So essentially you're saying we have two years for her to change her mind as to a career choice?"

"That's right. How many causes has she picked up over the last two years?"

Max smiled at her. "Plenty. So you're saying be patient and don't worry."

"Exactly."

"I'll try." Max settled back into the chair, then shut his eyes. "She sure did catch me by surprise."

Claire studied two robins pecking at the ground in the far corner of the yard. She saw no need to tell Max that in her gut she didn't think Rosanne would give up on her most recent cause any time soon.

The girl was genuinely awed by the effect she believed the Center's work created in people. And the determined gleam in Rosanne's eye when she'd inquired where to find an anal strap-on was a look Claire had witnessed many times. In Melissa's eyes, in Inez's, in Simone's, and even in the mirror.

Yes, Max was right when he'd once said it took a special woman to work at the Center. She could forgive him for not recognizing that look in his own granddaughter. Ultimately, Rosanne would have to find her own way. They all had.

Max stirred and grinned at her. "How is my nurse doing?"

"Just fine," she murmured, happy to see Max was no longer dwelling on his granddaughter. "I love you. How is my patient doing?"

"You know you haven't even modeled that nurse outfit you told me about?"

Claire shook her head. "No strenuous activity. I'm not going to have sex with you, Max, until after you recover from the surgery."

"Just because I'm on the shelf doesn't mean you have to turn into a desert wasteland."

She frowned.

"I still have ten fingers and a tongue," he said, waggling his tongue back and forth.

Her loins suddenly ached.

"I don't think getting a hard-on," he added, "is going to kill me."

She giggled. "No, I suppose you should be able to survive that."

"And I love watching you bring yourself off."

"Damn it, Max, you're making me wet."

His mouth curved into a grin. "That was the point." He slid his hand up the inside of her thigh. She smacked her lips when he fingered her pussy lips through her thin panties.

"Don't deny me the pleasure of watching you, Claire. Don't deny yourself."

"Jesus, Max," she moaned, as one of his fingers made its way beneath her panties. She sighed loudly. "Oh hell, it's been too long." She removed his hand. "Let's go upstairs to our four-poster bed. We'll both be more comfortable there." She gave him a quirky smile. "And me rubbing against your bald head shouldn't be overtaxing."

Max chuckled, got to his feet, then helped her stand. "We should have a few things left in our arsenal. Maybe eventually we should do a video for couples where a partner is bored to death waiting for surgery."

"Or," Claire quipped, leading the way toward the kitchen, "a split-screen video depicting phone sex."

"You liked that, didn't you?"

"Absolutely. I slept like a baby until Rosanne called." Claire glanced at the entryway door before turning toward the stairs.

"It's locked," Max said. "Trust me."

"I do." She squeezed his fingers behind her back as she led the way upstairs toward their bedroom.

"Damn, woman, you sure have an inviting ass." Max followed her up the stairs. "That reminds me. I'm positive I must owe you several spankings for what you've put me through these past several days."

Max pinned her to the wall as soon as they topped the stairs. Claire accepted his lips eagerly, then broke away and continued toward the bedroom. "We've got plenty of time, Max. We don't have to do everything at once."

"I know," he admitted. "I wish we could, but I know. What do you want to do first?" he asked as she guided him to the bed.

She reached under her skirt and yanked her panties down. "I'm already soaking." She placed one foot on the bed, then raised her skirt. "You might test your tongue out a little. And I'd love to wash your bald head with any leftover juices."

"Damn," he moaned, dropping to his knees. She inhaled as his tongue separated her folds.

Max leaned back and smiled at her. "This reminds me. I never formally asked you to marry me. This is the traditional position for asking. Claire, will you marry me?" He buried his tongue between her engorged lips before she could reply.

"Yes," she moaned, "I'll marry you. Kneeling might be the classical position for asking a woman to marry, but I doubt many guys mastered it quite the way you just did." Her head snapped back. "Oh damn," she muttered. "Give me your head." She straddled his bald pate, smearing her juices liberally. His hands cradled her butt. She gasped for breath.

"Baptism, by Claire," she whispered.

Max rose to his feet and gathered her in his arms. "I've never felt more blessed."

ABOUT THE AUTHOR

Adriana Kraft is the pen name for a married pair of retired professors writing erotic romance together. We like to think we've broken the mold for staid, fusty academics, and we hope lots of former profs are enjoying life as much as we are.

Having lived in many states across the Midwest, we now make our home in southern Arizona, where we enjoy hiking, golf, and travel, especially to the many Arizona Native American historical sites.

Together we have published more than fifty romance novels and novellas to outstanding reviews. We love hearing from readers at adrianakraft99@yahoo.com, and here is our website:

When It's Time to Heat Things Up https://adrianakraft.com

Find us at:

Blog: https://www.adrianakraft.com/blog

Twitter https://twitter.com/AdrianaKraft

Facebook: https://www.facebook.com/adriana.kraft.5

Facebook Fan Page https://www.facebook.com/AdrianaKraftAuthor

Instagram https://www.instagram.com/kraftadriana/

MeWe https://mewe.com/i/adriana1kraft

BookBub https://www.bookbub.com/authors/adriana-kraft

GoodReads https://www.goodreads.com/author/show/1578571.Adriana_Kraft

Extasy Books Page https://www.extasybooks.com/adriana-kraft

www.ingramcontent.com/pod-product-compliance
Lightning Source LLC
Chambersburg PA
CBHW071134170626
46809CB00002B/619